COASTAL CURRENCY

COASTAL ADVENTURE SERIES 10

DON RICH

Library of Congress PCN Data

Rich, Don

Coastal Currency/Don Rich

Florida Refugee Press LLC

Cover by: Cover2Book.com

This novel is a work of fiction. Names, characters, and incidents are either the product of the author's imagination or are used fictitiously. Any resemblance to actual persons, living or dead, businesses, companies, events, or locales is purely coincidental. However, the overall familiarity with boats and water found in this book comes from the author having spent years on, under, and beside them.

Published by FLORIDA REFUGEE PRESS, LLC, 2022

Crozet, VA

PROLOGUE

*S*everal days from now off the Eastern Shore of Virginia (ESVA)...

THE CAPTAIN FINISHED LOADING the noxious liquid into the large tank on the deck that was disguised as an insulated commercial fish box. He carefully replaced the fiberglass lid, using the built-in latches to secure it. Stepping up onto the seawall, he coiled the fill hose and returned it to the dock box. This box was also a disguise, intended to hide the hose from view. The supply pipe feeding it was buried underground. He removed his thick rubber acid-proof gloves and laid them on top of the hose before closing the dock box lid. Turning back to the boat, he could barely make out the unique lines of the drake tail deadrise in the dark night. There were lights in the shed over the covered slips, but he hadn't turned them on for fear of attracting attention. His only light came through the open back door of the corrugated metal boat shed. It came from a single security light outside of the old warehouse fifty feet away, but it was sufficient enough for his purposes tonight.

He stepped carefully over to the covering board, then down onto the deck. Entering the small deckhouse up in the bow, he started the big diesel engine. He went back outside to cast off the dock lines as the motor warmed up. Using the workboat's cockpit controls to ease the boat out of the slip, he then returned to the deckhouse to pilot her the rest of the way out into the bay, down a long, narrow, and meandering creek. A couple of hundred yards away from the bay he used a remote control to lower a heavy steel cable that was stretched across the creek, barring access by other boats. Signs attached to the cable warned anyone who approached that the area beyond was private property, and trespassers would be prosecuted. Once past the submerged cable, he hit the button for the motor, raising the cable again and securing the waterway.

He carefully navigated his way down the creek and into the Chesapeake Bay, idling out without using his navigation lights. Once he was well clear and had altered course to disguise his point of embarkation, he turned on the running lights. Now he looked like any one of the hundreds of commercial fishing deadrises on the bay, except for two things. The first was that ninety-nine percent of those other boats were tied up in their slips for the night, and wouldn't be leaving for another few hours. And the second was that rare drake tail design.

Unique to the early to mid-twentieth century, drake tails were originally built at Hooper's Island in Maryland. Instead of being built with a typical flat, straight, vertical, or even round stern, these were also round but protruded down from the aft covering board at a steep angle, extending the boat at the waterline. This was to add more flotation to the old, narrow workboats, allowing for larger cargoes of fish and shellfish, though only a few dozen were ever built before engines with larger horsepower became readily avail-able. This allowed boat builders to make their boats wider and longer to accommodate larger cargoes without the need for an extended stern.

The captain's boss loved both the look of drake tails, as well as their camouflaged extra buoyancy. This way when the tank was loaded, the boat wouldn't sit so obviously low in the water. He had this boat built at a small shop up in Maryland and was now keeping it in the shed, away from prying eyes.

Flipping the switch for the pump that drained the tank, the captain quickly evacuated close to a thousand gallons of toxic brew through a fitting in the bottom of the hull. This was the largest load yet, almost four times as large as he'd done before, as the plant had recently ramped up production. Since the captain knew the water around this area well, he hadn't bothered to turn on his fish finder to gauge the depth. If he had, he'd have seen that he was right in the middle of a huge school of menhaden, a species of fish that was highly prized for both bait and omega-3 oils. And he could have avoided causing one of the largest fish kills in the bay in over a decade.

His boss had instructed him to dump the liquid at cruising speed to minimize the concentration of the chemicals and to avoid any possibility of what would happen next. But the bay was so calm, and he was enjoying idling along in the dark. Besides, he figured his boss was just being overly cautious.

After using the tank's built-in saltwater sprayers to rinse the last of the toxic liquid from the tank, there was no trace of the smelly chemical left aboard. And this close to the mouth of the Chesapeake on an outgoing tide, he was sure it all would disperse quickly as it got drawn out into the Atlantic, just as it had on the runs he'd made before this one. On those, he had been at cruising speed during those smaller pump outs, just as he'd been directed. But that wasn't what happened this time. Not only had he dumped the chemicals in one spot, but he'd also misjudged the tide which was now slack. Quickly, over a million of the four to eight-inch-long menhaden swam into the murky cloud he'd created, long before it had a chance to become diluted and dispersed. Most of the fish never made it through alive, and the ones that did wouldn't survive for long, eventually sinking to the bottom like the rest.

Because of the warm summer water temperature, those dead fish immediately began to decay. Soon they would rise to the surface, as putrid gases began forming in their rotting bodies. By daylight, there would be a huge floating raft of fish bodies and oil, pushed and pulled by the tide and winds. By noon the rancid odor of the fish washing up on the beach would be strong enough to chase away anyone with a sense of smell. But that wasn't even the full extent of the environmental damage, as the toxins that killed the menhaden also now sickened hundreds of seagulls and other feathered scavengers that had seen the floaters as a free and easy meal. Soon they too would begin to succumb, adding to the number of floating corpses littering the beaches and the surface of the bay.

The economic damage would soon start, becoming even worse after the government jumped in, declaring this part of the Chesapeake to be a "No fishing or swimming area." The captain didn't yet know, but he was about to have a bad day. A very bad day after his boss figured out what happened and how it might affect his business. But as bad as it would be for the captain, his boss's day would be even worse.

1

THE TWO BEST DAYS...

Lindsay Davis looked concerned. "You're sure you want to do this, babe?"

Michael "Murph" Murphy nodded. "It's time. She's just sitting there in her slip, depreciating. And, she's a drain on our finances, having to maintain her. I'm pretty sure this buyer is for real, and besides, we'll still have *LNZ II* to fish from. Much less upkeep, and uses only a fraction of the fuel that she does." *LNZ II* was an older thirty-one-foot *Contender* center console outboard that Murph fixed up, and which they both used frequently.

The pair were just finishing breakfast, sitting on the awning-covered deck at the *Cove Restaurant*. Their table looked out over *Mallard Cove Marina's* charter boat row. Over on the right side of the marina basin out beyond the charter boats was the private dock, separated from the public by a fence and locked security gate. In the middle of that dock amongst the other boats was *Irish Luck*, the couple's sixty-foot Merritt sportfishing boat, and the subject of their current conversation.

As part of a tournament bet, they'd swapped their older, smaller Rybovich sportfish for the Merritt. They had found the Rybo in terrible shape down in Florida, and spent considerable time themselves renovating her from stem to stern, bringing her up to like-new condition. Enough that a country music superstar with a few Rybos of his own decided he wanted her for his collection, and he was willing to trade them the Merritt for the Rybo and a lot of cash.

Not being too flush in the cash department at the time, they proposed a wager. If they beat him in the tournament they were all signed up to fish, they would make an even swap. A steep bet, since the newer and much larger Merritt was worth almost three times what the Rybovich was, but the singer wanted her badly. The bet was made, and it turned out that the fishing gods were on their side.

Murph continued, "She was a means to an end, back when we were chartering. That was a tough life, and I like what we're doing now much better. You don't want to go back to chartering, do you?"

"Heck no! It was fun for a while, and we got so lucky with those two tournaments that we won ourselves. But I like this life much better."

The couple was the majority owner of the *Mallard Cove* complex on the southern tip of the *Eastern Shore of Virginia*, better known to the locals as *ESVA*. The complex consisted of a large marina, hotel, restaurant, two beach bar-and-grill combinations, a large tiki-style beach stage, and several water-related businesses. When they bought the property a few years ago, all that existed there was a marina with crumbling docks and an abandoned restaurant. At the time they had just won two of the richest fishing tournaments on the east coast, and the prize money was well into seven figures. The cash had been enough to purchase the run-down property without the need to take out a loan. Originally, the plan had been to continue their sport-fishing business and slowly fix up the marina and rent out the restaurant.

They'd approached Murph's old boss and friend, Casey Shaw, to see if he had any interest in renting the restaurant. By that point, they were almost out of cash. Casey was a very astute real estate investor with one of the hottest high-end properties on the Chesapeake called the *Bayside Resort and Club*. After a lot of persuasion by Casey and his wife Dawn, Lindsay and Murph finally agreed to let Casey and his partner group buy a forty-nine-percent stake in their property. Casey had a great talent for seeing what a property *can* be, rather than what it was right then. They got the benefit of his vision as part of their deal.

Another component of the deal was that Casey's group agreed to finance any of the future improvements that came about as a part of that vision. They would also handle the operation and development of all aspects of *Mallard Cove*. This would free Lindsay and Murph to continue their sportfishing careers, following the tournament circuit up and down the east coast. But it wasn't long before they were burned out and wanted to get away from the chartering business.

With the proceeds from the deal, they started investing in more waterfront properties, becoming members of Casey's group. They learned that passive investment was more their speed. They quit chartering and moved back to *Mallard Cove* full-time, giving up their nomadic tournament circuit lifestyle. So, for these last couple of years, *Irish Luck* had sat mostly unused and ignored in her slip.

Murph said, "Don't forget, it's not like we never get invited out on *Sharke* with the gang." *Sharke* was a new seventy-five-foot Jarrett Bay sport fisherman owned by Casey and Dawn, along with another member of the real estate partner group, Eric Clarke.

"I just don't want you to look back on this as a mistake in a year or two."

He shook his head. "Not gonna happen. You know what they say are the two best days in a boat owner's life..."

Lindsay smiled. "Yeah, the day they buy it, and the day they sell it."

Murph grinned back at her. "Exactly. We've had some great times on her, and she was our home for a while. But we've got other great times ahead, and I don't want to waste another second by having to keep scrubbing and oiling her teak decks. You know how little we've used her since we got *LNZ II*. And I can't single-hand a sixty-foot Merritt like I can the Contender. Plus, we've got a wedding coming up, and we've dumped all our cash into real estate and that catamaran business. They're great long-term investments for building a good income stream, but I'd feel a lot better with a fatter cash balance than we have right now."

Her brow furrowed, "That's part of it, babe. You don't need to spend so much on our wedding. We can have a smaller one here instead of such a big one up at *Bayside*. I don't want you resenting the expense. My parents would be happy to pay for a smaller one. But there's no way they can afford *Bayside*, and we don't need to have it there."

"And there's no way I'd ask your parents to pay for any of it. We're better off than they are, we're just temporarily 'cash poor.' After this Merritt deal closes we'll be flush again, and paying for the wedding won't be a problem. I want to have it at *Bayside* to make a statement. If we had it anywhere else, people might realize we've got a case of the 'shorts,' and that wouldn't be good for business. Perceptions are important. Think of it as a business expense."

"It's not a business expense! Don't try to deduct it; I don't want to spend my first anniversary in prison for tax evasion."

Murph laughed, "Neither do I. But it's the perfect opportunity to get even closer to our best business associates. I want them there as well as our other friends to watch me marry the prettiest woman in the world."

Lindsay was in her latter twenties and extremely attractive with long blonde hair and hazel eyes that changed depending on the lighting. Murph had shaggy brown hair, also with hazel eyes. At five feet ten, he was four inches taller than Lindsay, as well as ten years older.

Lindsay rolled her eyes. "Puh-leeze. We're already engaged, so you can quit doing the hard sell."

"Not doing the hard sell, I'm just stating a fact. And more than one of our friends and your family members never believed that day would ever come."

"I don't care what other people think, babe. I only care about the two of us. You know, the folks who do have the 'shorts.' And you especially need to quit worrying about what my family thinks because I sure don't."

"Your dad believes I turned you into a coastal vagabond, and I'm sure he can't get the image out of his head about how this place looked when we bought it. Neither he nor your mom has been here since then, and it's been over a couple of years."

She laughed as she said, "Well, can you blame him? You pried me away from my 'oh-so-glamorous' job as a bartender in that hotel in northern Virginia. Then you sweet-talked me into going with you and chasing dreams."

"Yeah, but you talked me out of chasing other women, so we're even. And remember, those weren't just *my* dreams, they were *our* dreams. When you take a look around here you've gotta admit they came true. Now your family will finally see it too when they come for the wedding. So maybe we'll spend a bundle up at *Bayside*, but I don't care. I want to make a point. For both of us."

"You don't need to. Really. That's a ton of money."

"Will you quit worrying about the cost? This boat buyer, Robert Outerbridge, is serious. So our low funds level is just a temporary thing," Murph said.

"How can you be so sure about him? You know that old saying all too well, 'buyers are liars.' What makes this Outerbridge guy so solid?"

"He asked if he could pay for her in gold Krugerrands. That's too far 'out there' to be part of some fake story."

"Krugerrands? Really? I've heard there are a lot of counterfeit ones. What do you know about Krugerrands?"

Murph pulled two small, black plastic tools out of his pocket and put them on the table. "Until yesterday, next to nothing. But you know Chris Luck who owns that sailboat named *Heavy Metal* over on the private dock? He also owns *Washington Coins* over in Virginia Beach. When Outerbridge brought up the coin idea, I went over to talk with Chris. He loaned me these and this." Murph pulled a large gold coin out of his pocket and picked up the first plastic tool. "This is a real Krugerrand. See how tightly it fits through the slot in this tool? And here, it has to fit perfectly in this indentation." He placed the coin flat in the round indentation and the tool dipped down on its end, like a see-saw with only one rider. "See how it's heavy on the coin end? That's how it should be if it's real. Fakes are usually much lighter."

Lindsay was far from convinced. "Okay, what if it's the perfect size but is a gold-plated slug of some other kind of metal, maybe some kind of heavy alloy? There's no way you can tell without drilling a hole in it, and I doubt your buyer would go for that."

He shook his head as he smiled slightly. "That's what I thought, too. But check this out." He took the other plastic tool that looked like a big clothespin and loaded the coin between the pincers. He pulled up an app on his phone and placed it next to the tool on the table. Using his finger to pull down a small, spring-loaded plastic hammer incorporated in the tool, he then released it, allowing it to strike the edge of the Krugerrand. A sweet tone resonated from the coin, and a second later the readout on the phone confirmed that it was indeed genuine.

"Whoa! That's pretty neat," Lindsay said.

"Hopefully neat enough to make sure the coins are the real McCoys. But the theory is nothing new. You know how all antique cash registers have marble shelves over the drawer part? That was so the clerk could bounce silver and gold coins on them to make sure they were real. Every type of metal coin makes its own unique sound."

She still looked worried. "But what kind of buyer uses gold coins to purchase a boat? That still sounds really sketchy."

"He said he's from Bermuda, and he'll be registering the boat there. I guess as a foreign national he's avoiding the US banks so as not to attract attention to himself, then have to deal with all that paperwork. Bringing in this much money from offshore could raise a lot of flags. In any case, I don't mind getting paid with over a thousand gold coins. We can keep them in the safe, and cash a few in at a time. Chris said he'd love to buy all that we want to sell; there's a drought in the market right now, and the price is moving up."

"I don't know..." Lindsay said, her brow furrowing.

"Tell you what. You go with us on the sea trial in an hour, and if after you meet the guy you're still not comfortable with the idea, we'll tell him he's got to do a wire transfer instead. But you have to admit, the idea of having a thousand gold coins is kind of cool, don't you think?"

"I think you've been watching those Scrooge McDuck cartoons again."

He laughed, "Hey, don't pick on Scrooge; he's my idol!"

Rolling her eyes she said, "That's what I'm afraid of."

ROBERT OUTERBRIDGE PROVED to be a smooth talker and an impeccable dresser. His boat shoes looked like they had come straight out of the box, and his khaki pants had razor-sharp creases. A polo shirt and aviator glasses completed his ensemble, making him look like he'd just stepped out of a preppy clothing catalog. Even after a run at wide-open-throttle with the wind whipping over the flying bridge, he seemed not to have a single blond hair out of place. *The guy must use hairspray*, Murph thought.

Outerbridge appeared to be somewhere between Lindsay and Murph in both age and height. When he spoke, he said all the right things to put the two of them at ease. He should've been really easy to like, but Lindsay's intuition kept silently screaming at her to keep her guard up.

Maybe part of that was motivated by the short, muscular guy who accompanied him. The guy who hadn't said a single word to them during the hour-long sea trial, giving Lindsay the creeps.

Outerbridge was now at the helm, a huge smile on his face as he backed the Merritt into her slip. He obviously had a lot of experience handling boats. Then again, being from Bermuda this wasn't all that unusual. They all went down into the cabin and sat around the L-shaped couch as Robert addressed Murph.

"She's everything you said and more. At the price we agreed on, and with the current price of Krugerrands, we're just two shy of 1,100 coins. What say you fill her with fuel, and I'll throw in those two." He nodded to his associate, who placed two stout-handled black cloth bags on the table, opening the zippers. Outerbridge reached inside the first one and pulled out a clear plastic sleeve filled with twenty of the bright yellow coins. "Fifty-five rolls, twenty coins each. About eighty-three pounds of gold." He carefully emptied each bag, arranging the rolls in rows on the table. "And I'll throw in the carrying bags as well." He smiled, flashing his over-whitened teeth.

Murph chose two rolls at random, one from each bag, and removed a coin from the center of each. Taking the two black plastic tools, his phone, and a small electronic scale out of his pocket, he looked at Outerbridge, who was unconcerned. "Nothing personal, Robert."

"No offense taken. I checked each one the same way when I acquired them. You can never be too careful these days." He smiled at Lindsay as if to reassure her as well. Or maybe it was a cover as he checked her out more closely.

The two coins that Murph had chosen at random proved to be genuine. He then weighed each of the fifty-five rolls, all of which were dead on in their expected weights. Each coin had one troy ounce of gold, and 0.197 troy ounce of copper, to make it more durable.

"Okay, looks like we're good to go." Murph slid a couple of papers across the table. "Here's your bill of sale, and if you wouldn't mind signing this receipt, saying you've taken possession of the boat."

Outerbridge nodded. "Assuming all liability from this point on. I completely understand."

Lindsay asked, "Will you be keeping her here?"

He repeated his shark-toothed smile as he once again focused on her. "As much as I'd like to since this is quite a 'happening place,' I have a private dock all ready for her, and we'll be leaving for there shortly."

He didn't elaborate beyond that, and Lindsay didn't push. The truth was that while she went along with the coin part of the deal, she didn't like nor trust Robert Outerbridge and was happy that he wouldn't be sticking around. She glanced over at Murph, who appeared almost mesmerized as he returned the rolls of coins to the two carrying bags. "Well, we had better go, Murph, and let these gentlemen get on their way."

"Hmm?" Murph looked up after loading the last roll. "Oh, right. I'll tell the fuel dock to top off your tanks and put it on my account. Well, good luck with *Irish Luck*; I hope you enjoy her as much as we did."

Outerbridge almost leered as he replied, looking from Murph to Lindsay, "I'm sure I will."

"Okay Linds, you take one bag, and I'll take the other."

Outerbridge watched the two leave, his gaze dropping down just below Lindsay's belt line as she went through the cabin door. Then he turned to his associate, who had taken out a tablet and was concentrating on the screen. "Is it working?"

"Yeah. It's showing forty-three pounds each including the bag weight, and they're heading down the dock on the other side of the marina. We'll know when and where they unload 'em." Each bag had tiny electronic scales and small wireless GPS tracking transmitters embedded in the handles.

"Perfect. See if you can link the tablet with the television." Outerbridge pushed a button on a remote control, and a "smart" flatscreen rose out of the countertop of the wet bar. A minute later an aerial view of *Mallard Cove* appeared on the screen. Two dots were moving in tandem around the marina basin. But instead of heading for the office as Outerbridge had figured, they split off and were moving toward the tree line at the eastern end of the property. And instead of stopping, they now were moving through and beyond the trees.

"What the hell is this? Give me that tablet." Outerbridge took it from the other man and expanded the view, revealing another, smaller basin and a handful of boats in slips. "I'll be damned, they've got another marina, a small private one." As they watched, the two blips moved onto what appeared to be a houseboat. A minute later the scale readouts went to zero, and the men still watched in silence. Two minutes later the readouts jumped, but this time only showed a pound each.

"They've unloaded the bags, Danny. Meaning they're storing the coins on that boat. Also means they have them stashed someplace aboard where they feel they're safe. Otherwise, they'd have gone straight to some bank's safety deposit vault. That's the thing about gold, most folks want to keep it close by. So those coins will be right there waiting for us to come and take them back."

The other man grunted in reply while intently studying what was on the television. He already knew he'd be actively involved in the operation to retrieve the coins. His boss widened the view, showing more details of the facility.

"Quite a place. From this side of the woods, you'd never know it's there. Looks like a helicopter pad and a pool with a huge pool house. That's quite a yacht at this other end of the basin. I wonder who belongs to all these boats, and how often they're around. That might complicate things a bit. You'll need to study this, and I'll come up with a plan.

"Since they've seen us both, we won't want to be seen around here again. I'll send Jerry over to snoop around. Since I doubt they'll be moving those coins, we'll want them to have time to forget about us, and maybe sell a few or show them off a bit. That way when they disappear, they won't connect it with us. Okay, let's go fuel up and head to our dock."

2

TIME OUT

Back aboard their houseboat home, *On Coastal Time*—or as their friends had renamed it, *"OCT"*—Murph unloaded the bags. He had installed a small built-in safe in their stateroom not long after they bought the houseboat. It was used mostly for emergency cash, along with a few handguns and ammunition. The gold now took up almost half of the safe's interior, crowding everything else. He pulled out one roll of coins before closing and locking the safe. Lindsay walked into the room, having been on her phone in the salon.

"Why didn't you leave that roll in the safe with the rest?" she asked.

"I figured on making a run over to Chris Luck's shop and cashing it in. Start slowly converting a few of 'em."

"In that case, let's pack one of those new bags with clothes for two nights, and we'll make a trip out of it."

Murph asked, "Where are we going?"

"The place where I just made a reservation, where nobody can find us. A getaway, just the two of us, and that's all you need to know."

"We're driving?"

She grinned. "You are. I'm navigating."

"More like nag-ivating."

"Keep it up and I'll be the one driving, and you'll be riding on the roof."

~

"Here you go, Murph." Chris Luck placed three packs of hundred-dollar bills with mustard-colored straps on the counter and began counting out several loose bills, which he placed next to them.

"Great, Chris, thanks!" Murph gingerly slid two packs, better known in currency circles as "straps," into his pants pockets and then handed the other strap and the loose bills to Lindsay, who put them in her purse.

"I'll be happy to take any more 'rands' off your hands when you're ready. Like I was telling you, they're a bit scarce now."

Lindsay asked, "Why is that?"

"Well, they're the most popular and recognizable gold coin in the world. And like yours today, they are easily convertible into other currencies. Plus, without serial numbers, they're next to impossible to trace," Chis replied.

"Sounds like they would be popular with the drug cartels," Murph suggested.

Chris nodded. "They used to be fond of thousand-dollar bills, back before the Fed quit printing them for that very reason. A million dollars in thousands was only ten straps. Now, as I'm guessing you already know, a million bucks in Krugerrands is around five hundred coins, and about forty pounds. Not quite as compact or light as a million in thousand-dollar bills, but harder to trace. So, there's a tradeoff."

Murph asked, "Are you going to be around your boat this weekend?"

"Hoping to. But I need to see what the rest of the week ends up looking like first."

"We're going out of town for a couple of days, but we should be back by then. I want to buy you lunch for loaning me those tools and the coin, as well as for the education."

"You don't have to do that; I appreciate your business."

Lindsay said, "We insist. And we appreciate your business as well."

"In that case, I'll make sure to come over to the '*Cove*.' Thanks, guys."

~

"SERIOUSLY? I've been driving for over an hour; you need to tell me where we're going," an exasperated Murph said.

The couple had made their way through Yorktown, then crossed the York River. They had passed through Gloucester and several small towns. Mostly endless farms and thick woods now lined the sides of the John Clayton Memorial Highway on Virginia's "middle neck." They were approaching the end of that road, coming up to the point where they had to go left or right at Buckley Hall Road. A road sign pointed to Gwynn's Island to the left, and Mathews to the right.

"Aha! We're going to our *Gwynn's Island Hotel and Marina*! Great, I've been wanting to stay there to try it out." The investment group had purchased the old decrepit marina and hotel last fall, having just recently completed the renovations.

Lindsay shook her head, smiling. "Nope. Take a right."

"We're going to Mathews? What's in Mathews?"

"We're going *through* Mathews, though we'll have dinner there tonight. We're going to Port Haywood."

Murph looked confused. "Never heard of it."

"Which is part of the point of a getaway, don't you think? Going to new places where you don't know anyone, and not a single soul knows you." Her smile became a triumphant one. "Back at *Mallard Cove*, everybody knows us or wants to, so we can never truly relax. And relaxation is what where we are headed is all about."

"What's this place called?"

"The *Talbot Creek Inn*."

Murph said, "Never heard of it, either."

"I know! I had to do a lot of research just to find it. Isn't it great?"

"We'll see. Heck, I haven't even been to Mathews. What's there?"

"Great little independent shops, and according to the online reviews, some of the best little restaurants going. In fact, those outnumber national fast-food restaurants ten to one in that area; there are only two chain restaurants in the whole county! The chefs of these great independent restaurants are mostly homegrown, though some have had some formal training outside the area. But they all either never left or they came back home, and they're building quite a following," Lindsay said.

"And all not that far from our *Gwynn's Island Hotel and Marina*. I like it! We didn't even know about this part when we stumbled onto that property, and this will be a great asset for it. Though we already knew about the *Bay Breeze Restaurant* of course. And by the way, I want to go back and eat there while we're here," Murph said. *Bay Breeze* was a fantastic little "dock and dine" restaurant on the water almost adjacent to the new hotel.

"It's on the itinerary for tomorrow, babe."

"Wait, we have an *itinerary*? I thought we were here for some rest and relaxation. I didn't realize we had a schedule to keep."

Lindsay nodded, "Yep. The best of these restaurants fill up fast for dinner. If you don't have reservations, on a lot of nights you'll be on a long waitlist, or maybe out of luck altogether. But wait until you see their menus. About as unique as you'll find outside of DC or New York. Just trust me, I've got a lot planned for us the next few days."

Five minutes later they were driving through Mathews, which turned out to be a quaint little town, just a few blocks long. It was obvious that most of the old downtown area had recently undergone an extensive renovation. Many of the boutiques and shops that now occupied the main drag looked new.

Murph commented, "Don't blink or you'll miss it."

"Yes, but what's here is really cool! And enough stores to make a day of it, shopping-wise."

Murph rolled his eyes, "Oh, goody." Shopping was not high on his list of fun things to do unless it had to do with boats or fishing tackle.

Lindsay swatted his arm. "I get to have a little fun too, you know."

"So long as there's a bar nearby, we're good."

"You're not just going to sit at some bar this whole trip. You've got to do at least some shopping with me."

The eye roll again along with a sarcastic, "Yes dear." Both earned him another arm swat. That's when he noticed the town had ended and they were once again bordered by woods. "So where's this Port whatever place?"

"Port Haywood, and it's a couple of miles ahead. We take a right on Terrapin Lane."

A few minutes later they spotted a handful of buildings on both sides of the road. Lindsay said, "Turn around, babe. I think we just passed it."

"What, that alley is the 'lane?' It's barely wide enough for one car!"

The narrow dirt road was easy to miss, sandwiched between a whitewashed block wall of a defunct service station and the side of a building that housed a deli. Murph backtracked and turned onto the road. A small sign tacked up on a telephone pole read, "Yes, this IS the turn!"

"Well, at least they have a sense of humor about it. And when you said it was 'a place where nobody can find us' you weren't kidding, Linds. It would take a bloodhound to pick up our trail down here."

"Quit griping and keep driving! The pictures on the website were adorable."

Over to their right, they passed the backlot of a construction company with decrepit supply trailers and various cast-off equipment. On the left side was an old abandoned house. Murph said, "You know, it's not too late to book a room over on Gwynn's Island."

"Trust me, babe, you'll love this place. I think being so remote is part of its appeal."

Murph grunted in reply, then a couple of hundred yards later turned onto an orange sand driveway with oyster shell patches where several potholes had been filled. Another few hundred yards ahead was a huge two-story home that looked to have been built at least as far back as the 1800s. A modern pool was beside it, and beyond that was a small boat ramp next to a nice wooden dock that extended out into Talbot Creek. An old deadrise workboat was tied up on the tee out at the end.

Murph nodded his approval, "Not bad. I dig the deadrise, too. Kinda adds atmosphere to the place."

"Well, it's not like this place lacks any of that! I think the inn is really cute. And I'm glad you like that boat because we're booked on the sunset cruise aboard it this afternoon," Lindsay said. "Grab the bag and let's go check in."

~

OUTERBRIDGE AND DANNY had tied up the soon-to-be "ex" *Irish Luck* in her new slip over an hour ago. After Robert left, Danny went back to studying the layout of the private marina and the interesting facility next door. He also was following the movement of one of the bags that had held the coins. It had started moving about the same time as *Irish Luck* had left *Mallard Cove*.

He'd identified the first stop in Virginia Beach as having been at a coin dealer, which was not all that surprising. But it was this second stop that had been concerning enough for him to text Outerbridge, asking him to come back to the boat.

"What is it?" Outerbridge asked as he came back into the boat's salon.

"I think they sold some of the gold. One bag left the marina, then they stopped at a coin shop. They just stopped again, and the bag is now half a kilo lighter. But where they stopped is why I texted you." He pointed at the screen.

Outerbridge's brow furrowed. "Across from the farm? Who *are* these people?"

"I don't know. But I'm gonna find out."

"Find out fast. I'm not a big believer in coincidences, and Jerry has to do a pick-up there tomorrow."

"I know."

"Well, if one or both of them are over on the west shore, tonight would be the best time to make a run at getting my coins back. We'll send Jerry over in the inflatable. It looks like that ramp next to the helipad would be a good landing spot away from most anybody. If someone spots him, he can claim engine trouble by pulling his fuel line loose."

Danny replied, "Yeah. Good plan. I'll tell him to get on it."

MURPH SAT in the cramped wheelhouse across from the old deadrise boat's captain, watching as he made their way around the bend in the creek and out toward the open water of Mobjack Bay.

"Smooth riding rig, Cap'n." He raised his bottle of beer in a salute.

The captain glanced over at Murph, "Thanks, Mr. Murphy. Wish I could take credit for it, but I only rebuilt her; the hull was already there. That's the nice thing about an old wood boat, you can keep repairing and replacing parts of it as they wear out or rot. Plus, the sound it makes going through the water is so much sweeter than a fiberglass hull."

Murph said, "Just call me Murph. I've had both kinds and you're right. I think a lot of wood hulls raise more fish, too."

"That may be true. 'Specially over those thin hulled 'glass boats that are so dang noisy. And my name's Red."

"Nice to meet ya, Red. I moved up to ESVA a few years back from Florida. There are fewer and fewer of the older wooden fishing boats down there now. Most are fiberglass, and they're getting bigger and bigger, pricing the smaller rigs out of the marinas. When I moved up here, I was really happy to find so many local wood boatbuilders still making the traditional designs."

Red sighed, "Not near as many as there used to be, and a lot of the younger ones have started building fiberglass boats now, too. Those are so much faster and cheaper to build, and you don't need as many real craftsmen. Back in the day, everybody in a building crew knew their way around wood. They knew how to pick it, cut it, laminate or steam bend it, and how to go into the woods and spot a tree with the right bends and curves for the shape and strength they needed.

"Nowadays, they just slap another layer of glass in the mold for more strength. The only real craftsmen are the ones who build the 'plugs' they use to make the molds, and some of them are even made with computers. Those kinda things don't have any soul. And there are fewer and fewer folks around here that can appreciate an old boat like this."

"Well, I sure do. I've been reading up on some of the old bay designs, both power, and sail. Went up to that museum in St. Michaels where they restore the old wood rigs. Bought a few books on those old designs." Murph had a faraway look on his face as if seeing back into the past.

The captain nodded and said, "This area used to be big in boat building. Over in Deltaville, too. Real craftsmen. Now there's some left, here and there, but as the fishing started dying out they didn't need that many new boats. A lot of the old small boatyards are gettin' bought up and replaced with houses, big'uns that no waterman can afford. Change is happening fast around here. Nice to run into somebody like yourself that's got an appreciation for the old ways."

"There's a lot to be said for them."

"There is at that."

Murph looked down at his now empty beer bottle, "I guess I better refuel, and spend some time with my lady. It's supposed to be a getaway, just the two of us, and she's sitting back there by herself with those other two couples."

"Yep, you'd better at that. But I enjoyed talkin' with you, Murph."

"Yeah, me too, Red."

Murph grabbed another beer from the boat's cooler, then sat back down next to Lindsay, who was in a conversation with an older couple and hadn't seemed to have noticed his absence. Then she turned to him and smiled before turning back and resuming her conversation.

He looked out over the side, locating the channel markers as they passed out of the East River into Mobjack Bay. It was something he did when on new water with someone else at the helm. Should anything happen to the captain, he'd be able to navigate their way back. It was an occupational hazard with Murph, never fully relaxing when someone else was running a boat he was on.

The dark water had only a light chop, and the breeze driving it was warm. He studied the low clouds to the west; they should make for a spectacular sunset. To the east, beyond Mobjack Bay, and across the Chesapeake lay Cape Charles, though it was just out of sight. A huge freighter was making its way north, probably bound for the Port of Baltimore or maybe the Annapolis anchorage. No doubt there were people over in Cape Charles that were watching this same ship just as he was, even if he couldn't see that land from where they were. He smiled at the irony.

"Penny for your thoughts, babe," Lindsay said, her head slightly tilted. She was wondering what had inspired the slight smile that Murph now wore.

"Hmm? Oh, just enjoying the ride, the scenery, and the company. I guess I needed this little getaway of yours more than I thought."

"Little getaway of *ours*. And yes, you did. We both did." She put an arm across his shoulders, leaning over against him.

MURPH HAD BEEN CORRECT, the sunset was indeed spectacular. It had been a long time since they'd seen one together out on the water. Too long. He made a mental note to take *LNZ II* out and watch future ones on calm afternoons.

As they headed back toward the East River, he also made a note of the steady white light of New Point Comfort Lighthouse, at the mouth of Mobjack Bay. It was one of the oldest lights on the Chesapeake and could be seen for over ten miles at night. A green flashing light marked the mouth of the East River, and a couple of others marked the channel well.

The turn into Talbot Creek wasn't marked, though it wasn't necessary since the captain had his GPS fired up, clearly showing the shoreline on the screen. All of these navigation features were now

filed away in the back corner of Murph's brain, added to his collection of mental charts of the Chesapeake. All of them were created
from experience; something you couldn't get from a screen or a paper
chart. Little did he know he'd be using this new knowledge much
sooner than he'd have ever thought.

~

Just before midnight...

Jerry killed the engine on the small rigid-hulled inflatable boat
(RHIB) letting its momentum carry him the rest of the way over to the
seaplane ramp. Rather than pull it up in the long wild grass on either
side to hide it, he pulled the bow up onto the concrete. If he was spotted, it would be easier to sell the "engine trouble" story if it didn't look
like he was trying to conceal the boat. He'd loosened the gas line
connector at the portable tank, which would take only seconds to
"fix" but would also explain the problem. He started walking up the
ramp, being careful not to make any noise.

Casey Shaw sat in a patio chair in front of his stone fire pit at the
Cove Club, or as his friends had nicknamed it, *C2.* This was the facility
he'd built for entertaining at *Casey's Cove,* the name of their small
private marina adjacent to *Mallard Cove.* It had a lot of features that
most of the boats here lacked. There was the helipad and seaplane
ramp, a hot tub and pool, and a two-story thatched chickee tower
built by a Seminole Indian friend of his. The building next to the
pool had a guest room, pool table, and indoor bar. But Casey's
favorite feature at *C2* was his outdoor kitchen. The fire pit was
between it and the pool and was a close second for being his favorite.

He stared into the fire, the final logs of the night slowly
succumbing to the flames as his last beer of the night was nearly
empty. Dawn had gone back to their floating home, the *Lady Dawn,*

almost an hour before. This was the large yacht that Outerbridge had seen in the satellite picture. While he loved that boat, he loved this fire pit almost as much. Sitting here earlier tonight with his wife, and now with only his Golden Retriever named Bimini, he was at peace with the world.

Bim was noisily gnawing on the leftover bone from a "tomahawk steak" —a ribeye with the bone still attached. Casey and Dawn had grilled and split the steak between them earlier, carving it off of the bone while leaving a nice strip of meat on it for Bimini. Ribeye bones to him were as much a favorite as this place was to Casey. That's why Casey was surprised to see him stop, turn and look in the direction of the helipad with a deep growl. Without any moon tonight, Casey couldn't see what Bim was worried about. Then the growl became a loud protective bark and snarl, sounds he very seldom made.

Like most Goldens, Bimini was more of a lover than a fighter, though he was very protective of Dawn and Casey. And ribeye bones. Whatever he was sensing now had him on high alert, and he was letting loose with a vicious-sounding string of barks.

"Who's out there?" When he didn't hear a reply, Casey added, "Answer me or I'll turn the dog loose." Which was a bluff, because Bim already had free rein of all twenty-one fenced acres of *Casey's Cove* and C2. This, and the fact he wouldn't leave Casey's side with a threat out there. He'd stay close to protect and defend his master at all costs.

A moment later they heard a small, quiet four-stroke outboard accelerate to full speed from over by the seaplane ramp, as Bim went silent again. Casey reached over and scratched him behind his ears. "Good boy, Bim. I don't know how you heard them over all that racket you were making with the bone, but I'm glad you did. Let's head back to the boat. I'll let the gang know in the morning that we had an uninvited visitor."

JERRY WAS SURPRISED to see the low glow of a dying fire over past the pool this late at night. Then he was even more surprised to hear a dog snarl and start barking. From the sound, he could tell it was a big dog, not one of his favorite things. He had always hated dogs ever since being bitten as a kid and having to endure a series of painful rabies shots. He heard someone threaten to release the dog, and that was all the incentive he needed to turn and race back to the RHIB. If Robert wanted those damn coins, he was going to have to figure another way to get them back. He wasn't about to risk getting bitten again.

3

THE GRAND ILLUSION

*I**n a suite at the finest waterfront hotel in St. Michaels, Maryland, a few hours before midnight...***

Jock "Jacques" Danville slowly caressed the face of the woman in the bed next to him as she sighed. The only light in the room came in through the windows facing the little harbor, a dim glow from the lights along the walkway leading to the hotel's dock. In the soft light, it was hard to see that she was almost fifteen years his senior. The low light as well as all the "work" that had been done by the best plastic surgeon in Switzerland helped hide much of the sun damage accumulated at the world's best coastal resorts. Most of it, but not all.

"I wish you could take me with you, Jacques," she said sadly. She knew it was impossible though, for too many reasons.

"You know that with what I have to do, Claire, and with the people that I am up against, it's far too dangerous for you to be with me when I leave. You mustn't even mention my name to anyone." *Especially anyone who knows your husband, who was away on an extended business trip,* he silently thought to himself.

"Where do you go from here? Will I ever see you again?"

"I hope we will be together again after I secure my true birthright. Then I will contact you and have you come and join me after I return our just rule to my people and I stop their exploitation by France and the Church.

"However, as far as where I am heading next, it's best that you don't know. I must raise more funds to hire the men I will need to fight alongside me. I'll be fighting for my people, but most of the men who will be with me do not fight for honor and justice, only for cash. But this is what must be done to free my country from such an unholy alliance."

Silently she reached over and retrieved something from the nightstand, turning back to him and pressing a cold metal and stone piece into his hand. It was what had originally caught his eye when he'd spotted her almost two weeks ago—her vintage eighteen-karat gold bracelet by Harry Winston. Absolutely stunning, with seven cabochon emeralds weighing almost seven carats, and just under two hundred diamonds with a combined weight of just under fifteen carats. He knew the retail value was close to $100,000.

"What's this?" he asked.

"Take it. Use the money it will bring to help free your people."

He thrust it back into her hand, "I can't accept this, Claire."

She shoved it back into his hand and said, "It's not for you to accept or decline, it's for your people."

He hesitated, just long enough before saying, "In that case, I'll accept it on their behalf. But how will you explain it to..." He wanted to show concern for her, but stopped short of saying "...your husband." Now was not the time to break the mood.

"I'll say that I lost it overboard on a boat. I'm sure that he... I'm sure it is insured, and I couldn't wear it now in good conscience after what I've learned about you and your people. But don't worry, and let's not waste time talking. You said you had to leave on the flood tide, and that will happen all too soon."

JUST AFTER MIDNIGHT, Jock followed the walkway down to the dock, then climbed aboard his inflatable tender. He cranked the small four-stroke outboard and headed for the tallest anchor light in the side harbor. He smiled when he recalled the line about "leaving on the flood tide," because he'd been reminded of that in an old movie he'd just watched. His sixty-eight-foot Palmer Johnson sloop *Mistral* did indeed have a full keel, and she drew a lot more water than similar-sized sailboats with retractable centerboards. But here on the Miles River, the natural channel was deep. In fact, he had plenty of depth out to the shipping channel in the Chesapeake, no matter what the tide.

The truth was that his flood tide remark had less to do with water depth than timing. *Mistral's* next port of call would be a place called *Bayside Resort,* farther down the Eastern Shore in Virginia. He'd learned that it was a gathering place for the well-to-do from DC and Northern Virginia. Numerous centimillionaires and the occasional billionaire or two were known to frequent the place. But more importantly, it was a hangout for the women of these men while they were away on business, as well as rich widows and divorcées. In other words, his idea of a target-rich environment.

Some of these women were extremely bored; they craved excitement and adventure beyond the spa treatments they would undergo there to pass the time. Many could be easily lured into trysts by a handsome, tan, and dashing man in his mid-forties who arrived solo on his sailing yacht. A man with an exciting story to tell, one that they would be eager to hear, believe, and promise to keep in confidence. Well, almost. Some of these promises would be broken, though the stories would be repeated only to their closest confidantes, women who were mostly as corrupt and/or bored as they were. The stories that Jock told would top most, if not all of the ones those bored women shared. Also in strict confidence, of course.

There was a private club at *Bayside*, with an exclusive member's list. This was to be Jock's next hunting ground. At an earlier stopover in Annapolis, he'd gotten into a poker game with a *Bayside Club* member on the fellow's yacht, and had taken the guy and his friends for quite a pile of chips. It finally came time to settle up, and after the other players had left, Jock magnanimously offered the man a trade. He could have his check back in exchange for having a glass of scotch with him on the yacht's aft deck, though he kept all the money from the man's friends.

One glass became many, stories were shared, and by the time he left, it was with a new "close friend" and the promise of a guest pass for the club waiting for him at *Bayside* whenever he arrived there this summer. Turning down the man's check had greatly added to his bona fides, though he knew his hunt there would likely net him a huge multiple of the amount that had been written on it.

By leaving St. Michaels tonight when he did, it assured he'd arrive at *Bayside* in the early to mid-morning. Most of the women he targeted were not early risers and were more likely to take their breakfast around then. In digging through the internet he'd discovered that the *Bayside Club* was famous for their breakfast brunch on the outdoor terrace, overlooking the Chesapeake. The channel leading to the club's private marina tucked in close to the shoreline right in front of that terrace, giving everyone there a grand view of his arrival. He couldn't have scripted a better entrance if he tried. In his business, research was crucial to success.

Jock was good at scripting and stories; it had been how he made his living for over the last decade and a half. Back then, in his mid-twenties, he'd worked on private yachts in the Mediterranean. During this earlier career, he'd seen his share of bored women of the idle rich that either owned the boats or were guests aboard them. Then by chance, he watched a movie about an older playboy con man working out of a villa in the South of France. The man pretended to be a prince in exile, plotting to retake his throne. In reality, this cad was only plotting to talk rich women out of their valuables, as well as their clothing. And he was very successful at doing both.

At first, he found it hard to believe that such a simple plot could be credible, that people could be this dense. But then he started studying the women who stayed on the yacht where he worked. He realized there were two types of them; the sharp ones who were successful in their own right, or the bored ones who preferred to enjoy the fruits of what they inherited, received as a settlement, or that others provided. Those were the ones he focused on, the bored ones. Especially the ones whose husbands were more busy making money than paying attention to their wives.

Boredom had a funny effect on many people, making them more susceptible to believing in fantasies. He quickly discovered how easy it was for these bored women to accept his wild stories. He found that the wilder the tales were, the easier it was to "sell" them. Many were so eager for excitement that they would do almost anything to get away from their existence, if only for a while. They saw themselves as being stuck doing the same thing, day in and day out. Granted, they lived in very luxurious surroundings that most other women would give anything for, but excitement can be the most enticing and intoxicating drug on earth.

Jock reasoned that while he had a natural ability to react quickly to different situations and talk his way out of most anything, it was important for his story to have a valid starting point. His tales must be based on facts that might be easily checked. During his days off he started researching the smaller principalities of Europe, searching for a place where he could set his latest story. He not only found the perfect place in Andorra, but someone in its past was also the perfect character on which to build his own story.

Andorra is a tiny country of 77,000 inhabitants on the border of Spain and France, created by Charlemagne. Its main industry is tourism, and with its numerous ski resorts as well as casinos, it hosts over ten million visitors annually. The governmental arrangement is very unique, technically being ruled by two "princes." The first is the Roman Catholic Bishop of Urgell, Spain, and the second is the President of France. It has been this way since the removal of a very short-lived king—"Boris the First"—back in 1934. This man, Boris Skossyreff, was a Russian immigrant who claimed to be a descendent of Charlemagne and also the rightful ruler of Andorra. He ruled long enough to establish a brief constitution, declare the country a tax haven and begin to lure foreign investment, then institute confidential banking services and establish the first casinos.

King Boris's mostly popular yet quasi-illegitimate rule might have lasted much longer if he hadn't declared war on the Bishop of Urgell.

Then again, it probably would have helped the war effort if Andorra had owned an actual army. Back in Spain though, the bishop did have his armed force which was quickly dispatched to Andorra to arrest Boris. He was brought to Spain where he was tried, convicted, then subsequently and rather rapidly deported.

In the years following Boris's reign, the dual princes established a business tax, which was favored by most everyone in Andorra except the business owners. But more recently they imposed a personal income tax, something that is now very unfavorable among the populace. Unfortunately for the people of the country, they had no recourse, since their leaders were chosen by the people of France and the Vatican, not Andorra.

Andorra's tale was all but custom-tailored to Jock's needs. A quick search of the internet would verify much of his story. Where it started veering away from the truth was when he claimed to be descended from Charlemagne and King Boris I. Also the part about planning to overthrow the dual princes' rule and abolish the income taxes. But the idea of getting rid of taxes was usually very popular with his target audience. This was designed to make himself seem both more trustworthy, as well as a valid reason for his having the support of the populace of Andorra.

Now imagine how exciting it would be to have such a crucial role in helping the rightful heir to the throne of Andorra take his place as the just leader of his people. All it took was a "small" donation of cash, jewelry, gold, or precious stones. This, and keeping it all in confidence until after "King Jacques" was successful in his mission, since his very life could well depend upon your silence. He was quick to tell you that he had such powerful enemies who would imprison him or even worse if they knew he was amassing a war chest.

But oh, what a story you will eventually have to tell at cocktail parties in Manhattan, Martha's Vineyard, DC, Palm Beach, or South Beach once he was successful. And there was little doubt that he'll be successful. Spend two minutes talking with him and you'll be certain of that. Spend even longer chatting and you could easily find yourself living out your very own fairy tale, if only for a short while.

~

BACK IN ROBERT'S OFFICE, Jerry gave him his embellished story. "I didn't have any choice, Robert, I had ta beat it out of there. That dog almost got to me before I made it back to the boat."

His boss replied sarcastically, "Wonderful, now they know someone was sneaking onto the place."

"Yeah, but they don't know who or why. I never saw the guy that sicced the dog on me, and he never got a look at me. I think it was the dog that let him know I was there. He might not even have been the guy you bought the boat from, and they might not figure me being there was about those coins."

Robert said sarcastically, "Unless they hate coincidences just as much as I do. Then Murphy will move those coins to some place where we can't find or get near them."

"But I thought you said one of the bags is at the inn across the creek from Cho's farm?"

"So what?"

"Then that wasn't him I run into. He might not hear about me bein' there when he gets back. An' whoever it was with the dog might not know about those coins. So, they'll still be on that houseboat. He don't have a reason ta move 'em. Probably thinks they're safe, bein' close to him an' his pals in that little marina."

Outerbridge stroked his chin in thought. "You may have a point. We know he was dealing with that coin shop in Virginia Beach. Why don't you go over there now and nose around? See if you can find out what they know about Murphy's coins, and if he mentioned having or even trading more of them."

After dismissing Jerry, Robert called Danny in. "What did you find out about why they're at Talbot Creek?"

"That gardener at the inn who keeps an eye on Cho for us says they're just there to relax. They haven't taken any interest in the farm. Even took the sunset tourist cruise on the inn's deadrise."

"I still don't like it. Tell him to keep an extra good eye on these two."

"Already did."

~

As usual, Jock's timing was right on the mark, as he passed by the terrace at the peak of brunch. *Mistral* was impressive, her shiny dark blue hull reflecting the small white bow wake as she slipped on by. Leaving nothing to chance, he had motored all the way down from St. Michaels, not wanting to be dependent on the wind to determine his arrival time. And by being under power she was also perfectly level, instead of heeling over like she would have been under sail. This gave everyone on the terrace an unobstructed view of her beautiful teak decks and Matterhorn white superstructure. And even more importantly, her solo, tan and toned, shirtless captain.

One of those who took particular notice was Andrea Coyne, an auburn-haired attractive woman in her mid-forties. The Bloody Mary on the table in front of her was her second of the morning. It had just started to dull the throb in her head, a souvenir of the previous night where she had tried liberally applying alcohol to make her date more attractive and entertaining. It hadn't worked. Sadly, the guy had been the pick of the unattached men at the club at the time, but she ended up stranding him at the club's bar. She had been considering going back to DC this morning, after last night's disaster.

But now Andrea was laser focused on the skipper of the beautiful yacht that was headed to the marina. He turned and looked over at the terrace, and for a minute their eyes met. Even at this distance, she saw him smile, and for a brief second, she forgot about her pounding head. She scanned the boat, expecting some young thing in a micro-tini to pop up through a hatch with an armful of dock lines. Then she noticed the pre-positioned fenders already hanging down the side of the hull, the coiled dock lines up on the bow, and more lines by the mid-ship spring cleats, and back at the stern. Apparently, he was single-handing this large sloop, a feat only someone with a deep depth of experience should attempt. Very impressive. She thought to herself that things might just be looking up around here after all. And DC wasn't going anywhere; it could wait.

"YOU COULD WORK off some of that breakfast by going into more stores with me," Lindsay suggested. Murph was parked on a bench next to the visitor's center on the town's main drag.

"Hey, I did three stores with you, that's my limit on shopping. You said this trip was all about relaxation. I'm relaxing. At least I'm not in a bar."

"It's only eleven o'clock! None of the restaurants that serve alcohol are even open yet."

"Don't remind me. But speaking of restaurants, don't forget that I want to eat at *Bay Breeze*."

"Kind of hard to forget babe, since you've reminded me every ten minutes. Don't worry, we'll go there today for lunch."

"Aw, gee, that means you'll only have time for one more store before we have to head over there."

Lindsay grinned slyly, "Three more, and only if you come with me. Otherwise, I might just keep on going. Don't forget, I'm the one with the truck keys."

Murph jumped up, "You make a valid point. Let's go shopping, and then we can eat!"

JERRY SAID, "I told the guy that I was interested in Krugerrands. He said they're hard to come by, though he'd just gotten ten in, but they were already sold ta people he's got on a waiting list. But he said the collector he'd gotten 'em from mentioned he'd be unloading more of 'em in a few weeks. He offered ta put me on the waitlist, but I told him I was outta town a lot, and I'd just have to keep checking back when I was around. I didn't wanna give him a fake name and number so he'd get suspicious when he called an' it wasn't me."

Outerbridge nodded. "Good move, Jerry. At least you can still pop in there if I need you to."

Jerry was pleased to have made up for the prior night's mess, at least in part. "Thanks, Robert."

"I want you to be extra careful tonight. We still aren't sure what Murphy is doing over across from the farm. Don't take any unnecessary chances. And if you see anything out of the ordinary, get the hell out of there."

Jerry nodded, "Got it. You can trust me."

"You aren't who I'm worried about."

4

THE PEGGY T

At the Bayside Club's terrace, later that morning...

"Nice boat. I was surprised to see you were handling something so big all by yourself," Andrea said.

She was still at her table, nursing a third Bloody Mary as Jock was walking past. He hesitated, then smiled. "Believe it or not, she was built to be single-handed."

She caught his ever so slight and heavily rehearsed accent. "I'd love to hear more about her. Won't you sit down, or are you meeting someone?"

Jock motioned to the hostess that he had been following that he would be sitting here instead of the table that she was leading him to. He pulled out the chair on the opposite side from Andrea and sat down.

"The truth is, I only know one member, Jack Martin. We played cards a while back, and he insisted that I come here and be his guest. I'm Jacques Danville."

"Andrea Coyne." She reached a hand across the table, but to her surprise he took it as he half stood, bending down to kiss the back.

"A pleasure to meet you, Andrea."

As he sat back down she said, "I saw by your boat's hailing port that you are from Marseille."

He gave her an enigmatic smile as he said, "That is my boat's home port."

"Not yours?"

He smiled again just as a server handed him a lunch menu, interrupting his answer. He glanced at it and asked questions about several items then ordered a Caesar salad with blackened North Carolina shrimp. Looking over at her glass he added a Kalik beer to his order.

He'd taken his time with the server intentionally since he'd seen that Andrea was irritated with the interruption. It was a ploy he used to keep control of the conversation. As he handed the menu back, he looked over at Andrea, giving her his most disarming smile, derailing her train of thought.

"I hear the chef has a wonderful reputation. I've been looking forward to this stop."

The phrase "stop" confused her. "Stop? You make it sound like you are on a train."

"I didn't mean to. More like a cruise, but without other passengers."

"So what's your itinerary if you are on a cruise?"

He shrugged. "There are places I'd like to see, and people I'd like to meet. Exactly when, where, and who is up to the wind and chance. Like now, for instance, meeting you."

"You never said if Marseille was your home."

The server reappeared, pouring his Bahamian beer into a tall glass before placing it and the bottle in front of him. Again he could see that Andrea was irritated by the interruption.

"To you, Andrea," he said, raising his glass.

She did the same, countering with, "And you, the wind, and chance. Also, to home, wherever it is..." She left the end of her sentence trail off, almost like the beginning of a period of dead air on the radio.

To avoid being rude he said, "As you saw, *Mistral's* home port is Marseille."

"But not yours." More of a statement than a question.

"At times, though I can't yet return to my real home."

"Why is that? *Where* is that?"

"The answers are... complicated. Perhaps when we know each other better, I can answer both. That is *if* we get to know each other better."

He saw she was a woman who was accustomed to getting whatever she wanted, when she wanted it, including answers. His refusal to provide them could go two ways; it might infuriate her, or pique her interest. He was determined to make sure it was the latter, he just needed to play his cards as well as he had on Jack Martin's yacht. Of course, on that night he'd been cheating, so it was easier. Then again, he was even better at this game.

"I think I'd like to, how about you?" She tilted her head slightly, in a silent sign of a challenge.

"Perhaps. Though you know so much more about me than I do about you."

Which wasn't really true, he thought. He knew she'd had brunch at the most exclusive and expensive club on ESVA, and the few pieces of contemporary gold jewelry she was wearing were all custom, and expensive. But they all paled in comparison to the antique gold pendant that hung on a chain around her neck. That was what told him he'd hit the jackpot.

It was a woven gold design, hundreds of years old, and was the setting for the most stunning Colombian emerald he'd ever seen. Fourteen carats in weight, with unbelievable clarity. He knew all of this to be fact because he'd seen the auction listing for it at the famous New York auction house that sold it several years ago. Estimated at $250,000, it had brought over $400,000 at the final hammer, with the buyer's name withheld.

While the piece's weight, workmanship, and quality of the stone represented much of the value, it was the provenance attached to it that helped demand such a high premium. The original owner had been the king of Spain, although the king had never laid eyes on the piece. It had been lost in a hurricane four hundred years prior, aboard a ship named the *Nuestra Señora de Atocha,* or, as it was better and more simply known in modern times, the *Atocha*—one of the most famous shipwrecks ever discovered.

Andrea being the current owner of this piece said several things to Jock about her. Not only was she exceedingly wealthy, but she was interested in treasure and undoubtedly the ocean as well. Things that made her one of the best marks he'd ever worked. It didn't hurt that she was attractive, and had what he would describe as "spunk."

She replied, "I'm not one of my favorite subjects."

"It would seem that we have that in common. I do not like talking about myself, either. At least, until I get to know someone."

"Which makes accomplishing that quite a challenge," she said.

"Perhaps we both know more than we think. Since you had brunch outside facing the Chesapeake, I'm guessing that you like the water. I'm also guessing that your favorite color is green, since that incredible stone in your necklace matches your eyes perfectly, and you were careful to only wear plain gold accessories with it. Nothing with stones of other colors that might distract from it.

"Let's see, the fact that you aren't wearing a wedding or engagement ring and since you invited me to sit down, I'd say you are in between lovers or husbands. They might not have been able to compete with your strong personality, a woman who is very secure in her own life."

She nodded her head slightly in agreement as she clapped her hands silently. "Bravo, and well done. Now it's my turn. Obviously, you also like the water. Many people paint their boats in their favorite color, so we'll go with blue. You showed up alone and admitted that you know no one that's here now, so we'll go with you being in between lovers since I'd have a hard time believing you're celibate. If you are, that's a waste, though I highly doubt you are marrying material. Not that I'm in the market for a husband.

"You won't talk about where you are from, and you have an eye for jewels. You're either an international jewel thief on the run from

Interpol, or you bedded some Russian oligarch's concubine harem and he has a hit team out hunting you down. How'd I do?"

"You were wrong on one point."

"Which one?"

"I've never stolen a jewel in my life."

It was in fact, the truth. All the jewelry he'd conned women out of had been *given* to him, albeit under false pretenses.

Andrea burst out laughing, partly due to the third drink, but mostly because she found Jacques the most entertaining man she'd met in a while.

"I knew it! The Russians are coming!"

"A gentleman never tells if they did or not."

This time she didn't just laugh, she roared.

AT *Bay Breeze*, the pair took a table next to the big window that overlooked the dock. Murph looked up at the tarpon mount overhead and commented, "Nice 'poon."

Their server had arrived with their menus and overheard the remark. "You're lucky that I fish, and know what you meant by that, fella. Not a lot of tarpon fishermen around here."

"We're from over on ESVA, and we have a few on the ocean side in the late summer," Lindsay replied. "We've both caught our share, here as well as down in Florida."

The server nodded, "That one's from over there, near Oyster. The owner took the measurements and released it, then got the fiberglass replica made."

"The best way to do it. We released all of ours, too. Who knows, we might have caught that same fish at some point."

"Maybe so. Anyway, what can I get you folks to drink?"

Lindsay said, "White wine and a Red Stripe."

"Be right back with those while you look over the menus."

Murph locked eyes with Lindsay, "Yep, I'm marrying the right girl. You knew what I was going to order."

She rolled her eyes, "Like that was so hard. It's lunchtime, and you said you wanted a beer. Lately, that's always been a Red Stripe. But yes, you're marrying the right girl. It's not like anybody else would put up with you."

"Ouch! That's vicious... wait, what the heck is that?" He turned to stare out the window at something that he'd seen out of the corner of his eye. A small, very unique-looking sailboat about sixteen feet long was heading for the dock. The lines of the boat were definitely old-school, from the straight vertical bow stem and low-slung sides to the dual sail rig itself. The freestanding main mast was raked slightly aft with a standard-looking triangular sail, but it was the headsail that was so different. About a tenth the size of the main, but unlike most jibs, it was attached to a small freestanding mast that was angled forward, away from the larger one.

An older, balding, and gray-haired man was at the tiller. He swung wide, bringing the bow into the wind but letting the boat's momentum carry it sideways to the dock, barely bumping the outer pilings.

"He really knows what he's doing," Lindsay commented.

Their server had just arrived with their drinks and overheard her. "He should. That's old Don, and he's owned that boat since it was built by that museum boatyard up in St. Michaels over twenty years ago. He'll talk your ear off about it if you let him; he loves that thing."

Lindsay saw that Murph was transfixed, focused on the boat as the old man tied her dock lines to the pilings. Then he furled the main and loosed the jib sheet, letting the small headsail spill all its wind. Climbing out of the boat, the heavyset older man used a cane to steady himself. He hobbled up the dock with a slow, painful-looking gait and limp.

Murph said, "I'd like to know more about it. Think he'd mind if I bought him a beer and picked his brain about it?"

"I've never known him to turn one down. But don't say I didn't warn you. Once he gets wound up, he usually stays that way. Full of stories, that one is."

They saw Don come through the door a few minutes later, and

their server approached him. His face lit up as she pointed to their table. As he hobbled over to them, they could see he had a brass casting of an oyster shell for a belt buckle.

Murph stood up and held out his hand. "I'm Murph, and this is Lindsay. We saw you coming up in that cool-looking rig."

"I'm Don, nice ta meetcha. Yeah, the *Peggy T*'s a replica of an 1800s crabbing flattie."

"Would you like to sit and have a beer? We'd love to hear more about her." Lindsay asked.

"Don't mind if I do," he said, pulling out the empty chair and sitting down heavily. "I don't recall seeing you folks around here before."

"We live over on ESVA, though we've been to Gwynn's Island a few times. *Bay Breeze* is our favorite place to eat when we're here," she said.

Don nodded, "Y'all have got good taste in restaurants, and apparently in boats, too. Yeah, building the *Peggy T* was the idea of the head shipwright at that museum up in St. Michaels, as part of a plan to save and teach all the old Chesapeake boatbuilding skills to another generation.

"There was this old fella named Chapelle back in the 1940s who went around documenting all the old wooden boats of the bay. Thank God he did; if it hadn't been for him, we'd have never known about most of 'em today since they're mostly gone now. This one is a Chesapeake, or Hampton Flattie. Used to be hundreds on the bay back then, crabbing and oystering. That's why she's got a low freeboard, she's supposed to work for a living by running trotlines and traps. Anyway, by the time Chapelle got around to measuring 'em, he could only find one in good enough shape to study."

Don sighed, then continued. "Back in the day, these were the pickup trucks of the Chesapeake. If you had one, you could use it to provide for your family, as well as use it for your basic transportation, too. It was an important part of Chesapeake life. These started dying out and were almost lost when deadrises with motors started taking their places."

Don's beer arrived, and he took a long pull off the glass.

"How'd you end up with her?" Murph asked.

"I love bay history. My wife and I saw it online and then went up to that museum to check it out, and there she was, sitting just outside of the boatbuilding shed. It wasn't just me; both of us fell in love with this gal on sight. They'd just lowered the price from nine grand to seventy-five hundred because they couldn't get anybody interested in her."

Don shook his head sadly. "Kids today, if they sail at all, they want something made outta fiberglass that you don't need to do much maintenance on. But a boat like the *Peggy T* isn't just a *boat*, she's more like a *lifestyle*. There's a lot of maintenance you need to do every year if you want her to keep floating and lookin' good."

Lindsay said, "She's beautiful. Such graceful lines for a working boat."

Don beamed. "Nice to meet a couple of kids like y'all that can appreciate her. Me and my wife never really thought of her as ours; more like we were caretakers and protectors of this little piece of history."

"Who is Peggy?" Murph asked.

"My late mother-in-law. Around here, workboats are usually named for important women in your family. Peggy and her husband Gene lived aboard their boat for years, and she was a damn good sailor in her own right." He winced, "Oh, sorry ma'am. Didn't mean to cuss in front of ya."

Lindsay laughed, "No worries, Don. We live and work around the water, so I've heard a lot worse."

"Yeah, but not from me." He sighed, continuing his story, "Anyway, my wife and I took on the responsibility that came with that little bit of history. Now it's just me left, and I'm getting so that I'm having a tough time keeping up with all the maintenance. Been looking around for somebody who would appreciate her like we did, but as the museum found out, folks like that are few and far between."

Lindsay looked at Murph and could see he had the same idea that she did. She asked Don, "So, you're looking to sell her?"

"Only if the right person comes along. I don't want to let her go to some goofball who wouldn't take good care of her. Like I said, she's the last of her kind, and history like that deserves to be protected. If I die before I find somebody, she'll go back to the museum."

Murph said, "Do you think we could talk you into taking us for a sail?"

Don leaned back against his chair, squinted a bit, and looked back and forth at the couple as if re-evaluating the two of them.

"A sail, like wantin' ta go for a free ride, or a sail meaning a sea trial? Are you interested in her?"

Lindsay replied, "We both love Chesapeake history, especially the bay boats. So, we might be interested, depending on how she sails. We're not looking for a free ride, how about we buy your lunch?"

"Throw in another beer with it, and you've got a deal."

"I STILL DON'T KNOW that much about you," Andrea said. This, despite having spent over two hours chatting over his Kaliks and her vodka rocks, after switching over from Bloody Marys.

"You know more now than you did a few hours ago."

"True, but not nearly as much as I'd like."

"Then meet me at *Mistral* around six if you are up for a sunset cruise with cocktails and hors d'oeuvres. There's no better place to learn about someone than aboard a boat."

"In your cabin, you mean," she said sarcastically.

"I meant on deck and at the helm. That's where you need to be if you want to learn about someone's soul. My cabin is for sleeping, sex, or both. Which is not where I was inviting you, at least not this evening."

She didn't know whether to be relieved or insulted. Though she realized it was a little bit of both. "Why not go sailing now?"

"Because I was up since midnight on watch, and I need to rest for a few hours if I'm going to be able to hold up my end of any conversation. And the kitchen here will need time to prepare a proper plate of hors d'oeuvres."

"In that case, I'll see you at six."

DON SAT on the bench seat amidship, Lindsay was aft on the tiller, and Murph was between them, long-sitting on the deck. Being down that low, he got to hear the water against the hull. It made a kind of whisper as the heavy wood boat passed through it. This was exactly what the deadrise captain had been talking about the night before. The sound was mesmerizing, almost lulling him to sleep as they made their way through the protected harbor at Milford Haven. They were heading for the bay through the channel at Hole In The Wall.

"I love the way this boat sails! So, Don, what would you want for her?" Lindsay asked.

"Uh, don't ya think Murph needs a turn at the helm before you decide to buy her?"

"Nope. See that almost comatose look on his face? That's all I needed to see. Trust me, he's in if you're willing to sell, and if we can agree on a price."

Don pursed his lips, looking back and forth between the pair. Murph seemed totally relaxed, and Lindsay had started glowing the second she'd taken the tiller. He realized from their lunch conversation that the two knew boats and boat maintenance. Murph had talked at length over lunch about his collection of books on Chesapeake boats and their history. Don had many of the same titles that he had mentioned.

"I'll sell her to y'all for exactly what I paid for her, seventy-five hundred bucks. I'm not looking to make money on her, I just want to make sure she gets a good home. And that's not a negotiable price, it's firm."

Murph nodded, coming out of his stupor. "It's fair, and it's a deal." He dug down into his pants pocket, pulling out one of the strapped bundles of cash, and counting out seventy-five of the one-hundred-dollar bills. He offered the cash to a now very suspicious Don.

"What the hell are you, some kinda drug dealer? I don't need dirty money or marked bills." Don held his hands up in refusal.

Lindsay said, "No, no, it's nothing like that. We sold one of our boats yesterday, and he happened to still have some of the cash on him. We own *Mallard Cove Marina* and part of *Gwynn's Island Hotel and Marina*. That's clean cash, not dope money."

"Ah. So, you two got that place away from the bunch that was makin' such a mess of the hotel remodel. Y'all have been doing a good job with it. Nice to see it getting done right." He reached out and took the cash from Murph. "Guess I'm the one who's going for that free sail now. I'll write out a Bill of Sale after we go back in."

"We're a small part of the group that bought that property, but with everything we buy, we do it right or we don't do it at all," Murph said.

"Good philosophy. Now I'm gonna follow your lead, Murph, and kick back. We'll let Lindsay do all the 'work' of sailing this rig."

"It's not like we could pry her hands off that tiller. See that look on her face? Guaranteed she has a death grip on it."

"Hey, I'm having fun, and she sails like an absolute dream! But we've got a few boats coming in ahead. How wide is the channel, Don?"

"Don't worry too much about the channel. As heavy as she is, she still draws less than a foot with the centerboard up. Even though it's down now, it's pin-hinged. So if you get in where it's too shallow, it'll kick up into its case until you get back in deeper water."

"That could come in handy in the Virginia Inside Passage over on ESVA. The Army Corps of Engineers and the Coast Guard have given up on maintaining the channel depth, and they're yanking the last of the channel markers," Lindsay said. "We'll still be doing a lot of sailing in that area. Maybe some rowing for exercise, too."

"Nice. Oh, and for as heavy as she is, she rows easy, too," the older man said.

"I'm too lazy to row," Murph said.

"I kinda doubt that, Murph, since you look pretty fit. But it's not like you have much of a choice when the wind dies. You're the only motor she's got." He pointed to the oars that were sitting in chocks on one side. "The original ones were too heavy, so I had these made out of ash. A lot lighter, and still real strong."

"Lindsay will appreciate that when she's rowing us."

"Hey! You said I'm the 'navigator,' remember? When it's rowing time, that's where you come in."

"In that case, we'll make sure we only go out when there's wind."

Don chuckled, "If you can do that a hundred percent of the time, you'd make a good weatherman, Murph. I've been out on days where I was sure there'd be plenty of air moving around, and I still ended up rowing home. It didn't take many of those days before I had those lighter oars made."

Don didn't seem to be in a hurry to get back and was enjoying having an audience that hadn't heard any of his stories before. He had accumulated a lifetime of Chesapeake adventures and was eager to share them with Murph and Lindsay. She let Murph take the helm for a total of ten minutes before reclaiming it, now completely bonded with the little boat.

"This is always what happens, Don, I buy a boat and never get to use it."

Lindsay said, "Not true! You use *LNZ II* all the time!"

Murph had told Don about refurbishing the Contender, and how it had led to them selling the Merritt.

Don smiled, thinking about how well the two of them got along. He knew that they both had made the right choice to be together, just as he had made the right choice to sell the *Peggy T* to them.

As they sailed back into Milford Haven, he said, "That dock over there on the right with the boat shed is me. Pull up to the end, and I'll go write out that Bill of Sale."

Murph noticed a fiberglass deadrise and a Boston Whaler floating in the two covered slips. "I thought you were getting out of boating, Don."

"I'm not dead yet, Murph. No, I said I needed to get away from all the maintenance this particular boat takes. Those two are 'plastic boats'; ones where you just turn the key and go. I'm getting to the stage of life where things need to be easier, and I've never had to row either one of those home," he grinned as he said it.

After disappearing into his sprawling single-story house for a few minutes, Don returned with the paperwork, which he handed to Murph. "Here ya go, she's all yours. Take good care of her, you two, and take good care of each other, as well."

"Don, you mind if I ask what you did before you retired? I mean, this is a pretty nice place you have here," Murph said.

"Retired? Who can afford to retire these days? I write novels. Who knows, maybe I'll put you two in one of them. Come to think of it, you might even make great characters for a series." He smiled and waved goodbye as Murph shoved the boat away from the dock.

Back in the channel, Murph took the helm, heading back to the restaurant to drop Lindsay off to retrieve their truck.

"I didn't realize we were out on the bay for as long as we were. You've got like a dozen miles back to the inn. It'll be dark in an hour and a half, and you don't have running lights," Lindsay said.

Murph had been thinking the same thing but didn't want to worry her. "No problem dear, I won't spare the horsepower on the way home."

"Funny, babe. You've got a good charge on your phone, right?"

"Yes, mom, I've got this," he said with a twinge of sarcasm.

"Just make sure you do. Kind of hard to become a mom without you around to do your part. And to change your share of the diapers."

KIDS, he thought, as he sailed solo back out into the Chesapeake. He hadn't given the subject much consideration, but obviously, Lindsay had. Then again, he realized it was logical. They'd been together for a few years, and since they were getting married soon, a kid might not be that far in their future. Or even kids, plural. He supposed he should have been thinking about the subject long before now, especially since he was caught so flat-footed when she brought it up. And changing diapers? Another part of the equation that he'd never thought about before. But how hard could that be?

He was almost always ready for anything that had to do with boating, from maintenance to seamanship and even rough weather. But all the stuff that came with kids, well, he didn't have a clue about it. What if he had a daughter or even daughters? How would he approach telling them to watch out for "players," meaning guys like he'd once been up until the time he'd met their mother? For almost an hour his mind was preoccupied with all kinds of new thoughts, so much that he hadn't noticed the wind slowly dying down, and with it, his speed.

He looked over at the oars and was glad that Don had bought the lighter ones since he was about to get a pre-dinner workout. It was time to rig the boat for rowing. Murph now wrapped the mainsail around its freestanding mast, securing it with the sheet line. Then he pulled the foresail's mast up and out of its stepped position where it passed down through the foredeck.

With the oarlocks in their sockets, he now sat on the bench seat, facing aft. With the first two strokes, he realized that Don had been correct about how easy she was to row. It was a good thing too, as he looked back and saw the New Point Comfort Lighthouse in the distance, about a mile behind him. That left another four miles or so to go. As he watched, the steady light from that tower kicked on in the growing dusk. It was going to be well after dark when he reached his destination.

He knew that Lindsay would be worried, so he called her. "Hey there. When I said I wouldn't spare the horsepower, I didn't realize that I was gonna be the horse."

"I felt the wind die out, and I was beginning to worry. Where are you?"

"Maybe an hour and a half out. I'm rowing for all I'm worth."

"Well, be careful and keep your eyes open for bow lights. There won't be any moon tonight, and it gets so dark out here without any city lights. But you can use the light on your phone to let people know you're there if you need to."

"Good idea."

"I'll push back our dinner reservations, and have a vodka waiting for you when you tie up."

"I am soooo marrying the right woman."

"Damn right you are, and I thought we settled this earlier." She laughed as she hung up.

The thought of both dinner and a waiting vodka spurred Murph on a tad faster. But soon the night finished falling, and only the few house lights that were shining helped define the shoreline. Still, the centerboard bumped across a few shallow bars that he encountered along the way as he hugged the shore. He was staying out of the channel in hopes of avoiding any boat traffic.

Looking out into a very dark Mobjack Bay, he was glad they'd taken that boat ride the night before. He remembered a few of the flashing green and red lighted channel markers, hopefully, enough of them to be able to find the East River, and finally, Talbot Creek. They were just small, colorful penlights off in the distance, but were still some very welcome sights.

He finally rounded the corner and entered the East River, less than a mile from the mouth of Talbot Creek. Now not expecting any traffic, he stuck to what he thought he remembered as being the channel. Then about a half mile in, Murph heard a boat coming but couldn't see it. The captain was running without lights, just as he was, and there wasn't enough time to row out of the way. He fumbled with his phone, trying to find the button for the flashlight on the lock screen, while also yelling at the boat to turn.

Murph found the light's button at the same time he saw the boat, now less than fifty feet behind him, and headed straight for his stern. He frantically flashed his light back and forth across the guy's bow, then trained it on his own boat's interior. At the last possible second the boat turned, missing him by a couple of feet, but still close enough that its chine hit his outstretched oar. The wake from the motorboat rocked the *Peggy T* violently. Murph heard the captain curse him above the noise of the engine, and he returned the favor, loud and long.

In the narrow beam of his phone's light, he recognized the boat as being a classic deadrise style. However, unlike most of the working deadrises that show their ages in trap dings or streaks of fishing grime on the side of the fishing cockpit, this one looked like it was brand new. Though he reasoned that it couldn't have been new because its unique rounded stern was that of a drake tail, a design that fell out of favor so many years ago.

The boat was quickly out of range of his phone's light, and it disappeared into the blackness of the night. Murph sat still for a minute, letting the adrenaline that had flooded his body work its way back out. Then he went back to rowing, though he now angled out and away from the channel. While he didn't expect to run into any more traffic, he hadn't figured on running into that deadrise either and having it almost run into him, literally.

5

———————

MAKING HIS PITCH

Andrea was amazed at how easy *Mistral* was to "single-hand" for such a large yacht. By the time she'd arrived, Jock had her tethered to the floating dock with only a stern and spring line. He quickly released both himself, and they motored out into the bay.

Once in deeper water, Jock started stepping on several small, round, black rubber domes that were built into the teak deck at the helm. These covered switches controlled the roller-furling systems for both the mainsail and the jib, as well as the hydraulic winches that worked the sheet lines wrapped around them.

As *Mistral* heeled over in the wind, Jock noted that this didn't bother Andrea in the slightest. Most non-sailors would find it disconcerting, especially on a boat this size, so she obviously had some sailing experience.

"Not your first time under sail," he noted.

"Not even close. I started sailing when I was six or seven, in a pram over at Annapolis."

Prams are the most simple form of small plywood sailboats that are the perfect trainers for little kids.

"Care to take the helm?"

She smiled, "I was hoping you would ask."

Taking the large wheel in hand, she looked as confident with it as Jock was. He pointed out which of the deck switches operated the winches for both sails, then sat on the bench seat next to the helm.

"She is amazing, Jacques!"

He smiled at her, "She absolutely is, even more than *Mistral*."

"Cheesy lines don't become you."

"I didn't mean it that way. It's just that I haven't seen any woman take her helm as confidently as you just did. You're obviously quite comfortable with it."

"Sexist lines don't become you, either."

"That wasn't intended to be sexist, it was supposed to be a compliment and not one that I give easily."

"In that case, you're forgiven, and I guess that I'm flattered."

She looked up at the mainsail, then tapped the deck switch to activate the winch, hauling in the main ever so slightly. Jock had just been about to suggest she do that.

"And I'm impressed. You have a real feel for her."

She slowly turned and looked at him with a slight smirk. "I think the same might be said about you, and I'm not talking about the boat."

"Now who is being cheesy and sexist?"

She laughed, "And to think I was about to go back to Washington this afternoon. This is the most fun I've had at *Bayside* so far this summer. I'm glad you came along."

He smiled at her in return.

She looked perturbed. "This is the part where you are supposed to say that you're glad you showed up as well."

"I didn't realize we were playing parts and sticking to a script."

"Sure we are. It's the age-old story of romance and seduction. Or maybe you'd like to skip the romance part and skip straight to the seduction scene. Though you are doing so well at both. And not that I'd mind terribly if we skipped ahead a bit."

He figured this was a test; Andrea trying to read him. Jock figured that he could indeed "skip to the seduction scene" and she wouldn't mind. But then things would likely be over. He needed to get closer to her than a one-night stand would get him if he was to be able to take a shot at the big score. He was certain he could con her out of his biggest take of the year, if only he was patient enough. But before that could happen he had to take back control of the narrative.

"When I was in my twenties, I'd have already taken you up on that. But if all someone wants from the other is sex, they miss out on so much that life has to offer. What other people have to offer. Others that are interesting, as I thought you might be. Whether it is romance, or just spending time and communicating with each other. That's the true art of living which seems to be disappearing fast these days, and what can make life so enjoyable.

"Perhaps we've both made a mistake. Why don't we come about and head back to *Bayside*." He was about to find out if the con was completely blown, or if he'd taken back control of the situation.

Andrea couldn't decide if Jacques was interesting or infuriating. He was a much better candidate to spend time with than any other man she'd met at *Bayside* so far, and any in DC of late as well.

"I wouldn't say that either of us has made a mistake. It's more like we don't know each other yet. You're right about the lost art of communication. But you didn't look like you fit the mold of someone who was more into communication than seduction when you pulled in shirtless and strutting as you passed the terrace this morning."

He looked at her as if trying to make up his mind about something. "When we sat and talked on the terrace, you didn't sound like someone who was looking for a new 'boy toy.' You sounded like you had so much more depth than that. And again, who is the one being sexist now? I do not strut; I leave that to peacocks. I do, however, like to sail shirtless on my boat when it is hot, as it was earlier today. You should have plenty of depth here to be able to come about, by the way."

"What about if we keep the boat going straight, but we change the direction of our conversation instead? Maybe we do have some depths of our own to explore."

He intentionally crossed his arms, feigning disinterest. "I thought so a while ago, but now I'm not so certain of it."

"I'd like to keep going, Jacques, I haven't even found out where you're from yet. We do have so much to talk about. I apologize if I insulted you with that 'strutting' crack. Look, if you still want to go back, you take the helm."

He leaned back on the bench. "You seem to be doing well enough, I'll leave it to you as to where we are heading."

She smiled, then again looked up at the main sail before scanning the water out in front of them. "I love this so much."

"Then why don't you have a boat of your own?"

"Well, I do have a friend with one. Though so far, he's more of an acquaintance. But he might become a friend, I guess time will tell."

A LITTLE MORE THAN an hour later the wind began to drop. Jock noted that Andrea had kept on a steady direction north, as the west wind had allowed them to stay on a reach without having to tack back and forth. This also meant that it would take at least an hour and a half to get back to *Bayside* under power. He figured that had been intentional on her part.

He took the helm, showing her how to use the roller furling system to stow each sail, then he cranked up the engine. He deliberately kept the throttle at barely over idle speed as he reversed course. After asking her to take the wheel again, he ducked down into the cabin, returning with the tray of hors d'oeuvres, a bottle of vodka, and two glasses of ice.

"Much easier to bartend under power when we're not heeling over," she said.

"Very true." He poured the vodka into each glass, then handed her one. "We still have to keep a watch out ahead, but this is very pleasant."

She raised her glass, "To making new friends afloat."

"And to sharing a fantastic sunset." He motioned to the west where the sun was now lighting up some low clouds in a spectacular display of color.

"I was concentrating on sailing, and almost forgot what we came out here for."

He nodded. "So easy to do when you take on the responsibility of being the captain."

"More like when I get lost in the joy of wind, sails, and water. Responsibility, yes, but I put the joy part first.

"So, Jacques, my man of mystery, you've entrusted me with your waterborne home, are you now willing to trust me enough to talk about your land home?" She cocked her head slightly in an inquisitive, yet challenging look.

He paused a beat, took in a deep breath, and began the first part of his story, being hesitant enough to really sell it. When he finished, he tried to figure out just how successful he'd been.

"So, this is why I'm clandestinely raising funds in America from loyal friends of Andorra. But I'm also keeping somewhat of a low profile, being cautious about who I contact. While the government of France and the Church sound so above board and innocuous, they are as dangerous as any enemy you could imagine. And it can be difficult to judge where someone's loyalty may lie when talking about the Church."

Andrea was amused by what she deemed to be a total cock and bull story. "So you say that you are the last descendent of Boris the First, and these people want to kill you for it. All over ski resorts and casinos," she said, her voice dripping in sarcasm.

He knew this was a pivotal point, where his story would be believed or rejected. "Partly, yes. Though think about your own country's history of murder and violence that happened during the battle for control of Las Vegas. Control of my country's tourist attractions, while very lucrative, also pale in comparison to its largest asset. That would be our secretive banking system, which in Europe is second only to Switzerland's in assets."

"Next I guess you are going to tell me that some Catholic Bishop and the president of France are conspiring together to steal all the money in those banks." She seemed to be losing patience with his story and was about to tell him to speed up and take her straight back to *Bayside*.

"The money isn't the most valuable part; it is the information that's key. The 'two princes' have access to the records of who owns the accounts, and who makes deposits into those accounts. Some of the account holders have included five of the last six presidents of your country, and many of the current and past leaders of your Congress. The list of their secret depositors to those accounts includes some of the most powerful companies in the world. Ones who have had laws enacted in their favor by these recipients. And these are only the ones from your country. There are thousands of other politically connected account holders from across the globe, as well as many wealthy tax evaders. All told, tens of billions of US dollars are in the accounts of your countrymen alone.

"Knowing the identities of the account holders and the depositors can be used as leverage by those that have the proof. Careers and lives could be at stake. Trust me, I know. The president of France and some of those within the Vatican walls will stop at nothing to keep this information to themselves. The list of those who have disappeared for them to keep these secrets is much longer than the list of those that were killed for control of your casinos in Las Vegas, as I mentioned before."

She stared at him, then shook her head. "I've got to hand it to you, when you come up with a fairy tale, it's a world record whopper. Secret bank accounts of the presidents and Congress, as well as a conspiracy to kill by the Vatican and the French president. And yet you have no proof but want me to believe this crap. You know, I've heard enough. Speed up and get me back to *Bayside*."

He sighed. "This is exactly why I don't trust many people with the truth because they don't believe me. But I never said I don't have proof."

He turned on the deck lights around the helm station and raised his shirt. In the dim light, she saw two details that she'd missed in the distance as he passed by the terrace earlier. Two old scars on his abdomen, obviously from large caliber bullets. He heard her sharp intake of breath.

"How did you survive that?"

"As far as they know, I did not. I would like to keep it that way, too. Even though we are parting ways, please keep what I told you in confidence. My future safety may well depend on this."

He switched off the lights and the autopilot, then gave the engine more throttle, staring ahead into the dark bay. He thought back to the time he received those bullet wounds. Of course, they weren't from an assassin sent by either the Church or France, but instead a cheap American hit man with bad aim who was hired by the husband of one of his first marks.

He'd barely survived, and it was a lesson he'd never forget. The woman was very promiscuous, so her Russian husband kept someone watching her at all times. From that point on, Jock was extremely careful in choosing his marks, never again making such an amateurish mistake.

Andrea wasn't as certain now that his entire story was fake. Her mind raced as she tried to figure out which parts might or might not be true. The bullet scars definitely were. But the bit about the King of Andorra sounded like so much crap. She wondered if Andorra even existed since she'd never heard of it.

"Where is the head?"

"Down below, all the way forward by my stateroom."

Once she was out of sight of Jacques, she looked up Andorra on her smartphone. The Wiki post confirmed much of what Jacques had said about Andorra, which was a real principality. Though it lacked a list of Boris's descendants and obviously had nothing about any banking conspiracy.

So, she reasoned, no matter how fantastic it sounded, there was a possibility that parts of his story might be true after all. She could be walking out on the most interesting man she'd ever met. That, or the biggest cad. Only time would tell, and only if she was willing to spend some with him. She had already decided before she went back up on deck.

"So, the internet confirmed what I said." He still looked straight ahead instead of at her when she returned.

"Pardon?"

"You checked out what I told you, or at least most of it. That's what I'd have done as well. So I'm glad that we will be parting on good terms, without you thinking of me as a liar. I meant it when I asked you not to repeat what I told you, by the way. That's also the truth."

"Okay. You're right, of course. I did check out your story, at least as much of it as I could. Andorra sounds lovely."

"It is. Though it was a much better place to live before the two princes began their oppression of my people. Which is why their liberation has become my life's work." He glanced over at her briefly, his grim-looking face dimly lit by the light from the instrument panel.

"You know, this sounds like a movie I once saw about a con man on the coast of France who claimed to be raising money to liberate his people." She wanted to see how he'd react.

"I saw that same comedy. Brilliant actors. It made me wonder how they came up with that plot. Sadly, it helped to considerably narrow my list of potential contributors to this cause by casting a shadow of doubt on my own truth. Now I can only approach those who know and trust me; it's next to impossible to expand my reach beyond them."

"You're right, they are great actors. Of course, neither had been shot in order to be cast in their parts, at least that I know of."

He chuckled. "That would be taking method acting to the extreme, wouldn't it?"

"I'd like to make it up to you, my doubting your story. Would you care to have dinner with me tonight when we get back, Jacques?"

"I'm sorry, it has been such a long day, and I don't feel much like getting dressed for dinner at your club."

"Neither do I. What about someplace where we can go as we are? I mean, you do have to eat, and there's a cute little beach café with great food right next door at *Bayside*'s public marina. We can make it an early night, no strings attached."

"That sounds perfect."

~

HALF AN HOUR after his encounter with the deadrise, Murph approached the dock at the inn. It was dimly lit with a series of solar walkway lights, but there was still enough light for him to see Lindsay's silhouette out at the end. She was waiting with that promised vodka, along with one for herself.

"I was starting to get worried," she said as she put the drinks down and helped him tie up.

"Not half as much as I was. I almost got run over by a deadrise that was running with no lights."

"About half an hour ago?" She asked.

"How'd you know?"

"I heard a boat that was coming down the creek, but I couldn't see it because it didn't have any navigation lights. I think it tied up at that farm across the way."

The creek was about three hundred yards wide at the point where they were. Murph recalled seeing the farm that she mentioned earlier in the day, and he knew there was an enclosed boat shed over there. But right now there wasn't any light coming from that direction; there weren't even any security lights burning.

Murph stepped up onto the dock. "You know that I run without lights sometimes because it makes it easier to spot channel markers, other boats, and floating hazards. But I only do that when there's enough light coming from the moon or the shoreline to outline any obstacles. Where that dude was running was as black as the bottom of a well. The only reason he would be running 'dark' there is to avoid being seen by anyone else. And that's not all that's hinky about that boat." He told her about the rare design, and how it appeared to be brand new. "Definitely not a real working deadrise."

"Yes, but neither is the *Peggy T*. Maybe that guy is a fan of old

Chesapeake boats just like you are. I doubt all those old crabbing flatties were kept like yachts in their day, though Don sure kept her that way."

"Maybe. But I still think that there's something 'off' about this whole thing."

He'd no sooner finished his sentence than they heard the sound of a boat motor starting on the other side of the creek. As still as the night was, they were able to follow the boat with their ears, even though it wasn't visible in the blackness of the moonless night. Once again, it was running without navigation lights.

Murph continued, "Definitely something shady about this. He must've been in that boat shed, but he didn't use any lights under there or we'd have seen them. And after almost running me over, he's still not using his nav lights."

The sound of the boat receded into the distance. Lindsay handed him his drink and sat down in a dock chair with hers. "Don't worry about it. Let's just drink these, and then we need to get a move on if we're going to make our reservation. I got them to push us back to the last of the night, but if we're late, we'll be going to bed hungry."

LATER THAT NIGHT, over on ESVA...

Outerbridge was waiting in his plant's boat shed when the deadrise backed into her slip. After tying up the boat, Jerry stepped over onto the dock with a backpack which he held out to his boss.

As he reached out to accept the pack, a worried Outerbridge asked, "How'd it go?"

Not wanting to admit to almost hitting the idiot in the unlit rowboat, especially since he was sure exactly what Robert had been worried about, Jerry replied, "Came off without a hitch. Coins look right, the package is intact, and Cho was happy with the bills."

"Good. He should be, it's not like he can get those anywhere else, especially with the infused compound. I'll check the coins to make sure they're all genuine. Meanwhile, you go get some sleep, I'll need you to make a pump-out run tomorrow night. The chemist wants to make another batch with a change in the formula. He's getting closer to creating an even better bleaching agent."

"Why even have him mess around when you've got such a good thing going?"

Outerbridge was irritated over the question, "You just stick to running the boat, and let me worry about what I do or don't want to be involved with. I've now got to come up with a new plan to get my Krugerrands back from that Murphy character since you botched that up so badly the other night. As it is, we've wasted the perfect opportunity." He turned and walked away, leaving a chastised Jerry standing on the dock.

Jerry mentally kicked himself, since he'd now blown what had been his chance at redemption, by running his mouth. Robert got irate when people questioned his plans or ideas. Especially when it was Jerry that did it.

~

THE NEXT MORNING over breakfast at the inn, Murph asked the owner about the farm across the creek.

"They grow a variety of Chinese vegetables that get shipped all over the country, and some even go overseas. I've never actually met the new owners though. They bought the place a couple of years ago and have kept to themselves ever since. I think they're Asian, from what I've heard."

Murph was surprised. "Chinese vegetables in the middle of Virginia? I'm used to seeing corn, soybeans, and even cotton over on ESVA, but not bok choy."

The inn owner shrugged, "I guess the soil over there is right for it, and apparently there's a big market out there for their product. All I know is they're quiet neighbors, and that's a plus for us over here, with running an inn."

"I guess so. Well, thanks for the hospitality, we'll be heading out after breakfast. It won't be the last time you'll see us though; this place is so relaxing." Murph didn't want to share the events of the night before, and he wanted to change the subject away from the neighbors.

"Anytime. We'd love to have you both come back."

AFTER CLEARING out of their room after breakfast and picking up sandwiches and bottled waters for their lunches from the deli at the turn-in, Lindsay walked with Murph down to the *Peggy T* to see him off. "Looks like you won't be using the oars today. Nice steady breeze from the south."

"Yeah, I'm hoping to make it to the *Cove* in time for cocktail hour. You weren't kidding, she is such an easy boat to sail."

Lindsay laughed, "Just make sure you don't fall asleep at the tiller on the way over." She handed him the bag with his lunch.

"I'll do my best. But I think *Peggy T* could almost find her way to her new home all on her own if I did."

"Don't test her, babe. See you at home."

6

———

HOMECOMING

E*arly the next morning...*
Andrea walked out on the floating dock, spotting Jock on the bow of *Mistral,* wearing only loose-fitting shorts as he moved through a series of yoga poses. She watched patiently, waiting as he finished up his session. Then he rolled up his mat, spotting her when he turned.

She smiled. "Good morning."

"Good morning to you as well. You're up early today."

"Yes, and thanks to that 'early to bed, early to rise' adage, I have a clear head as well. It helps since I didn't have company last night, nor too many drinks."

Jock laughed. "As you saw by the end of dinner, I was fading fast. I couldn't have handled too many drinks either, or anything else for that matter. I desperately needed to catch up on my rest. Come aboard, I have coffee brewing. You do drink coffee, correct?"

"I've already had one cup so far this morning, but that only primed the pump, so I'm ready for another. And breakfast. Have you eaten?"

He shook his head. "Not yet. I prefer to do yoga on an empty stomach. I don't usually eat much for breakfast, just some fruit and perhaps a croissant. Unfortunately, I'm out of bread and pastries, but I'll happily share some fruit with you."

"That would be perfect. I usually only have more than that if I'm having brunch instead of breakfast."

She followed him through the hatch and down into the cabin, watching as he stowed his rolled mat in a side compartment. He motioned for her to take a seat on a bench beside a beautiful varnished teak cocktail table. Then he brought two bowls of fruit from the galley and followed up with two cups of coffee. After setting both on the table, he pressed a hidden button and the tabletop was raised to dining height.

"Very impressive," she said.

"I can't take credit for it since didn't have the boat built, but the person who did was very inventive. The table lift uses the same hydraulic source as the winches and roller furling system." Jock knew that by not taking the credit, it further added credibility to his other stories. Humility sells, or so he thought.

She looked around. "Quite the floating bachelor pad that you have here."

"It is a comfortable home, and serves my purposes well." Now warning bells were starting to go off in his head.

"I'll bet it does," she said with a slightly sarcastic tone.

He crossed his arms and leaned back against a counter instead of joining her on the bench. "Why?"

"Why, what?"

"After last night's dinner and the accompanying conversation, I thought we had gotten to know each other quite a bit better. But now you use an almost accusatory tone when I said my home serves me well. I don't understand why."

"Because in thinking it over, I get the sense that you're playing me. Or at least trying to."

"I think you are misunderstanding me."

She smiled wanly, "I'm not so sure."

He chuckled, but in a frustrated way. "I don't know what I can do or say to prove that I'm not. Then again, I shouldn't have to, and frankly, I'm not sure that I want to. After all, you're the one who showed up here this morning."

"Because I'm still curious. Cautiously curious."

"At least you are honest. Though I don't know how happy I am about not being taken at my word over what and who I am. Again, I thought we'd settled that last night."

"It's a new day, and the sun is shining. Things can look different in daylight. And your table reminded me of something I've seen in a movie."

Jock was trying hard not to overanalyze the things Andrea was saying, hoping to stay a step or two ahead of her. But this woman was a bit of an enigma; much more cautious, and so hard to read. He thought he'd already sold her on his story, but it looked like he might have to do it all over again. And then she laughed.

"Sorry, I can't help it, this hydraulic table is too much. And the confused look on your face right now is priceless. In the movie, this man had a bed that would raise and lower, so that he could adjust it to the perfect height to…"

Jock held up his hand, "I understand. But this table is where I eat, and that's all I do on it. I seriously doubt that lying across those fiddle boards would be very comfortable."

Fiddleboards are raised wooden edges on a table or countertop that prevent plates and cutlery from sliding off in a rocking boat. She chuckled, reaching out and putting a hand on the nearest one.

"No, I don't think it would. Just to be clear, you don't happen to have the same mechanism under your bunk though, right?"

This time he saw her eyes twinkling as he replied. "No. It's just a regular bunk, with no mechanisms." She was far more complex than he'd originally given her credit for. Actually, not just complex—challenging. Challenging was a far more accurate description. Every time he thought things were settled, she tossed him a new curveball.

"Just as well. In the movie, the bed went haywire at… a most inconvenient moment. Think of it as a tandem ride on a mechanical bull, but naked."

"You are a very surprising woman, Andrea. I never know what

you are going to say next. I am very glad that I decided to make a stop here."

LATE THAT AFTERNOON, at Mallard Cove...

"Looks like I'm just in time to have you buy me a beer."

Lindsay looked up from her beachside table at the *Cove Beach Bar* and focused on the man. He was about five feet, nine inches tall with shaggy gray hair and a matching scruffy beard. His left earlobe boasted a gold circle earring. Sanford "Sandy" Morgan was a best-selling author and neighbor who lived aboard his fifty-five-foot trawler, *Epilogue* over in *Casey's Cove.*

"I guess you are at that, Sandy. Have a seat." She motioned to a chair next to hers.

He sat down and told their server he'd like a Red Stripe. Then he asked Lindsay, "Where's Murph?"

"On his way over from Mobjack Bay in our new boat. Well, not new, but new to us."

"I thought you two were in the 'selling mode' instead of adding to the fleet."

She chuckled and said, "Well, it kind of followed us home." She told him about their chance meeting with Don, and how they'd both fallen in love with the boat.

"Oh, Baloney is just going to love this!"

"I'm gonna love what?"

Another man had walked up to the table but he didn't wait for an invitation, quickly taking a seat in an empty chair. He was somewhere around sixty years old, short, and mostly bald except for a strip of short salt-and-pepper-colored hair around his head just above his ears. Strangely, an unlit cigar was sticking out of his mouth. As odd as this was, his two even more defining characteristics had to do with his voice. The first being that it was very loud. The second was that despite living on ESVA for over two decades, he'd lost little or none of his thick New Jersey accent.

Sandy replied sarcastically, "Well, don't wait for an invitation, Gilligan, just take a seat."

"I told ya ta quit callin' me that, ya hack! We runnin' a tab here or what?" He motioned to the server that he needed a beer.

Sandy said, "Lindsay's buying me a beer, but you're on your own."

Lindsay rolled her eyes, knowing that she'd be stuck with the entire tab, Baloney's beer included. Sandy could certainly afford to pay for his own, but so could Baloney. Captain Bill "Baloney" Cooper owned two charter boats based out of *Mallard Cove* and was also the highest-paid cast member of the popular cable show, *Tuna Hunters*. Though he seemed like just another dock bum, he actually brought in just over seven figures annually.

After their server delivered the two beers, Baloney's cigar disappeared into his shirt pocket. The only time this happened was when he was either drinking beer or eating. It was his wife Betty's strict rule that he couldn't light up until his boat was out beyond the marina's jetties. At no time was he ever allowed to light up ashore.

But those rules didn't prohibit him from mouthing the unlit stogie. It was also a barometer of his temper. When he was angry or irritated, it would quickly swap sides of his mouth, seemingly all by itself. When he was happy and telling tales, it bounced up and down like a maestro's baton.

Baloney used to buy the cheapest, most putrid-smelling stogies available, but after the viewers of *Tuna Hunters* took notice of his signature tobacco stick, he was approached by a cigar company. "The Baloney" was the result, a special blend of tobacco leaves that was a vast improvement over what he used to smoke, and they were now available in various lengths and gauges in many ship stores in marinas up and down the coast. These cigars cost several times what he used to pay, but as part of his compensation for licensing his name and likeness to them, he received several boxes for free each month.

Again he asked, "So, what are you two talking about that I'm gonna love?"

Lindsay had been scanning the water, finally spotting the *Peggy T* clearing the Fisherman Inlet Bridge. Murph was now paralleling the beach that ran past the bar. As she smiled, Sandy followed her gaze and then matched her smile. Baloney's back was to the bridge, so he had to turn around to see what the two were so happy about.

"Ain't that thing ugly! Looks like that front sail's broken."

"Beauty is in the eye of the beer holder, Gilligan. And this beer holder loves her classic lines," Sandy commented.

"Since when are you a blow-boat fanboy, ya hack?"

"Since I've heard the backstory behind that one."

"How'd ya hear about that? And what'd ya hear about it? What's with ya two grinnin' lunatics anyhow?"

Lindsay had been doing her best to avoid laughing, but it was a losing battle. She knew there would be an explosion coming, and she didn't have long to wait as the boat came closer. She saw Baloney staring, and then the realization of who was at the tiller hit home.

"Ya gotta be kiddin' me! Tell me that ain't yours and Murph's, Lindsay," he said, in an even louder voice than normal.

More than one sailboat and their captains in *Mallard Cove* had prior run-ins with Baloney, who would've preferred that all vessels in the marina be propelled by engines, not sails.

"I could, Bill, but I'd be lying."

"The man gets rid ah that bee-uteeful Merritt, an' brings home *that thing?* This some kinda midlife crisis or what?"

"If it is, then it's affecting both of us. Wait 'till I take you for a sail, Bill, you'll love her."

"Nope! That ain't happenin'. Even if I was dead, I wouldn't want either ah youse two takin' my ashes out in that thing. It ain't like we don't have too many blow-boats around here already, ya had ta go an' add another one."

"Don't worry, we'll keep her over in *Casey's Cove.* She'll be totally out of your way. Though she doesn't have a motor, so she'll always have the right of way over you stink-boaters!" Having quickly tired of Baloney's criticism of her new boat, she purposely brought up the issue that really irked him.

There is a maritime rule that sailboats solely under wind power always have the right of way over all powerboats. The only exception is those vessels that have a "restricted ability to maneuver." Unfortunately, too many sailboat owners aren't aware of this last part, though common sense should let them know to avoid these mostly larger vessels. Around ESVA these were mostly large freighters, barges, and military ships. Since neither of Baloney's sportfish boats qualified as a "RAM vessel," by law they had to give way to all boats under sail, no matter their size.

"Yeah, well, maybe your after-hours visitor will love it too, and it'll get swiped," Baloney said.

"What are you talking about?" Lindsay asked.

"While ya were gone, Case was sittin' by the fire late at night with Bim, and somebody pulled up at the ramp an' tried sneakin' up on him."

"What!"

Sandy interjected, "You don't know for certain that he or she was 'sneaking up' on Casey."

"Well, they sure didn't say anything. Had plenty of time to, from what Case said, and when Bim went off they hauled boogety. Didn't answer when Case called out to 'em. Left in an outboard." Baloney puffed out his chest like he had been an eyewitness to the whole event, instead of just repeating what Casey had told him.

"'Hauled boogety?'" Sandy rolled his eyes. "You are the star example of the failure in the English curriculum of the Garden State's public school system."

"Yeah, 'hauled boogety!' What's wrong with that? Ya know, if you started writin' like people talk, ya might sell more books."

"Uh huh, and chase away the millions of readers that already buy my books..."

Lindsay jumped back into the conversation, "Wait! So, did Casey get a look at the person or the boat?"

"Nah, just heard 'em leave. Said it was a small outboard, probably a four-stroke engine 'cause it was real quiet."

"Not much in the way of crime around here lately. Word has gotten around the waterfront that we take care of our own at the *Cove*. But maybe they didn't get the memo," Sandy said.

"Or are from out ah town. Mebbe Virginia Beach. Mighta been lookin' ta rucksack the pool house," Baloney suggested.

"That's 'ransack,' Gilligan." Sandy shook his head.

"Whatever. But probably lookin' for stuff that's easy ta pawn."

Lindsay countered, "Or, maybe trying to sneak into the pool for a midnight swim. It could have been somebody off a boat, or that has done work here in the past, or even a couple of kids, who knows? But it sounds like they weren't expecting to run into a dog. Word might get out about that, too, which is a good thing."

Sandy had been watching the *Peggy T* as Murph passed by, and wanted to switch the conversation back. "I do love her lines, especially the square 'deadrise' style bow. But as much as I hate to, I have to agree with Baloney, that foresail's mast looks wrong."

"Ya see what I mean there, right? Kinda like a knight on a horse, lookin' for a jest."

"That's 'joust,' Gilligan!"

"Whatever, ya hack."

"Don told us that the 'jigger' or 'stick-up' sail was more common back then. The builders and watermen were always trying new rigs to improve the way their flatties sailed. This reverse angled sail helps it point higher in the wind, which might have come in handy when the captain was running a crab trotline, and he was dip netting the crabs that hung off of it." Lindsay clearly loved the history behind the boat just as much as Murph.

"I bet it would run good with an outboard hangin' off the stern," Baloney said.

Sandy asked, "Have you ever been sailing, Gilligan?"

The thought of it was enough to make him ignore the nickname. "No! I've got a perfect record goin' with that, and I ain't about to wreck it now."

"Well, if you gentlemen will excuse me, I think I'll go meet Murph and help him tie her up."

"See you later, Lindsay," Sandy said.

After she left, Baloney looked worried. "Now what, we have to pay for our own beer?"

"Maybe somebody will show up, and we can duck out and stick them with the tab."

"I like the way ya think!"

They had another couple of rounds without anyone showing up that they knew, and Sandy excused himself to go "make room for more beer." Two minutes later their server came over and put their tab in front of Baloney.

"Sandy said to give you this, Baloney." She smiled, knowing the history between the two.

As he begrudgingly reached into his pocket he said, "That blow-boat loving son of a…"

Back at *Casey's Cove*, Lindsay hurried over to the seawall in front of where *LNZ II* was tied up. Murph was just coming through the narrow inlet. He swung wide, letting his momentum carry him over to the wood pilings where he tossed Lindsay his bow and stern lines.

"Hey babe, you made good time," she said.

"And I didn't nod off once," Murph grinned. "Though it was so relaxing. Luckily I had such a clear day. We need to add a compass to her in case we get caught out on the bay in fog."

"Not a bad idea. But I don't know how many times we'll be making that crossing."

"True, but it's cheap insurance if we decide to. And speaking of crossing, what do you say we make a run up to *Bayside* tomorrow in *LNZ II*? We need to get with Cindy about our wedding plans," Murph suggested. Cindy Crenshaw was the manager of the *Bayside* complex and a good friend of the two of them.

"Haven't you had enough of the water for a while? We can run up there in your truck instead."

"Yeah, but you can't catch flounder from my truck, and I've heard there are some around the cement ships at Kiptopeke."

Nine large World War II cargo ships made of cement were sunk in the shallows off the old ferry depot, forming a breakwater. The ferry had quit running when the Chesapeake Bay Bridge-Tunnel (CBBT) opened in the 1960s, and the area was made into a park. But over the years the crumbling ships had become a great habitat for many of the birds and fish of the area.

Lindsay asked, "Are you thinking crabmeat stuffed flounder?"

"I'll probably dream about it tonight."

"Then so will I. Let's plan on it!"

JERRY prepared to make his late-night run to dispose of the chemical brew that Outerbridge's chemist had created. Little did he know that when the sun rose tomorrow, a lot of things on ESVA will have changed...

7

GOVERNMENT "HELP"

The next morning after a leisurely breakfast at the *Cove*, Murph and Lindsay boarded *LNZ II* with their fishing gear and a cooler full of ice. As Murph warmed up the engines, he switched on the VHF radio and turned it to the local fishing channel. Baloney was talking to another boat.

"I'm thinkin' it's from one ah them damn menhaden boats, gettin' over their limit an' dumpin' these so they don't get caught an' fined."

"I dunno, Baloney, there's cobias an' rockfish floatin', too. Way too many of 'em to have been netted with the menhaden."

Baloney replied, "Ya mebbe right about that, Cap'n. I know this, I ain't keepin' ah one of either of 'em until we find out somethin' more. Could be some kinda algae bloom like that red tide thing they get down in the Gulf. I ain't gonna let my charter take a chance on gettin' sick on bad fish. I'm gonna run down off the beach out front an' see if we can't get on some ribbonfish instead."

"Yeah, I gotcha good there Bill. Catch 'em up!"

"Will do. *My Mahi* out and standin' by."

Murph and Lindsay looked at each other with worried faces as Lindsay grabbed the microphone. "*My Mahi, LNZ II*. What are you talking about, Bill?"

"Hey, Lindsay. You guys still at the dock?"

"Just leaving now."

"If yer headin' into the bay, you'll see. Huge fish kill, startin' about Fisherman Inlet Bridge and goin' north. Mostly menhaden, more than I've ever seen before. Wind's startin' to push 'em up on the beach."

"Roger that, thanks."

Murph firewalled the throttles as they cleared the inlet at *Casey's Cove*, their Contender jumping up on a plane as it leveled out on top of the water's surface. They quickly passed the entrance to *Mallard Cove Marina* and then the *Cove's* beach. So far, there was no sign of the fish kill.

"Maybe he's exaggerating, and it's not that bad," Murph suggested hopefully.

Lindsay shook her head. "For Baloney to burn extra diesel to get from the bay over to the beach, it's got to be bad. And that looks like it straight ahead."

The floating raft of fish corpses started under the bridge, just as Baloney had said. A breeze had kicked up from the south, and already many of the fish were beginning to be pushed ashore. The tide was now ripping outward, bringing with it more of the putrid-smelling fish bodies that would end up on the beach at *Mallard Cove*. Murph stopped the boat at the edge of the raft, as they both stared in horror.

"This is bad," Murph said.

"Way worse than bad. Look at that gull." Lindsay pointed to a seagull that was floating on the water in amongst the fish, about fifty feet from their boat. From its jerky movements, it was obviously in distress. As they watched, it lost the ability to hold its head up. Its head pitched forward, the beak dropping below the water, and then it stopped moving.

Other seagulls were diving on the raft of fish, scavenging a free meal. The one that would be their last. As Murph and Lindsay scanned the raft, they saw a few floating rockfish and cobia like

Baloney's friend had mentioned. But they also saw a few dead rays mixed in as well.

"Baloney's wrong," Murph said. "Look at their bodies, they aren't crushed like they had been caught in a seine net and sucked up into a transport boat. And if they were dumped as bycatch, that gull wouldn't have gotten sick. Look, there's another that's acting the same way." He pointed to a gull that had just crash-landed on the water a little farther away, exhibiting the same symptoms as the first.

Murph pushed the throttles forward again, steering as far upwind as he could from the floaters while still staying in deep water. As they passed under the bridge and broke out into the open Chesapeake, they were both stunned by what they saw. The raft of dead fish stretched as far north as they could see, and the shore was covered, up to the high-tide line. Murph dropped back to idle speed.

"The breeze must've been coming from the west last night, and now it's shifted south," he said.

Lindsay agreed, "Which means a lot of this line that's being pulled down and out of the bay will get pushed up on the shore around *Mallard Cove*. We've got to get out in front of this."

"I'm on it." Murph hit a speed dial number on his phone as he put it on speaker. "Mimi? Murph. We're about to have a nightmare end up on our beach. There's a massive fish kill on its way down the bay. We need to close the beach until they figure out what caused it. We don't want anybody getting sick, especially since we know there could be an issue with the water."

Mimi Carter was the hospitality manager of the *Mallard Cove* restaurants and bars, as well as being in charge of the beachfront. She hardly missed a beat before coming up with suggestions.

"I'll tell Barry that he's going to need someone with a dip net and a dingy to scoop up any dead fish that make it into the marina." Barry was the *Cove*'s Bahamian-born dockmaster.

"Good. We can also use the tractor with that hay rake for cleaning up seaweed on the ones that hit the shore, but we're going to need to dig a big, deep pit where we can bury them. The smell from the dumpster would knock you over in no time if we used that. And I don't want to dump any of them out farther in the water if they're contaminated. It looks like some seagulls that ate them are already dying."

"We've got a regular customer that has a heavy equipment company. I can get him to bring a backhoe over here."

"Perfect, Meems. But no matter what we do, our tip of ESVA is gonna get clobbered, from a business standpoint," Lindsay said.

"That big, huh?"

"Afraid so. Until these all get cleaned up, and I don't mean just in front of us, all of southern ESVA is going to start to reek."

"I'll get right on it." Mimi hung up.

They watched as the breeze fought against the current, bunching up groups of fish. Those were then sucked out into the channel between *Mallard Cove* and *Fisherman Island* by the outgoing tide, forming what looked like silver-colored weed lines as the increasing breeze now pushed them shoreward. It was the perfect nightmare scenario for *Mallard Cove*.

Off in the distance, they saw a Virginia Marine Police boat arriving, and farther up the coast, they saw a Coast Guard boat making its way south, parallel to the raft. Within the hour more boats from a handful of other agencies would be on site. There would be squabbling over which agencies had jurisdiction over the disaster so that they could all prove their own relevance to help to justify the dollar amounts of their budgets. Environmental groups would also be joining the fray, volunteering to help with the cleanup as well as taking photos for their fundraising efforts.

An hour later at *Mallard Cove*, their crew was already making progress on the cleanup. Or at least they were holding their own against the onslaught of the floaters. That was, until two opposing alphabet soup agencies showed up, each trying to outdo the other by asserting more authority. They had one thing in common, ordering the *Mallard Cove* crew to "cease and desist," and telling Murph and

Lindsay the government was going to handle the cleanup from that point on.

"Really? When are you going to get started?" Murph asked.

The first guy from the larger agency said, "We should have our crew down here by tomorrow morning, or tomorrow afternoon at the latest. We had to get them started farther up in the bay."

The second guy said, "These fish might become evidence of a crime, so by dumping them in that pit, you could be destroying evidence or interfering with a criminal investigation, or potentially even contaminating this property."

"Then just what do you suggest we do with them then?" Murph asked, in a very sarcastic tone.

"Leave them alone! Like he said," jerking his thumb at the first government guy, "our crews will be coming to take over the cleanup at some point. Until then, you need to stop."

Murph's eyes narrowed as he addressed the two. "Do you smell that? It's twice as strong as it was an hour ago. Multiply it by ten times, and that's what it will smell like by the time your crew gets here tomorrow afternoon. I won't have any customers left by then, but my employees will still need to get paid even though I won't have any money coming in."

The first government guy looked at him like he was daft. "If you can't pay them, just send them home. They're not part of the cease-and-desist order, so that's on you, and not our problem. But we can't have you destroying evidence."

Typical government geek, Murph thought. No clue about how business works, or about the responsibility that he felt to his employees. Heat was now rising up the back of his neck as his anger increased along with his frustration. Then he saw the backhoe coming towards them, the front bucket loaded with dead fish, and he had an idea.

"So, this is all evidence, right?" He pointed to the pile of dead fish at the bottom of the pit.

The smug guy nodded. "It sure is."

Murph held up a finger for the backhoe operator to stop. He went over and had a quick conversation with the man, who then got a huge grin on his face. Murph walked back over to the government guys as the backhoe bypassed the pit and headed for the parking lot with its smelly load still in the bucket.

"Hey! Where's he going with those? I told you to stop!" The guy exclaimed.

Murph smiled. "He's preserving your evidence."

The government guys watched in horror as the backhoe operator raised the front bucket over the bed of a pickup truck with a government agency's logo on the side. The bucket tipped forward, dumping the load as its driver screamed, "Noooo!" and then ran to his truck.

Murph looked over calmly at the second guy, "Where are you parked? We'll make sure that you get your share of this evidence as well."

Without a word, that guy started running toward the parking lot, passing the truck whose driver was now trying to figure out what to do with his stinky cargo. He stormed back over to Murph.

"You have to clean that crap out of my truck!"

"I thought they were evidence," Murph said sweetly.

"They are!"

"Then they're your responsibility. You don't want to break that chain of custody, right?"

"Just get them out of my truck!"

"Where do you suggest I put them? Do you want them in the hole? Because they're not going in my dumpster or back on my beach."

The guy was exasperated, "Dump them in the hole, I don't care! I just want them the hell out of my truck!"

"Then back it down to the pit," Murph directed. He sent a text as he went over to retrieve a shovel while the man went back to his truck.

Once the truck's tailgate was even with the edge of the pit, the man climbed out and demanded that Murph empty the bed. Instead, Murph handed him the shovel.

"I wouldn't want you to accuse me of scratching your truck and damaging government property." He smiled widely.

After the truck bed was empty, the man thrust the shovel back at Murph. "Here. And I mean cease and desist, or I'm going to hit you with every fine I can think of."

Murph wagged a finger side to side. "I don't think so, at least not unless you want to pay those with me. You just did everything that we've been doing, and we have you on video." He pointed over toward the *Cove Beach Bar* where Mimi had been capturing everything with her phone's camera.

"You son of a..."

Murph interrupted him, pointing toward the parking lot. "Hey! Get back in your damn truck, then get the hell off of my property. I'll keep cleaning up my place, you just go and worry about everybody else's properties. The day I need the government to step in and do my job is the day I put *Mallard Cove* up for sale. Now get out of here! Go somewhere else to justify your damn salary."

The guy started to object, but he saw the backhoe coming with another load of fish. Quickly, he got in his truck and sped off, passing Lindsay who was walking toward Murph with an armful of signs.

"Who was that?" She asked.

"Some self-important idiot. How'd those come out?"

She held one out for Murph to see. On both sides, it read *"Beach Closed Temporarily. No Trespassing or Swimming."*

"Nice," he said. "Make sure you get pictures of them after they're in place."

"*You* make sure to get pictures after you help me place them! You don't work for the government, you know." She thrust half of the signs at him and he reluctantly accepted them. "And the smell is a lot worse now than when I left to go to the sign shop. It's all the way up and down the main road, too."

He shook his head as he placed the first sign. "We'll be lucky to have any customers back in here in a month."

"WHERE DID YOU FLUSH THE TANK?" An irate Robert Outerbridge had awakened Jerry, who was in a berth in the Merritt's crew quarters. He was trying to catch up on the sleep he'd lost the night before by doing the dumping run.

"Huh? Down by Kiptopeke, why?"

"In one spot, or did you spread it down the bay while running as I told you to?"

The fact that he was asking the question jolted Jerry into almost complete consciousness. He realized that something must've gone wrong. He thought about lying outright, but he had seen Robert's fury when he caught someone doing that before. The guy hadn't been seen since. Jerry wasn't sure if he'd just been fired, or if Robert had done something far more drastic. Right now, he didn't want to chance making that same mistake and to find out what might happen.

Jerry hung his head, "In one spot. It was so nice and calm out on the bay..."

Robert exploded. "All you had to do was follow orders! You've caused the biggest fish kill in recent memory! Now every government agency, as well as non-profit environmental group, is either on ESVA or on their way here. They'll be snooping around all over the bay and ESVA to find the source. I've had to stop the chemist's work until after this dies down since we can't take a chance on getting spotted dumping another load. And we can't risk making another run across the bay to the farm in the deadrise until all these Feds are out of here. Cho is going to be furious."

For a split second, Jerry thought about his earlier comment about questioning the necessity of Robert "...messing with that stuff" referring to the ultra-bleaching compound. But fortunately for him, he kept those thoughts to himself.

"I could drive it over," Jerry suggested.

"Why do you think we transport Cho's powder by boat? If you get stopped on the highway there's no way to ditch the evidence. Get stopped in the boat, and you can throw it overboard. That stuff instantly dissolves in liquid, not that they'd know what it is anyhow.

No, we'll wait until the heat is off the area. But I'll have to tell Cho in person about the delay." Robert never called or texted Cho, avoiding any chance of a phone tap or electronic trail.

He went silent as he thought, finally saying, "If we can't go back to working on the bleaching agent or transporting the powder right now, then we can concentrate on finding a way to get my coins back from Murphy.

"What's done is done. Get out of the rack and ready to cast off. We'll have to take this boat over and back to Cho's because it's clean. The water is crawling with Feds."

"WELL, I'm glad that you didn't have one of those hydraulic lift things in this bed, since we did so well without it." Jock smiled at Andrea, who laughed. A little bit of early morning light was peeking in between the curtains, illuminating her face. They were in bed at her waterfront home at *Bayside Club Estates*.

"I agree, it would have been overkill, especially if it had malfunctioned like the one in the movie. Though that might've made for a fun challenge." She chuckled and pulled him closer. "But speaking of hydraulics, do you think we could put *Mistral's* to use and go for a sail today? I'd love to get some sun out on the water."

Jock replied, "I can think of nothing better that I would like to do."

"Well, I don't know whether to be pleased or insulted," Andrea said, smiling.

"Then let me rephrase that. I can think of nothing better that I would like to do than to please you."

"In that case, I'm definitely not insulted."

JERRY SAT SILENTLY on the navigator's seat next to the one at the helm, sulking since Robert was running the Merritt. Jerry had always run whatever boat they were on, at least until Robert bought this one. Granted, it was the fastest and most fancy of all those he'd ever owned, and a lot of fun to run. But Jerry suspected that there was more to it, and this was punishment for disregarding orders. It was also a subtle reminder that he could be replaced, like the crewman before him who had disappeared without a trace.

Robert had been right about the water being covered in Feds. They'd no sooner left their creek before a Coast Guard boat pulled alongside and told them to stop. A young petty officer and a seaman transferred over to their boat, then asked where they were headed after they climbed down to the cockpit to join them.

"Over to Mobjack Bay to fish, since we heard about the fish kill over here," Robert replied.

"Good, we're just making sure that all boats know that this section of the bay is closed to both fishing as well as swimming or any human contact until further notice. I'd like to see your registration and have a look down below. Are there any others aboard besides you two?"

Jerry had already retrieved their temporary registration and handed it to the officer as Robert said, "Just the two of us aboard, and you're welcome to look anywhere you'd like."

The petty officer looked surprised. "Bermuda, eh? Can't say that I've ever seen any vessel's paperwork from there before. You're a long way from home."

"I have a second home here. I figure that hurricanes can't hit both places at once." He smiled and chuckled, as the officer did as well.

The seaman made a cursory and quick examination of the cabin, then rejoined the higher-ranking man who said, "Well, enjoy your stay on this side of the Gulf Stream. And good luck fishing on the other side of the bay."

The two crossed back over to their vessel and waved as they pulled away.

"That's exactly why we can't risk another run for a while," Outer-bridge said as he scowled at Jerry. Then he climbed back up to the flybridge and resumed their route across the bay.

8

CAUSE & EFFECTS

The Chesapeake Bay has often been described by environmental groups and others as a "national treasure," a very accurate description. For years several non-profit groups and government agencies had been working to reverse the damage to this irreplaceable resource, most of it caused by decades of overfishing and pollution. Because of this, water quality has been a huge focus, so there were numerous labs around the bay filled with people that have the expertise and equipment ready to help in determining the cause of the fish kill. While it wasn't easy to extract the chemical compound from those dead fish that caused the disaster, these people, unfortunately, had a lot of prior experience with fish kills in the bay and the surrounding waters. What they discovered this morning, though, came as both a shock as well as a source of anger, setting off alarm bells all over DC.

Learning that it was a manmade catastrophe was bad enough, but one of the trace elements they found in the chemical compound extracted from those fish was something entirely new. Well, almost new, as it was an element that had first popped up on the radar of the scientific community a year before. Before that, there had only been twenty-four elements in the group known as "synthetic elements."

These make up a section of the Periodic Table of Elements that do not occur naturally here on earth. All of the original twenty-four were created between 1944 and 2010. The mechanism for the creation of these elements involved human manipulation of their fundamental particles inside a nuclear reactor, a particle accelerator, or an atomic explosion.

Then last year, traces of a new kind of highly addictive drug called Rescentol began showing up in counterfeit prescription pills on the streets of the US and in various countries of Europe. Ten times more addictive than Fentanyl, and just as deadly in even smaller quantities, it was rapidly becoming an epidemic as it became more widespread. It contained another new, nuclear-event-spawned element, and to date, this was the only known use of it. Another part of why it raised such concern within the halls of government is that the only source for this element so far is the country that originally discovered it—China.

That traces of Rescentol were now being found in these fish was puzzling enough by itself. But the researchers discovered this fish-killing compound contained a mixture with an ingredient that was well known to certain government agencies, most notably the Treasury Department. They knew that this second rare ingredient, when combined with the others in this compound, was often used to bleach out the special ink used in the printing of modern US currency. And the compound that killed the fish was also loaded with dissolved ink.

The most advanced modern counterfeiters can mimic almost all of the printed features of today's bills. But there are still a few things that have been added in recent years which have proven too difficult for even the best of them. For instance, the color-shifting ink changes from copper to green as the bill is tilted by forty-five degrees. This was added in the early 2000s on all but the one and five-dollar bills.

Another of the almost insurmountable obstacles to counterfeiting today is the blue 3D ribbons that are woven into one-hundred-dollar bills. These are printed with bells and "100" that move up and down when the bill is shifted from side to side. And a huge hurdle on all five-dollar bills and higher are the clear security threads inscribed with the bill's denomination, which is woven into the paper. These were added in 1990.

But the biggest obstacle counterfeiters have to overcome is sourcing the paper itself. Everyone knows the feel of the paper used by the Federal Reserve to print money. It's a proprietary blend of twenty-five percent linen and seventy-five percent cotton, with little red and blue security fibers randomly embedded in the paper stock. It is only allowed to be supplied to the Federal Reserve. Without this authentic paper and its unique feel, a counterfeit bill can stand out like a streaker at a black-tie dinner.

Although the Treasury Department tries its best to keep the details about them secret, there are several cases where advanced counterfeiters have bleached one-dollar bills. They later reprinted the dried notes in higher denominations. It was now obvious that somewhere around the Chesapeake, counterfeiters were currently in operation. The obvious first question is where? The second question is why would Rescentol also be included in the solution? Then the largest, most explosive question of all: what was China's involvement?

Several government agencies were about to become involved in the case, and their joint investigation would begin by looking on ESVA. One FBI special agent in Virginia Beach had a lot of ties over on the peninsula, and she knew the best place to start asking questions. She took the lead in this part of the investigation and decided to start with a friend of hers who had his finger on the pulse of ESVA businesses and commercial real estate.

"Hi Casey, thanks for meeting with us." FBI Special Agent Stephanie Baker walked into the salon of the *Lady Dawn*. Stephanie was a pretty brunette, roughly Casey's age, and best described as one cool customer, even when she was under fire. Casey knew this for a fact, since on separate occasions she had shot and killed two men that were trying to kill him.

Stephanie had become part of a group recently nicknamed *Casey's Crew*. This handful of highly trusted people had unrestricted use of all the amenities at the *Cove Club*. Today Stephanie was accompanied by a tall, slender man, somewhere in his mid-thirties. "Casey, this is Special Agent Jim Randall of the Secret Service, in from DC."

Casey shook the man's hand and motioned for the two to have a seat on the sofa across from his. "How can I help you?"

"Agent Baker tells me that you have several businesses in the area and that you can be trusted to keep things in confidence. Because of this, she thought that maybe you would be a good place for us to start asking around. We think that there might be a counterfeiter operating on ESVA, or somewhere around the bay. Have you seen any fake bills showing up in your businesses lately?"

"I haven't heard of any, but I don't deal with any of the cash personally. I can tell you though that the vast majority of our business transactions are paid for either by credit cards or checks; very little of it is in cash."

Baker asked, "Does anything suspicious come to mind? I know through your real estate dealings you have a thorough knowledge of waterfront properties on ESVA. This might be in a commercial location where seeing truck traffic loaded with crates, boxes, or barrels coming in and out could be expected. Though they'd probably want to be somewhat secluded. Does any location like that stand out to you?"

"Yes, about a hundred of them. Wholesale fish houses, small manufacturing companies, any one of dozens of warehouses. I mean, we are more rural farmland than anything else, and that means there are small pockets of properties like you're describing. When I moved up from South Florida a few years ago, that was part of what was such a culture shock to me. Down there, every inch of waterfront has been developed. But up here, so many farm fields border the bay and its tributary creeks. There are thousands of miles of shoreline along the Chesapeake Bay and its tributaries."

Randall nodded, "I thought it might be a long shot, but it was still worth asking. We're also checking with all the local banks about any reports of counterfeit bills, and they're supposed to be turned in of course. But many of those bills never make it to the bank if they're spotted by a retail business. They're either destroyed or passed along, depending on if the business is willing to take the hit or not. Usually, it's the larger establishments like yours that won't pawn them off on their customers."

"Absolutely not. Not to mention, we train our people to scrutinize the larger bills, and to refuse any that don't look legitimate."

Stephanie said, "It was worth a try. Though counterfeiters don't normally try to pass off bills in their backyards, especially in places they might frequent like restaurants and bars."

Casey looked surprised. "So, you think this person might be a regular customer of ours?"

She replied, "Not necessarily, but you do quite a business here and up at *Bayside* and the *Bluffs*. Chances are if they do live on ESVA, they might have had a meal or a drink at one of your places."

The *Bluffs* was another marina and restaurant combination that Casey's group owned on the Atlantic side of ESVA. He looked thoughtful as he mulled over what they'd said. Then he asked, "You mentioned barrels. Does this have anything to do with that fish kill?"

Randall quickly answered, "We aren't ruling anything out. But we won't know for sure until after we find them. This means we need to find the money trail. Thanks for your time." He stood up, signaling an end to their meeting. He didn't want to have to field more questions about how the two things might be linked.

Stephanie and Casey also stood, and he walked his two visitors out, stopping at the top of the gangway. "If this does turn out to be related to the fish kill, I hope you catch the bastards who caused it. Not just for the money they've cost everyone around here, but for the damage that's been done to the fishery. It's going to take a long time to recover."

Randall said, "Just to be clear, Mr. Shaw, I never said those two things were related."

"I know. But you didn't deny it, either, and you mentioned barrels. Last time I checked, chemicals came in those."

~

"WHAT YOU MEAN you cannot ship for a week or two? We have a schedule, Robert!" As Outerbridge had expected, Cho was livid. "I receive another shipment of special element from China, and now have many more boxes of dollar bills. You must take it back to factory with you."

The bills were singles that an associate of Cho's collected from his large vending machine business. He sold them to Cho at a forty-percent premium, which ensured an uninterrupted supply, no questions asked. This was another key part of the counterfeiting business, acquiring a steady flow of one-dollar bills for bleaching without attracting attention. Outerbridge couldn't very well walk into a bank and request a hundred thousand one-dollar bills without raising all kinds of flags. But Cho and his connection were both part of the Chinese triad mafia and were sworn to keep silent under threat of death.

"You'll just have to sit on it all until we can get back to regular runs. We were boarded right after we left today, so there is no way we could risk it. There are more government boats out on the bay than private ones right now."

"You were *boarded*? Yet you came here anyway? Are you *insane*? You may lead them here!"

"Relax, I handled them. It was Coast Guard kids. I told them we were going to fish in *Mobjack* since our side of the bay is closed. If they watched us on radar, that's what they would've seen. But there's no way I'm taking any of the special element back with me, or shipping any of either the bills or the powder back over here, at least until things cool down." As Outerbridge finished saying this, he could see Cho's jaw clench in anger.

"This your mess. You create supply problem, and now I pay for it." When Cho got angry, his Chinese accent became more pronounced, and his sentence structure more choppy.

Robert made a patting motion with both hands, trying to calm him down. "It probably won't be more than a week or so before we're back to making normal runs again. And we had good results from the larger batches we ran, so we'll be back on schedule and even beyond it in no time."

"You must make certain we are. You have two days, no longer."

~

OUT ON THE BAY, the day had once again upheld the Chesapeake's reputation for great summer sailing. The steady breeze from the southwest gave *Mistral* a great run to the south, without having to "pinch" too high into the wind, or needing to tack back and forth.

Jock went down below to fix lunch for both of them and was greeted with a surprise when he returned to the cockpit. Apparently, when Andrea had spoken about getting some sun, she had meant on every square inch of skin. Seeing the shocked look on his face, she laughed.

"Jacques, you can't tell me that this is the first time you've had a naked woman on deck! You're European, for goodness' sake. Isn't this the normal 'uniform' for the Med? And besides, it's not like you didn't get a good look at everything up close in person last night!"

"In many places in Europe, this is true. But here on the Chesapeake, with as much boat traffic as is around, and with every American having a cell phone with a camera, there is a high probability of a picture of a naked you 'going viral.' I would not ordinarily have any issue with that. But I do have to be extremely careful about such things.

"If I were by chance caught in the same picture, with the attention that it could draw, and completely deserve I might add, this could fall in the hands of the wrong people. The ones that I do not want to find me. However, if we end up offshore in the ocean at some point where there is so little traffic, I might even join you."

"You're right, of course. I'm sorry, I hadn't thought it through, and I don't want to create an issue for you." She relinquished the wheel to him, then put her bikini back on.

"No apology is necessary. I'd love nothing better than to have the freedom to not have to worry about such things, but it is a small price to pay if I am to be able to free my people."

"Hey, I'm the one who had to cover back up."

He smiled, "Yes, but I'm the one who is deprived of such a stunning view."

Still not certain about the validity of his story, she didn't mind the compliment, however. Partly because of it, she was more inclined than ever to give him the benefit of a doubt. She had no plans to return to DC anytime soon, at least as long as he was still at *Bayside*.

$$9$$

AN UNINVITED VISITOR

M*id-morning, the next day.*

"MURPH? Robert Outerbridge. Did I catch you at a bad time?"

"Not really, Robert. Things are kind of slow around here at the moment."

"Ah, yes, I've heard that they closed the waterway down near you. I imagine that's had a bit of an impact on your business."

"That's putting it mildly. But we've cleaned up the last of it, and we're just waiting for the 'powers that be' to issue their 'all clear' so we can open our beachfront back up. Until that happens, things will probably stay slow. But you didn't call to hear me moan and groan about business. What can I help you with?"

"I have a few questions about some of the systems on the Merritt, and I wondered if I might ask you and your lady about them over dinner, say at the *Rooftops* grill at *Bayside* later tonight? My treat, of course. Maybe brighten your day a bit."

Rooftops was one of Murph and Lindsay's favorite restaurants.

Located on the second-floor end of *Bayside Resort* overlooking the marina and the Chesapeake, the views were almost as good as the food. A chef cooked some of the best steaks on ESVA over a charcoal-fired grill in a corner of the large, screened, open-air restaurant. Still, Outerbridge wasn't one of Murph's most favorite people, but paying over two million dollars for the Merritt qualified him as one very large customer. And a free steak dinner at *Rooftops* wasn't to be sneezed at.

"We'd be happy to take you up on that. We'll pick you up on the way. What time would be good for you?" In truth, Murph didn't know exactly where Outerbridge lived, just that it was somewhere farther north on ESVA.

"Actually, I have some errands farther up the Shore that I need to take care of this afternoon. What say we meet at the restaurant around eight? I'll make a reservation under my name."

"We'll see you then."

AFTER HANGING UP, Outerbridge looked over at Danny and Jerry. "That should give you at least a two-hour window, starting around dark. Assuming the coins will be in some kind of strongbox or safe, you should have plenty of time to find and open it, Danny. Jerry, you drop him off next to their inlet, then standby in the Inside Passage to pick him back up."

He started pulling tools out of a waterproof satchel on the table in front of him. "This mini crowbar should get you through the door, and this battery-powered grinder is equipped with a cutting wheel that will make short work of whatever they've got them in. I've attached a small diving lift bag with a CO_2 cartridge to this mesh bag. It will allow you to equalize the weight of the coins underwater, so they won't drag you down."

Danny asked, "What if the dog that went after Jerry is aboard?"

Robert's eyes narrowed slightly as he pulled a small semi-automatic pistol with a tiny silencer out of the satchel. "It's a .22 caliber, loaded with short cartridges. With the silencer, it shouldn't be louder than someone snapping their fingers. It will take down any dog, or any person who might get in the way, with a head shot."

Danny took the pistol from him, feeling the weight and balance of it as he smiled cruelly. "Nice. I hope I get a chance to use it."

"If you do, just make sure it doesn't get left behind, and that it doesn't make it back here."

Danny nodded while Jerry remained silent, realizing that he was in a lot deeper than he'd originally bargained for. Counterfeiting and drugs were one thing, but he was arguably now a co-conspirator in a plot that might include murder. Any doubts he had about what happened to the other crew member who disappeared had just vanished as well.

AFTER MURPH HUNG up the phone, he had a twinge of regret about not checking with Lindsay first before committing to the dinner. That regret got a lot bigger after he caught up with her over at the *Cove* restaurant for lunch.

"Babe, I wish you hadn't agreed without talking to me first. There's something about him I just don't trust. And the guy that was with him was even worse. Majorly creepy."

"I doubt he'll bring him to dinner. I got the feeling it's only going to be the three of us. Besides, we still need to talk to Cindy about the wedding, so we can go a little early and take care of that."

She sighed, "I guess so. But I'd still rather have it here, and save the money."

"I'm only going to get married once, and I want to do it up right."

"Darn right you are! But this is so backward, it's usually the bride that wants a bigger, fancier wedding."

"Yeah, well, I want to show off by showing you off."

"You don't need to, babe. We've accomplished a lot together, and everyone knows that."

"It's just nice to remind them now and then about how far we've come, and that together we're a success." He paused a minute then added, "A decade and a half ago I was Casey's boat washer back in Florida, jumping from one beach bunny to the next. This wedding says I'm not that guy anymore. I don't need to depend on Casey, and you're the one I want to be with, period. And I want us to make as big a splash as we can when we make that statement, okay Linds?"

She smiled and reached across the table for his hand. "Okay, babe."

HE WATCHED as the drake tail deadrise disappeared into the darkness of the "ditch" section of the Virginia Inside Passage. Then Danny took one final bearing at the mouth of the inlet before he submerged. There was just enough light coming from the power pedestals on the docks to backlight the boats in *Casey's Cove*. This had allowed him to identify Murph and Lindsay's houseboat. His rebreather, the empty lift bag, as well as the tool satchel were all strapped to his compact electric diving scooter which would pull him along faster than if he were wearing fins.

His rebreather was a device that recirculated his exhaled breath after first scrubbing it of carbon dioxide and adding oxygen. It is completely unlike a typical SCUBA setup which utilizes compressed air in a tank. With those, when the diver exhales, the air bubbles rise to the surface. A rebreather eliminates both the bubbles as well as the "Darth Vader" noise of the regulator.

Danny had a small digital compass and depth indicator console glued onto the scooter. The scooter also had a bright LED floodlight built into the nose, but he didn't dare use it for fear of being spotted. Dropping down to a depth of eight feet, he figured this would be deep enough to avoid detection, yet shallow enough to stay above the bottom while still well under the houseboat's hull. He reasoned that the large yacht at the end of the basin must draw at least eight feet of water, so there shouldn't be any obstructions at that depth between the inlet and the stern of the houseboat.

The basin was about three hundred feet across, and he'd calculated it would take the scooter fifty seconds at its four miles per hour to propel him from the inlet to the houseboat. He'd been correct about both the time as well as the unobstructed run, with one exception. As the dark water began to brighten from the dock lights, he suddenly spotted a dark shadow looming directly in front of him. At the last second, he managed to turn and miss colliding with a twelve-inch steel piling. It was situated at the end of the finger pier which ran between both the houseboat and *Sharke*, that large sport fisherman. Carefully, he finished the last of his run under that same finger pier, then moved over and surfaced behind the stern of *On Coastal Time*.

As expected, there weren't any lights coming from inside the houseboat, and the dock lights barely illuminated the stern and doorway. Danny stayed motionless with just his head above the water as he listened and watched the edge of the seawall for any sign of movement. Just as he thought it was all clear, he heard a voice over beyond *Sharke*, and whoever was talking was coming his way.

"C'mon, Bimini, I don't want you doing any 'business' behind the boats. Hold it until we get up to C2, pal," Casey Shaw said.

Danny realized by the content of the one-sided conversation that it was someone who was walking a dog. Maybe even the aggressive guard dog that had gone after Jerry. He moved his head back into a small void between the edge of the float under the finger pier and the houseboat's hull. While he couldn't see anyone go by, it also meant they couldn't see him. But he was still able to hear the man occasionally say something to the dog. His voice faded as he moved down the walkway that abutted the seawall.

Danny waited until he didn't hear the voice any longer before moving from his hiding spot. Then he attached a line from the scooter to a stern cleat on the houseboat, then removed the waterproof satchel and the mesh bag. He left the scooter to dangle from the line, just beneath the surface.

Pulling himself up onto the houseboat's small aft deck, he then studied the door to figure out the best place to apply the crowbar. He was about to jam the point between the doorjamb and the door but first decided to try the handle. To his surprise, the door wasn't locked. Moving inside and pulling the door shut behind him, he almost fell down a short flight of steps that led down from the doorway. Using a small diver's penlight, he scanned the interior.

Danny found that he'd entered the salon or, he thought, maybe they call it the living room since it was part of a houseboat. It was larger than he'd expected; almost sixteen feet wide. At the far-left end of the salon was the head, and to the right was the galley. Or maybe the bathroom and the kitchen. Again, he wasn't sure what to call them, but he chose to check the galley first. He wanted to get as far away from the seawall as possible so that his light would have less chance of being spotted by anyone passing by.

As he entered the galley, at the rear he saw a ladder that led up to a hatch in the ceiling, and he figured he'd save that for last. There was a set of sliding pantry shelves that served as the back galley wall as well as a bedroom door, and these had been left open. Again, he wanted to put more distance between himself and the seawall, so he went in, sliding the shelf-door shut behind him. The small bedroom was about ten feet deep and the same distance wide. There were two large windows that he could open and escape through if he were to be surprised. He pulled the draperies across both so that the light from his little flashlight couldn't be spotted from outside. Now with relative privacy and an escape route pre-determined, he allowed himself to relax slightly as he got to work.

As part of his preparation, he'd done a lot of thinking about where he would keep the coins if he were Murphy. The obvious choice was a safe or a strong box, just as Robert had suggested. But where would you put one of those? Danny decided that if someone kept a couple million in gold at home instead of a bank vault, it was because they wanted it kept as close to them and as easily accessible as possible. And if it were his gold, he'd want it either in or near his bedroom. As far as boats go, this one had a very simple layout, as did the bedroom itself. But with the boat being over sixty feet long, there could be plenty of other places to hide things. More than he'd want to think about. Though small, this room had the feel of being the master bedroom, he couldn't see them having to climb that ladder every night.

He hoped he was right about this being where the gold was stashed, and he began a careful and methodical search of the room. Almost immediately he spotted a small hatch outline in the carpet under the front edge of an upholstered chair. He pushed the chair back and opened the hatch lid, but it turned out to be the deck access point to a bilge pump. There wasn't any sign of the gold in the recess, or of anything that it might be kept in.

After returning both the hatch and the chair back where he'd found them, he scanned the rest of the room. He spotted something peculiar about the large bed. While it was perched on four legs like most other beds, at each of the four corners was a wire cable that led up and through the ceiling. And in the center of the wooden bed frame was a long horizontal metal handle. On a hunch, he grabbed the handle and found that the bed lifted straight up with little effort; the cables apparently led to hidden counterweights. Once up in the air, a row of open cubbyholes in the wall down by the floor that had been hidden by the bed was now exposed. They were loaded with shoes, the majority of which were women's. He pulled the shoes out of each of their cubbyholes, shining his light into the spaces to ensure that they were empty.

After he replaced the shoes, he noticed that what at first he'd thought was an architectural detail that resembled Japanese rice paper screens above the cubbies was actually a pair of sliding doors. Opening the left one, he found that it was a hanging closet, loaded with clothes. Checking under, above, and behind the clothing, he didn't find anything that might hold the gold. Closing that door, he opened the one on the right and discovered it concealed a set of shelves. His heart skipped a beat when he saw that the one on the bottom had half of its space taken up by a small, built-in safe. Next to it were two stout-handled black cloth bags that he recognized as being the ones Outerbridge had given them to carry the gold.

Finding the bags was a bonus since Robert wanted those back as well. If the electronics in the handles were discovered after Danny had taken the gold, it could easily point a finger back at one or both of them. He pulled both bags out of their storage place, then studied the front of the safe. It wasn't as formidable as he'd feared, and the grinder with its cutting wheel should quickly give him access to the mechanism. He started cutting but worried that the noise it was making might be heard by someone on one of the neighboring boats or the dog-walker. Danny grabbed a thick beach towel from a shelf above the safe, folding and holding it so that it enveloped the grinder without getting caught in the wheel. It muffled the noise significantly, while also containing the stream of sparks that were generated.

Ten minutes later, the electronic keypad mechanism and part of the front of the safe door were on the floor. Danny then removed the mechanism which kept the door handle from retracting the round locking bars, and he was able to open the safe. Inside was the gold, a small stack of hundred-dollar bills, and a few handguns in soft cases.

Quickly Danny loaded fifty-three of the rolls of coins into their original cloth bags, then put those into his mesh bag. He had left the fifty-fourth roll out of the bags. Lifting his diving rash guard top and shoving the cash into his bathing suit's pocket, he considered doing the same with the extra roll of coins, but he decided it would be too obvious. He'd find another way to carry and keep them.

Robert had said to leave any cash or weapons behind, for fear that they could be traced or identified through their serial numbers. But he wasn't the one taking the risk by stealing the gold back, so what Robert didn't know wouldn't hurt him.

He reached back in and pulled out the first case, which turned out to contain a vintage Colt Python. Even through his heavy nitrile gloves, he could feel how well it fit his hand. He checked the other cases, which turned out to hold modern Glocks, all of which he dismissed. He put the roll of coins in with the pistol and zipped the bag shut.

"Screw Outerbridge," he thought, as he shoved the Colt into the waterproof satchel along with the grinder. He folded the towel, placing it back on the shelf. Closing the safe door, he then slid the closet door shut and lowered the bed back into place.

Danny hoped that with any luck, the theft might not get discovered for a day or two. What he hadn't factored in was that by finding the coins so quickly, he'd already used up a large part of his quota of luck, which was rapidly running out. Since he'd used the penlight in one hand and replaced the towel with his other, he'd missed spotting the telltale smoke that had begun rising from the section of towel which had caught all the sparks.

He retraced his steps, peering out the small window of the front door before opening it. There was no one in sight as he moved to the corner of the small deck, setting the satchel and mesh bag near the edge. Once back in the water, he pulled the satchel down and reattached it to the scooter. The mesh bag with its heavy cargo proved to be a lot trickier. He used the built-in CO_2 cartridge in the small lift bag, but its buoyancy still wasn't enough to completely neutralize the weight of all the gold. He was going to have to counter the added negative buoyancy by running the scooter at more of an upward angle to help take the extra weight and keep him level. He knew that transferring to the deadrise was going to be even trickier because of it.

Releasing the line from the cleat, he energized the scooter simultaneously. Fortunately for Danny, the boat basin was much deeper than the eight feet he'd hoped for. It took him half the width of the basin to find the perfect angle to hold the scooter and be able to maintain a steady depth. At one point he had dropped down to fifteen feet but still hadn't collided with the bottom. However, his porpoising up and down had thrown his time and distance calculations off. When he surfaced he found he was barely out of the basin and into the narrow inlet, and much closer to its shore than he would have liked.

Readjusting his course, he aimed for the shallow north corner of the entrance so that he could hover with his head barely above the surface, the gold resting on the bottom, as he used his penlight to signal Jerry. The original plan had been for him to do this from the middle of the channel, but there was no way he wanted to have to fight to keep the gold from dragging him down. This way he could use the scooter to take him directly to the boat where he could clip everything to a line while he pulled himself aboard.

When he reached that corner, he had an unexpected and unwelcome surprise that would once again force him to modify his plan.

10

UNINTENDED CONSEQUENCES

"C'mon, Bimini, I don't want you doing any 'business' behind the boats. Hold it until we get up to *C2*, pal," Casey Shaw said.

Bimini looked up at him while lowering his hind leg, annoyed at the rebuke. He'd been poised to "salute" the power pedestal behind *Sharke*, but went back to his walk. Then he slowed down behind *On Coastal Time*, staring at the houseboat for a moment before continuing behind his master. Something about the boat bothered him, just not enough to investigate further. The two of them passed several other boats as well as the enclosed boathouse before he finally split off from the concrete path and trotted over to the grassy area by the perimeter fence.

"Good boy, Bim," Casey said as he walked over to the outdoor kitchen to retrieve a beer from the refrigerator. It was a routine that he and Bimini had repeated over a hundred times before. He pulled up an app on his phone, using it to turn on the pool lights. When Bim was finished relieving himself, the big Golden Retriever walked down the pool steps, launching himself out into the deeper water to take a couple of laps.

Casey sat down on a patio chair as he watched his furry pal swim while he drank his beer. He knew Bimini would have his fill of the water in another five minutes or so. Then he'd get out and shake off as much water as he could before Casey would use a towel to absorb the rest of it. Then the two of them would start to walk slowly back to the *Lady Dawn*, a routine that neither seemed to tire of.

But tonight after Bimini got out of the pool and shook, he turned away from Casey and ran across the pool deck and over toward the helicopter pad. At first, he was growling, then finally barking and snarling as he ran. Casey went running after him, recalling the recent incident where he'd seen him act this same way. The day after that, Casey had some high-intensity floodlights installed along the shore-line. As he ran toward Bimini, he used another switch on that same phone app, this time turning on the new lights.

Bimini had stopped at the base of the seaplane ramp and was barking at a boat that had been far too close to their shore but was now accelerating out of range of the floods. Casey watched the boat as it cruised out into deeper water, soon becoming enveloped by the darkness of the night.

As much as the actions of its unseen operator were suspicious, it was also a very intriguing boat. Casey recognized it as a drake tail deadrise by that unique stern. But this wasn't all that was strange about it, since that transom also lacked a name. And despite the vintage design, the boat appeared to be quite new. Either that, or it had recently been painted, as its hull reflected the light from the floods.

"Good boy, Bim." He patted the dog's still head, his hand getting covered in loose, wet fur. "You've chased them off. I wonder if that boat had anything to do with the other night? But that was another boat, a small outboard, not a large deadrise."

Bimini turned and looked at him with a confident, soft bark. It was as if he was saying that of course, it was and that he could sense it was the same guy. He turned back toward the water, still on alert.

After a few minutes Casey said, "Well, whoever he is, he's not coming back. Let's go get a towel and dry you before we head back to the boat. I've had enough excitement for tonight."

He used the app again and set the timer on the floodlights to shut off in a half hour, then the two went over to the pool house to get Bim toweled off.

~

JERRY SILENTLY CURSED himself for getting so close to the shoreline and attracting the dog's attention yet again. While he was sure that the man with the dog hadn't seen him since he was in the safety of the wheelhouse, he must've at least gotten a good look at the deadrise. If he was connected with Murphy, after the break-in was discovered he may remember the boat and connect the dots. This wasn't good. And neither was the fact that he'd had to move farther down the passage to stay out of range of the lights. Which meant it was going to be harder to spot Danny's signal.

Fortunately, the line of floodlights didn't go all the way down to the little inlet, so he should still be able to pick him up under the cover of darkness. He hoped Danny hadn't run into any problems and had not been forced to use that silenced pistol. The way he'd looked at it and almost caressed it gave Jerry the creeps. And if he *had* used it on someone, Danny might now consider him to be a loose end. One that could tie him to the murder, and he might decide that Jerry needed to go as well.

While he was pondering this, he spotted Danny's signal. But instead of it being out in the middle of the channel like he expected, the light was over closer to the shore. After getting spotted at that ramp, he wasn't happy about having to pick up that close to shore by the inlet. He swung wide as he headed back, getting as close to the opposite shore and as far away from the reach of those floodlights as possible. Once past them, he killed the navigation lights, hoping to blend in with the darkness.

Moving back to the cockpit, he dropped a line with a clip over the side, securing the other end to a cleat on the covering board. Using the cockpit controls, he maneuvered the deadrise in as close as he dared to the shoreline, stopping opposite where Danny was waiting.

Danny could barely make out the boat's outline as it got closer.

Unfortunately, seeing the floodlights had been an unwelcome surprise. At first, he could make out the deadrise on the other side as it approached, but then it melted into the darkness once its nav lights were extinguished. Finally, Jerry was opposite his position, and he could hear the boat's exhaust as it idled in neutral, then spotted it as the low deck lights came on. He used the scooter to close the gap between him and the boat, clipping it and its tethered cargo to the line.

Danny had barely climbed over the covering board when Jerry turned off the deck lights and put the boat in gear, accelerating to a fast idle.

"Hey!" Danny hissed, "Stop. We gotta get the gear aboard."

Jerry replied, "Never mind that, look over in the cove!"

Danny had a clear view straight down the inlet for a few seconds before the jetties obscured it. The side of *On Coastal Time* that faced the basin was now ablaze. He realized Jerry was right, they needed to put a lot of distance between them and that cove. There was going to be a lot of attention paid to that area in a short amount of time.

"At least give me a hand with the line. It's gonna be like pulling a whale with all that drag."

"I'll stop us in a minute. I want to get out of sight of that fire first." He paused before saying, "I didn't know you were gonna torch it."

Danny shook his head. "Neither did I. Must've been some sparks from the grinder that started the fire. But that isn't such a bad thing, either. It'll keep them from finding out the safe was cracked, at least for a while."

A minute later Jerry put the boat in neutral, and the two men hoisted the gear and the gold aboard then retreated into the wheelhouse. Jerry took the boat up to cruising speed then flipped on the navigation lights as they entered Fisherman Inlet Channel. Now they looked like any other fishing boat, returning from a long hard day out on the water.

Danny asked, "What was the deal with those floodlights? You didn't tell me about seeing them the last time you were there."

"That's because I didn't see them." Jerry figured the less he said about the encounter, the better.

"Did they get a look at you?"

"Nope, I was here, in the cabin. No way they could see in."

"But they saw the boat?"

"Probably, but I'm not sure. By the time those lights came on, I was almost past them."

Danny looked thoughtful and concerned. "Must not have been the motion sensor kind then, those would've come on as soon as you got near 'em. Somebody had to turn 'em on."

"Might not have had anything to do with me or the boat. Maybe they're fishing or netting some shrimp, who knows? But I wouldn't worry about it. That fire will take their minds off everything else."

Danny sat down across the small cabin from Jerry and opened the satchel. He wanted to make certain that the Python was dry. He pulled the gun case out and turned it so that Jerry couldn't see what was in it when he opened it. But Jerry knew what a soft-sided pistol case looked like.

"I thought Robert said to leave any weapons if you found them."

Danny glared at Jerry, then reached in and opened the roll of coins, pulling out two which he held out for him. "What weapons."

Jerry hesitated then took the coins out of his hand, putting them in his pocket. "I didn't see any weapons, and that's the truth."

11

FIRE SALE

Casey and Bimini headed back to the *Lady Dawn* after toweling off Bim in the pool house. Halfway down the concrete walk, Bimini took off at top speed, barking as he ran.

"Bim, where are you going," Casey yelled after him.

But the dog didn't slow down at all until he got to the ramp that led to the finger pier between *Sharke* and *On Coastal Time*. That's when he stopped and turned to look back at Casey, barking urgently for him to catch up. By the time Casey reached him, he spotted the glow inside the cabin windows. There was no one else in sight to help, and Lindsay's car wasn't in its space behind the houseboat. He figured that she and Murph must be out somewhere. But still, he had to check.

Casey jumped over onto the small entrance deck and tried the front door, which opened easily. Smoke poured out of the doorway, and he couldn't see too far into the salon because of it. What he could see though was the orange glow through the smoke, and he knew the houseboat was already too far gone to contain it with a handheld extinguisher. Besides, there would be no going into that smoke-filled cabin.

"Lindsay! Murph! You guys in there?"

The only reply was the sound of glass breaking as the heat took out the windows in the back bedroom. Bimini was barking even louder now, concerned for his master's safety.

Casey retreated to the dock and dialed 911, reporting the location of the fire. But he knew that it would be at least ten minutes before the volunteer fire department could assemble and reach him. He also knew that there was a large propane tank under that back deck that fueled the furnace and the range. When the fire reached that tank, it would explode with the force of a bomb.

"Casey, what the hell? Did Murph and Lindsay get out?" Sandy asked as he came running up, eyes wide as he surveyed the scene.

"I don't think they were in there. If they were, there's nothing we can do for them." Casey looked left at Marlin and Kari Denton's vintage Chris Craft, *Why Knot*, in the next slip and then back across the finger pier at *Sharke*. He had to get them both away from the fire before it spread to them or when that tank blew. Then he had another idea.

He turned to Sandy, "We've got to cut *OCT* loose and let the breeze carry her across the cove. There's that big propane tank under the aft deck that Murph just added. If it explodes here, it'll take out this whole line of boats."

Sandy nodded grimly and raced over to the power pedestal on the seawall, unhooking *OCT*'s power, cable, and water lines. Casey went to work on the three short dock lines with a sharp pocket knife, not taking the time to try untying them at the cleats. As he worked on that third and final line at the outer end of the dock, the heat from the fire was so intense it was singeing his hair. In another minute or two it would undoubtedly start blistering the paint and varnish on *Sharke*; the two boats were separated only by that six-foot-wide finger pier.

Back at the stern, Sandy and Casey began pushing the hull out and away from the dock. The slight southwest breeze helped by pushing against the superstructure, which acted like a sail. She slowly cleared the end of the dock just as Dawn and some of the crew of the *Lady Dawn* came racing down the walk. The fire was rapidly advancing through the cabin, fueled by the breeze and the wood and fiberglass construction of the houseboat.

Dawn asked, "What happened? Are Lindsay and Murph okay?"

Casey put his hands out wide, urging everyone back. "I don't think they were aboard. As to what started it, I haven't got a clue, but we all need to get back. If the fire hits that propane tank, we don't want to be anywhere near it."

Sandy added, "You mean when it hits that tank. Thank God the wind is blowing it in the right direction."

OCT's stern was now about twenty-five feet away from the end of the finger pier, on a course toward the shore to the left of the inlet. Casey kept herding everyone back up onto land, away from where the fiery hull was headed. He used another app on his phone to open the electric gate for when the fire trucks arrived.

"Bimini was the hero," Casey said, as he patted the dog's large head. "He saw the fire and started barking. I might have passed by if it hadn't been for him, since it wasn't showing outside the cabin at that point. I'd hate to think what would've happened if we hadn't gotten it away from the dock."

He looked up and watched as the hull had now drifted almost halfway across the basin. The fire had engulfed most of the super-structure and was advancing rapidly toward the back deck and that tank. In the distance, he heard a siren approaching.

The first fire truck came through the gate just as the tank exploded. Bits of flaming wood were thrown almost all the way back to the boats at the dock. A huge mushrooming orange column of flame raced skyward, bathing the cove in an eerie light. They could see that the aft bulkhead was gone, as was the entire stern.

Water was now rushing into what was left of the hull. With no transom left to keep it out, she began to slowly slip below the surface. Not that there was much left to sink. The upper deck, which contained a small guest quarters and sundeck, had already collapsed down into the lower deck area. Only the lower portions of the salon's side walls were left. It took less than two minutes for it all to disappear under the water. Everyone on shore watched in stunned silence until one of the firemen approached them.

"Which one of you owns that boat," he asked the crowd. "Did everyone get off safely?"

Casey replied, "My friends, Murph and Lindsay do. Did. And I'm pretty sure that no one was aboard. Their car is missing, and when I opened the door to look, I couldn't see anything or anyone. We were so busy trying to get it off the dock before the fire could spread, I didn't get a chance to call them, but I will now."

Before Casey could dial his phone, Lindsay's car came through the gate. Murph and Lindsay jumped out of the car and raced over, surveying their empty slip.

"What happened? Where's our boat," he demanded.

Casey told the stunned couple the story as they stared dumbfounded out into the cove. Only a few charred pieces of wood floated on the surface.

"We're just glad that you two weren't aboard," Dawn said.

"Everything else can be replaced, Murph. Insurance should cover most of it," Casey added. He could see that they were in shock.

"We've lost... everything. We don't have anywhere to live, we don't have any clothes, our computer, everything's gone," Lindsay said sadly. "There's nothing left."

Dawn put a hand on her shoulder, "Again, insurance should replace it all, and your computer was backed up on the cloud, right? We'll take you guys clothes shopping in the morning, and you can move into the guest quarters at the pool house until you get a new boat."

The fire chief asked Murph, "Do you have any idea what would have caused the fire?"

He shook his head. "No. Everything was in good shape, all the electrical... and we put in new propane lines when we replaced the tank last winter. There was no reason for it to have caught fire. But I'll need to raise it as quickly as possible, and get it over to the slab at Albury's Boat Works."

"Good. When you do, we'll want to inspect it and see if we can determine a cause. Give us a call when you get it pulled out. There's nothing we can do here until then."

"I DIDN'T WANT to say anything in front of strangers, but we've got two million in gold Krugerrands and a few grand in cash in the safe," Murph said to Casey and Dawn. They were all in the salon on *Lady Dawn*, where Casey had mixed them all drinks. He wanted to help Murph and Lindsay calm their nerves.

"If it was a fireproof safe, it all ought to be fine," Dawn suggested.

Murph nodded. "It is, and you're right, it should. But I won't rest until we get what's left of her raised, set up on the hard, and those coins are back in our hands. I'm guessing the electronic lock will be ruined, but Carlton Albury should have some tools that will help us open it. I already called him, and he has a salvage guy lined up to raise and tow her down to his boatyard. He'll be here at first light."

"Good. You two stay aboard here tonight. Casey and I will loan you some clothes until you can go shopping. You can worry about moving over to the pool house tomorrow."

"Thanks, Dawn, we appreciate this. And we'll get out of the pool house as soon as we can rent a place or find a new boat," Lindsay replied.

"Nobody is scheduled to stay in the pool house anytime soon," Casey said. "So you kids stay in there as long as you like. Insurance can take a while to settle up, and you two have enough things going on as it is. This is one less thing for you to worry about."

Murph smiled ruefully. "Thanks, Case. Fortunately, we have that gold, so we don't have to wait for the insurance check before we start looking to replace *OCT*. We'll get those coins back tomorrow, and put them in a vault at the bank. It's going to be one busy week."

ROBERT OUTERBRIDGE STRODE across the dark yard between his warehouse and the Merritt's slip over next to the boathouse. He stepped down into her cockpit and hurried into the salon where Danny and Jerry were waiting.

"Chingas, boys! Well done," Outerbridge said as he opened both of the cloth bags containing the Krugerrands.

Jerry looked at Danny and asked, "Chingas?"

Danny nodded, "Means he's happy. It's a Bermuda thing."

"Damn right I'm happy! And you got the bags back as well. Good job! I was hoping that I had stalled that pair long enough for you to get it all done. No troubles, right? Where was it? Was there anything else with it?"

Jerry glanced away as Danny said, "It was in a safe in the closet. There were some guns and a few grand in cash with it. One little bit of trouble though, the houseboat caught fire after I left."

"What? Damn it, Danny!"

Jerry was looking down now as Danny said, "This might not be a bad thing. It'll wipe out any DNA evidence, and maybe it'll take a while before they figure out the gold's gone."

"They'll know by now, trust me! If my boat burned with this much gold on it, the first thing I'd do is get it out of the wreckage. Damn it! Now they'll know exactly when it was stolen, and that they were both with me at the time. I'm connected to it because I knew they had it."

Danny said, "But they didn't know that you knew where it was. Or that you know where they live. Make that, lived. They'll be guessing, and they don't have any proof."

"They won't need much to start digging around. I'm going to find out what those favors I give to the sheriff are really worth. Tell me you at least left the guns and the cash."

Danny nodded. "Yeah."

For the first time, Jerry looked up. "Good thing the new sheriff likes them China girls that Cho gets him."

Outerbridge looked at Jerry as if seeing him for the first time today. His eyes narrowed as he said, "You've been quiet. Too quiet. So, what about you, were there any problems on your end?"

"Uhhhh, nope. Easy drop off, and fast pickup. Nobody spotted me dropping him off or picking him up."

"Dropping off and picking up? What about the rest of the time?"

Jerry nervously shifted one foot. "Well, some floodlights got turned on by the water a little after I went by that ramp..."

"HOW MUCH 'after?' Soon enough to have seen the boat and that's why they turned them on?" Any elation that Outerbridge had left was now gone, replaced by growing concern.

"Dunno. They were still on when we left. Like I told Danny, musta been a coincidence, and they were goin' fishing or something."

Outerbridge winced at the mention of the word "coincidence" and he glared at Jerry. "Now we have to figure that they've seen the boat, and maybe you, too."

Jerry shook his head. "No way they saw me, Robert, I was in the wheelhouse the whole time. But maybe they mighta seen my stern as I was going away."

"Maybe, huh. So I'll take that as fact. They can't connect any of us to the deadrise, and we need to keep it this way. The best way to do that is to keep running her only at night, and undercover in this shed during the day." He went silent, thinking about the best way to react to what he'd just learned. "Okay, here's what we're going to do to throw them off the track..."

12

UNHAPPY SURPRISES

The salvor was good to his word, his boat and crew showing up at daylight. It took less than two hours for them to get several straps under what was left of the hull and attach lift bags to them. Once the top edge of the hull was level with the surface, they began towing it slowly out of the cove, up the ditch, and out into Magothy Bay. Albury's Boat Works was located about midway up the bay, a couple of miles north.

Murph, Lindsay, Casey, and Dawn followed along close behind in *LNZ II*. At Albury's, they tied up at the floating dock by the "slab," a large concrete pad loaded with boats that were hauled out "on the hard." Carlton Albury joined the four of them as they watched while the salvage crew maneuvered the burned-out hull over the straps of the travel lift which was waiting out on its twin concrete piers. The operator slowly lifted it above the water, pausing to allow the water to drain out of the now open stern where the transom used to be. The salvors used long boat hooks to retrieve their straps and lift bags.

Once the majority of the water had drained out, the operator finished raising the hull. He then drove the lift over to where several large wooden ties were lying on the ground and lowered the flat-bottomed hull down onto them. After all the travel lift straps were removed and the gantry rolled away, Murph and Lindsay used a small ladder to climb into the charred wreck.

The salon walls were only half as high as they had been, and there were no walls or bulkheads left in the stern. Up forward, the bulkhead and the sliding pantry doors were also gone. The only thing left of their bedroom was the hull below it. What little was left of that deck had collapsed into the bilge, which now was filled with a charcoal-looking muck.

Murph estimated the area where the safe had been and spotted a square shape among the debris. He carefully made his way over and started digging out the heavy fireproof box with his hands. It turned out that what he'd seen was the back of the safe, which had fallen through the weakened deck when the closet structure collapsed.

When he rolled it back upright, he didn't understand why part of the face was missing, leaving the locking mechanism exposed. He recalled that the front had been metal, not plastic or anything flammable that the fire could have consumed. A sudden dread overcame him as he wrenched the now bent locking handle, opening the door. His worst fears were confirmed.

He made his way back into what had been the galley area where Lindsay and Dawn were salvaging some of Lindsay's cast iron cookware. She looked up at his ashen face, not realizing the depth of his anguish. Her face was smeared with black soot where she'd wiped away tears. She said, "It's all gone, babe."

He nodded. "I know. And so's the gold. We've gotta call the cops. We need to figure out who could've stolen it, and get it back. But we've got to get out of here and let the cops at it, this is a crime scene now."

～

"So, Jacques dear, I've managed to get us an invitation to my neighbor's home this evening for cocktails. You'll love meeting him, he's Eric Clarke. And his daughter and his girlfriend are both dolls. They're choppering over from Northern Virginia tonight and bringing a friend with them." Andrea was excited about showing off her latest beau.

Jock tried not to show his excitement at recognizing Clarke's name. "Who is this Clarke person, an American actor?"

"Seriously, dear? He's a well-known Virginia billionaire! I can't believe you haven't heard about him."

He continued to feign disinterest. "Sorry, but I'm not too well versed on American 'monetary royalty.' I pick my friends by their deeds and personalities, not their net worth."

"You aren't even the least bit curious about mine?" She smiled slyly.

"It's not something we do in Europe. Things like these magazine lists of the wealthy that are so popular over here are frowned upon back at home."

"Oh, he's in them all. Want to know if I'm in any?" She batted her eyelashes in an exaggerated and teasing way.

"No. I have learned all that I need to know about you from our long talks during our days of sailing. That, and committing to memory every square centimeter of your body like it was a navigational chart." He put an arm around her waist, pulling her close as she pretended to protest at first. Then she put both arms around his neck and grinned.

"Well, the truth is I'm not in as many as Eric. But I like your standards. And just so you know, there will be a navigation test on that chart later."

He shook his head. "I would prefer to take that test now."

Rikki Jenkins stood with her partner, Cindy Crenshaw, on the patio behind Eric Clarke's home. His lot was the largest and best situated in all of the *Bayside Club Estates*. The Chesapeake bordered one of his property lines, and the creek leading to the club's private marina another. The view from the property was the best of all the homes there.

While Cindy was in charge of everything at *Bayside* including the club, Rikki was the majority owner and head of *ESVA Security*, a low profile, national security firm which handled a lot of government problems that politicians would rather forget about. Her office was located in the *Bayside* compound.

Rikki was fond of saying that her company provided "plausible deniability, which comes with a very large price tag." But when you were a politician who can't afford a scandal and the government has stepped in yet another mess, as it so often did, Rikki and her team were who they called to make things "go away."

They also handled security at all of the properties Casey Shaw's investment group owned, including *Bayside*. Clarke, Rikki, and Cindy were all friends and also partners in that group, so the two women's presence here tonight was only partially business, and mostly pleasure. Though those two reasons tended to overlap a bit.

Rikki Jenkins was what can best be described as "a severe beauty." In her early thirties, she had short platinum hair, ice-blue eyes that you could see from across a room, and a slightly athletic build on her five-foot, nine-inch frame.

In slight contrast with Rikki, Cindy was very shapely, with soft curves, shoulder-length curly blond hair, and bluish-gray eyes. Roughly the same age as Rikki, she was an inch shorter. The two had been a couple for a few years, living together on their older Hatteras, *Hibiscus*, in the *Bayside Resort's* marina.

"Hello, you two!" Clarke walked up and kissed each woman on the cheek.

"Hello, Eric. I saw that you had landed a bit earlier than normal this afternoon," Cindy said.

"Well, that's one of the benefits of hiring a CEO, the chairman can get a few hours head-start on the weekend and the cocktail hour!"

Rikki looked at him and said, "I'd hire one for *ESVA*, but once she knew everything that I know, I'd have to shoot her. Rule one is to not leave any loose ends." She winked at Clarke.

He laughed, "I'm glad that I know you well enough to be able to tell that's a joke."

She cocked her head slightly and raised an eyebrow before

breaking into a grin. "Are you sure?" Then the three of them laughed, though the other two knew a lot about Rikki's past. A past that included more than its share of dead bodies, all of them having belonged to some very bad people. In addition to being beautiful, she was also very lethal when necessary.

Clarke had dark hair but was slightly balding, and was a couple of pounds over his "fighting weight." He was in his early forties and the same height as Cindy.

"So, where are your two favorite women?" Cindy asked.

"Missy took Candi and her friend out for a ride in *'Lil Miss* a while ago. They should be back soon; the sun is getting ready to set."

"Missy" was Eric's very cute, mid-teenaged daughter, Elaina, by his ex-wife. She preferred living with her dad and "Candi," who was ex-Congresswoman Candace Ryan. Roughly Eric's age, Candi had a striking build and was very toned, with shoulder-length auburn hair.

In addition to his half interest in *Sharke*, Eric owned a mint nineteen-fifties, seventy-five-foot Trumpy yacht named the *MissE* which is tied up beside the house. He also owns an eighteen-foot Winter custom center console named *'Lil Miss* that Missy all but lived in for most of the summer.

Eric already owned *MissE* when he met Casey, who thought of Eric at first as an overbearing jerk. He showed up overdressed in Palm Beach preppy style at a very casual get-together. As it turned out, both he and Eric had an aversion to crowds. His mannerism and dress were part of Eric's way of compensating. After overcoming initial misconceptions, they'd become fast friends. Along the way, Casey taught him about "Chesapeake Casual" dress, which meant fishing shirts and khakis or shorts. The polo shirts were then relegated to the back of his closet when he was on ESVA.

Missy and Rikki were both avid fisherwomen, and the two friends often shared the same boat. Lately, that meant either *Sharke* or *'Lil Miss*. The two were teaching Eric, who built *Sharke* in partnership with Casey so that Missy would have the opportunity to fish with both Casey and his crew. Not that she wouldn't have had a permanent invitation anyway, but Eric liked paying his way for his family.

"Eric! I'd like to introduce you to my new friend, Jacques Danville. Jacques, this is Eric Clarke, Cindy Crenshaw, and Rikki Jenkins." Andrea had arrived with Jock on her arm, and he was doing his best to be nonchalant.

"Ladies... Mr. Clarke." He bowed his head slightly to the women and extended his hand to Eric, who shook it.

"Eric, if you don't mind. Especially since you're a friend of my best next-door neighbor."

Andrea chuckled, "Since you only have two neighbors that live next door, I had a fifty-fifty chance of being the favorite."

Rikki had a sixth sense that had served her well over the years, even saving her life on more than one occasion. Right now, with this new guy, it was screaming at her to watch out. It hadn't helped that he had shown up with Andrea Coyne, who was not one of her favorites among the residents here. And despite what Eric had just said, he was only being ingratiating to her since she was his neighbor. Rikki knew that invitation for cocktails was at her request, not at his offering.

In Rikki's opinion, Coyne was someone who used people until she squeezed all the usefulness out of them. She had enough money so that she could do that and even get away with it for a while. Though she was quick to grow bored with people, especially men, playing with them and then casting them off like old ragged clothes.

Fortunately, there usually weren't enough new and interesting targets for her here. Her stays were typically short before she became bored and returned to DC where the hunting was better. Not that she hadn't shown up with a new "boy toy flavor du jour" on occasion. Kind of like how a female crocodile will bring a fresh kill to an underwater log, jamming it underneath to let the meat "season and tenderize." Then she can enjoy it at her leisure before completely devouring it.

But despite his seemingly contrite exterior, Rikki felt that there was something more about this Jacques and that he wasn't like so many of the others. Whatever it was that set him apart, she was certain it wasn't good. Then again, maybe this one might be someone who could turn the tables on Andrea. The brief thought brought a slight smile to her lips, and too late she realized that Jacques had been looking at her. Not curiously, but more in a cool appraisal, the way a thief might look at a store's security cameras as he cased the place right before a big heist.

Oh yeah, this was one to keep an eye on. Not for Andrea's sake, since she could care less about her. But she intended to look out for Eric. It wasn't just that this was part of her job, but as her business partner and friend, it was also personal.

Breaking eye contact with Jacques, she looked over at Cindy, who had recognized the subtleties of "the look." The one of Rikki's that said things were not quite right, and more than they'd seemed. It was part of why they were so good together; they could almost read each other's thoughts at times. Cindy glanced at Jacques, who was now focused on Eric. Then she looked back at Rikki, who gave her an almost imperceptible nod. Confirmation that something was off about Andrea's new guy. Now both women were on alert.

Rikki's vigil was interrupted by the silent vibration of her phone. She pulled it out of her pocket and looked at the caller ID. She mouthed, "Back in a minute" to Cindy, and took a few steps away from the others.

"What's going on, Case?"

"They hauled what was left of *OCT* this morning. It wasn't an accident, they were robbed. Their safe was broken into before the fire."

"In the *Cove*?" Rikki wasn't often thrown off balance, but this came as a shock. They all considered *Casey's Cove* to be a very safe and secure place. Between Casey and Dawn's crew and the rest of the gang there that were liveaboards, there was almost always someone around. A stranger would have stuck out like a sore thumb.

"So, what did they get? Guns?"

"One pistol, a Colt Python. A little over ten grand in cash, and two million in Krugerrands."

"Two *what*?"

"Two million dollars. Proceeds from selling the Merritt."

"I'm on my way. Why didn't you guys call me earlier?"

Casey sighed, "The new sheriff was keeping a lid on things, threatening everyone with arrest if they said anything to anyone."

"That *hack*? Tell me you're kidding."

"Wish I was. He said we could be charged with 'impeding an investigation' if we shared information with anyone else. And there's more, but I don't want to tell you over the phone."

"On my way."

"Meet us on my boat."

Rejoining the others, she apologized for having to rush off. Eric and Cindy knew not to ask questions. They understood this just came with the territory with Rikki.

Eric replied, "No worries, I see reinforcements arriving." He smiled as he pointed out into the bay. Missy was on her way into their private dock, along with her two passengers.

Then before Rikki could leave, she noticed a very strange thing happening, as Andrea's friend's face went ashen. He turned and looked in the other direction, away from the arriving boat, and clutched his stomach.

Andrea noticed and asked if he was alright. He said quietly to her, "A bit of an upset stomach. I'm afraid I need to go back to your house for a while."

"I'll take you over there."

"No, stay and enjoy your friends. This has happened before, an unfortunate lingering side effect from these." He touched his shirt over where the two bullet scars were. "I'll probably be indisposed for a bit and I doubt I'll be back for more cocktails. I'm sorry."

"Are you certain that you don't want me to come with you?"

"Positive. Though if you wouldn't mind checking on me in a while..."

"Of course, dear. I'll finish this one drink, say hello to the girls and then I'll be over."

He hurried away and was out of sight down the driveway before Missy had finished docking. Part of what made him such a good con man was his ability to rapidly react to changing situations, and steer the outcomes. The upset stomach bit explained why he had to hurry away. It also ensured that he'd only be mentioned in passing, because Andrea wouldn't want to explain why he had disappeared. Which also meant there was less chance of his name being dropped in front of Claire Fisher, the woman from St. Michaels. He'd recognized her as a passenger on the arriving outboard before she'd had a chance to spot him. A fluke of bad luck, and a very disturbing one.

Rikki asked Andrea, "Is your friend all right? He looked as if he'd seen a ghost."

"He'll be fine. Sudden onset of a stomach bug."

"I hope he gets better soon." She turned to Clarke, "Eric, please say hello to your ladies for me, and thank you for the invitation."

As she turned to leave, Rikki couldn't help but think that Jacques, or whatever he called himself, was lying about the sudden illness. Probably his name as well. Something about *'Lil Miss*, or more likely someone who was in it, had spooked the hell out of him. So, her initial intuition had been correct. She was determined to find out what was behind it, but first, she had to help Lindsay and Murph find out who took their gold, and hopefully get it back.

13

EXODUS, PART 2...

"Oh, I thought you might be camping in the head," Andrea said, surprised at seeing Jock sitting on the couch in her living room when she walked in.

"I'm sorry, I lied about being sick. I saw someone on Eric's outboard that I had to get away from before she saw me."

"What? Who, and why?"

"Her name is Claire Fisher, or at least that's the one she's using now. Remember how I told you there were people that I didn't want to find me? Dangerous people, that have friends in high places? She's one of them."

"What? Nonsense. I talked to that woman, and she didn't seem dangerous at all. Although you're right, she did say her name was Claire. She's a friend of Candi's, and very sweet."

"Oh, she's very sweet. Until she puts a bullet in your brain when your back is turned. Don't you think it's a funny coincidence, her showing up here right after I did? She tracked me to St. Michaels, and now she's here. That's not a coincidence, Andrea. Remember how I had motored all night to get here? I spotted her up there, and then I left in the middle of the night before she could find me. Now she has tracked me all the way down here. You didn't mention my name, did you?"

"No, I did not. I only said that my friend had fallen ill suddenly, and I needed to go check on him, which was why I wasn't staying." She paused a minute, thinking. Then she shook her head slightly and said, "You must be wrong about her, maybe you have her confused with someone else."

"Trust me, I do not have her confused with anyone. She's a cold-blooded killer. Whatever we do, we can't let her know I'm here. Fortunately, they were going to tie up at Eric's dock and not continue down the creek to the private marina. If she had seen *Mistral*, she'd have known for certain that I am here."

"They use the house docks for their boats, so there's no reason for them to go over to the marina. So you're safe so long as you stay here in my house until she leaves."

Jock nodded while silently congratulating himself on selling the story since apparently, Andrea had now bought into it.

"Well, I cannot think of anyone I would rather be housebound with since I need to stay out of sight. I'll make us some drinks so that we can relax, and call the club to order dinner delivered. We'll have a nice, cozy evening at home."

Jock went over to Andrea's bar and poured two vodkas, keeping his back to her so she couldn't see that two-thirds of the drink he poured for himself was water. His plan was to keep making drinks and get as much vodka into Andrea as possible until she finally fell asleep. He needed to get out of there before Claire discovered him, and then Armageddon happened when she found out he was with Andrea.

Jock couldn't believe the irony, he was finally in the middle of what could be the score of a lifetime, but he couldn't stick around long enough to pull it off. He knew he couldn't risk it. Rich people know a lot of other rich people, and if he was exposed, his story would be told from Boca Raton to Martha's Vineyard. He'd be finished on the east coast.

His ability to rapidly adapt as the situation changed came into play once more. He had a plan. Rich people love things being about themselves. Jock would again take control of the narrative by making his departure not about himself, but Andrea. This would ensure her silence, and endear him to her even more. Then he would lie low in some place off the beaten path just long enough. Finally, he would invite her to join him on some island somewhere. One that was far enough away not to run into any of his old marks, but still fancy enough for her to want to bring along plenty of jewelry. He smiled as he turned back to her, delivering the first drink, the plan now put into action.

RIKKI WALKED STRAIGHT into the *Lady Dawn*'s salon, not bothering to knock. Casey, Dawn, Lindsay, and Murph were seated on two of the couches. She sat down in one of the matching chairs.

Casey said, "Hey Rik, thanks for coming right over. I'm afraid this is something we're going to have to end up dealing with ourselves."

He told her about finding the boat in flames, then how it sank in the cove. Murph took over the story at that point, explaining how he and Lindsay had been at dinner with Outerbridge at his invitation.

"The guy kept stretching out the dinner conversation, taking forever to finish his food, and at the same time trying his best to look down my blouse," Lindsay said. "I should've worn a higher neckline."

"So you think he was stalling to keep you there," Rikki asked.

Murph exploded, "I damn well know he was! Making sure that whoever broke in had plenty of time to get the job done."

Rikki held up a hand to try and calm him. "Okay, that sounds plausible. Did you close the deal over on *OCT*, and did he see the safe?"

Lindsay said, "That's the part which makes no sense. We dealt with him over in the marina, on *Irish Luck*. The Merritt's registration address was the marina office's. He didn't follow us when we left, and there was no way he should have known about *Casey's Cove*, *OCT*, or the fact that we put the gold in the safe. Nobody but Murph and I knew where it was."

"How did you move it from the Merritt over to here?"

"Murph took one bag, and I took the other. They were pretty heavy."

"Where did you get the bags?"

Murph answered, "Outerbri... it was the bags, wasn't it?"

Rikki nodded. "More than likely there were trackers in one or both of them. He'd have known the gold was on the boat, and then it was just a matter of searching it."

Murph hung his head, "I left the bags in the closet next to the safe. I might as well have left them a neon frigging sign saying 'Come rob us.' Damn it, I'm sorry Linds." She reached over and put a reassuring hand on his.

Rikki continued, "Have you called your insurance company yet?"

Murph looked disgusted. "Yes. The pistol is covered because it was detailed on a schedule. They're denying all but fifty grand of the gold claim because the coins weren't listed, and neither was the cash. If we can't prove Outerbridge stole it all, we're out two million bucks. And we won't be able to replace *OCT* with a damn rowboat after they take out all the deductions on the settlement. I've got to get those coins back."

Casey said, "But here's the strange part, and why I say we'll probably need to take this on ourselves. As soon as that new sheriff, Bromwell, heard Outerbridge's name, that's when he shut us down about sharing what we knew with anyone else."

Dawn added, "You could see the change in his face. He's not the friendliest guy by any means, but all of a sudden we were getting treated like *we* were the criminals."

Rikki nodded, "I haven't heard too many good things about him. He cleaned house after he was elected, and unfortunately, all the deputies he ran off were the real straight arrows."

"You think he could be tied in with Outerbridge?" Lindsay asked.

"I don't know enough to say for sure, at least right now. But let's just say I wouldn't be shocked if he was. So, where does this Outer-bridge live?" Rikki asked.

Murph looked chagrinned as Lindsay answered her, "That's the thing, we don't know for certain, since we never got his address. But I get the feeling it's on ESVA somewhere. He said he had his private dock all set up and ready for the Merritt. When he left here, he was headed toward the bay." She paused a minute, "So you think this whole thing was preplanned as a swindle from the start." The way she said it was more of a statement than a question.

"Feels that way. The big tipoff is the form of payment, those gold Krugerrands. No serial numbers, and no way to trace them. If he had them sitting on a table in front of him, you couldn't swear for certain that they were the ones that were taken from you. He'd have been screwed if you'd have taken them to a safety deposit box at a bank. But owning gold has a strange effect on a lot of people. They want to keep it closer to them than at a bank somewhere. I'd say he was counting on that, and why he had that tracker or trackers with them. Why don't you call him, and see if you can find out where he lives. He probably likes to keep his gold close by, too."

"Good idea." Murph took out his phone and dialed, then a sour look came over his face as he listened. "Disconnected."

Rikki said, "Makes sense, he wouldn't want anyone being able to track his phone."

"You couldn't anyway," Lindsay said. "It was one of those cheap ones you can buy in convenience stores, the ones that don't have a GPS built in. Said he'd lost his regular one overboard and hadn't had a chance to go over to the phone store in Virginia Beach to replace it yet."

Rikki nodded. "Using a burner phone. Sounds more and more like he was behind this. Casey's right, this is something we're going to have to handle by ourselves since I doubt we'll get any further help from the sheriff. I'll get my people working on trying to find out where he lives." She paused while she thought then said, "I'm guessing whoever he sent after the coins came here by boat."

Casey said, "Couldn't have, at least not pulling up to *OCT* or into the cove, I'd have seen them. The only boat I saw was in the ditch out front, headed toward Magothy Bay. Though it *was* running without lights. What caught my attention was Bimini started barking at the water, like he'd done the night after you guys sold the Merritt. But that boat was an outboard, and this was a new-looking deadrise that I saw when I hit the floodlights. One of those rare drake tails."

"A *WHAT*? You didn't mention that part! What was the name of it?" Murph demanded.

"That's part of what was funny about it," Casey said. "It didn't have a name, at least not on the stern."

"Sonofabitch! I almost got run over by that same boat, or one exactly like it, over on Talbot Creek on the west side of the bay. But you said you'd have seen it if it had pulled into the cove."

"Yes, but he wouldn't have necessarily seen a diver being dropped off and picked back up," Rikki mused. "Maybe they had already loaded up by that point."

"That was over eighty pounds of gold! No way one diver could handle that much. Maybe there were a few of 'em," Murph replied.

Rikki said, "Don't forget the two-thirds rule. That eighty pounds would weigh less than sixty pounds underwater because of the density and displacement."

"That's still too heavy for one diver."

"And how did they raise your hull this morning?"

"Lift bags and strap... Of course! A single diver could've used some lift bags to compensate for the weight. So when you saw 'em Case, they were loaded and heading home."

He shook his head. "I don't think so, Murph. When Bim started barking, the boat was barely idling along up near the shore, like they were waiting around for someone. If they'd had already picked up their diver, they'd be hooked up and running, wanting to get away fast. Plus, there was nobody in the cockpit. I bet that they were waiting for a signal. And when I was on my way over to C2, something around OCT was bothering Bim. Could've been that he sensed someone was aboard who shouldn't have been." He paused, thinking. "I didn't stay on the ramp for that long after the deadrise went past.

They could've easily doubled back and picked up a diver and the gold."

"Well, I know one other place where that deadrise has been. It's a Chinese vegetable farm over on Talbot Creek. We can be there in a half hour in *LNZ II*. Let's go!"

"Hold on, it's dark outside. If that farm is related to Outerbridge, I don't think you want to go barging in there after dark," Dawn argued.

Murph looked across the salon and through the windows, realizing Dawn was right. He had been so focused on trying to figure out who had ripped them off, that he'd lost track of time.

Rikki spoke up, "And we're going to have to be very careful if we're going to get any information about the boat or its owner when we get there."

"You'll help us then?" Lindsay looked hopeful.

"Of course, I will. I'm going over there with you, but in the morning, not now. Let's all sleep on this tonight, and meet for breakfast at the *Cove*."

It was almost one o'clock in the morning before Jock was able to sneak out and take off in *Mistral*. Andrea was making small noises that were a combination of a snore and a purr, so he knew she would sleep straight through the night. He'd penned a note explaining why he couldn't put her in any more jeopardy than he already had. And that once he found the perfect place where they could be together again safely, he'd contact her.

Once out on the Chesapeake, he motored south, hoping to reach his destination around sunrise. He'd picked out a spot for a layover while he decided on his next move. It was the perfect place with plenty of tourists, lots of smaller boats, and not as many yachts. Not the kind of place where he'd expect to run into any of Claire or Andrea's friends. But the pictures on the internet showed that it had a bit of an almost Caribbean vibe, so it could be fun, especially the two beach bars. Some place named *Mallard Cove*.

14

BACK TO THE CREEK

It was just before sunrise when the group met up on the big outdoor deck at the *Cove Restaurant*. There were a few other tables already taken, mostly by regulars and tourists that would soon be boarding the charter boats docked in front of the deck. It was a popular early morning breakfast place for the fishing crowd, partly because they opened so early, and also because the food was so good.

Casey was the first to arrive, choosing one of the less desirable tables away from the ones that overlook the marina so they'd have more privacy. Those other, more popular tables got claimed the fastest by the regulars after the offshore fishermen left. The only other occupied table near Casey's had some bleary-eyed guy who was eating a croissant and some fruit. He looked like he'd had a hard night, and didn't seem interested in anything or anyone around him.

"Hey, Case." Rikki took a seat next to him.

"Morning, Rik. You find out anything?"

"Very little. It's like the guy never existed, at least here in the US. What I did find was an address in Bermuda, and that's about all. No vocation, banking, nothing. And here's the weird thing, all the property records over there connected with that address have been erased. No sales records, nothing."

"Is this all that unusual for Bermuda?"

Rikki nodded. "Extremely. They're very meticulous about their record keeping over there. The archives go all the way back to when the English Virginia Company created the first permanent settlement there, in 1609."

"So, Outerbridge has some pull back home."

"Looks that way." She paused, then asked, "Isn't Dawn coming with us?"

Casey shook his head, "We have a large enough landing party as it is, and she had meetings already scheduled. Better if we keep it to just the four of us."

Rikki glanced over at the restaurant's floating dock where Murph and Lindsay were pulling up in *LNZ II*.

"Here they come. Everyone knows to be carrying, right?"

"Oh yeah, we're all armed. It's not likely that he'll want to give back a thousand Krugerrands without a fight. If he's even around there. At the very least, he'll know we're onto him, and bad things can happen fast when you kick a hornet's nest."

OVER AT THE OTHER TABLE, Jock had been quietly sipping his coffee, keeping his back to Rikki. He'd already waved off his server once when she tried to give him a warmup since he'd intended to go straight back to *Mistral* after breakfast and get a nap. He'd been at the helm for over six hours straight. But that was before Rikki showed up, and now he signaled the server that he had changed his mind. Suddenly he wasn't in such a hurry to get back to the boat. Overhearing a conversation about a thousand gold coins can have this kind of effect. He did the math in his head about what they would be worth, and he liked all the commas and zeros in the sum. He also didn't want to draw Rikki's attention to him by getting up and leaving.

"GOOD MORNING, GUYS," Rikki said.

Murph had his grim face on as he walked up and merely nodded. Lindsay smiled and returned the greeting.

"Hey! Good mornin' youse guys! Up early to go fishin'?" Baloney had walked up with Sandy in tow. The pair were planning on having breakfast before going out to take advantage of the now reopened cobia season. Baloney proceeded to pull out a chair without being asked or invited. Sandy looked questioningly at Casey, who indicated he should do the same.

Casey replied, "No, we have something to take care of."

"Hey Murph, Lindsay, I been meanin' to tell ya how sorry that Betty and me are about you losin' your boat like that. If there's anything we can do ta help you kids, all ya got ta do is say so." For all his faults, Baloney was a true friend and was very fond of the couple.

"Thanks, Bill, that's so sweet of you two. But we're good for now," Lindsay replied.

"We'll be even better when we catch up with the sonofabitch that caused..." Rikki put a hand on Murph's arm, stopping him in mid-sentence.

Baloney was confused, "Wait, what? I thought the fire was an accident?"

Sandy looked at the serious faces of the four and said, "Bill, I'm getting the feeling that this isn't the right time to start asking questions."

"Whattayamean? If somebody did it ta them, I wanna know about it. Nobody does stuff like that here, not ta my pals."

Rikki smiled and told him, "Baloney, you know you'll hear all about it later. But as Sandy said, it might not be in your best interest to get those answers right now. Legally speaking."

Baloney silently weighed what Rikki had said before he answered. "All right, Rik. But ya know if ya need me and Sandy, we're there for ya like we've always been. Ya can count on us."

Ordinarily, Sandy might've objected to someone speaking for him, but in this case, Baloney was right. Both of them would be glad to help, no matter what might be involved.

Casey deliberately steered the rest of the conversation over to fishing, which was where it stayed until their food arrived. However, Murph was unusually silent and sullen the entire time. Finally, the four departed, leaving just Baloney and Sandy sitting at the table.

Jock signaled for his check, then left enough cash to cover it as well as a hefty tip. Servers know a lot about what goes on around their restaurants and are more likely to be chatty with big tippers.

"Good luck out there today guys," Jock said as he passed the remaining pair's table on his way out.

"Yeah, thanks," Baloney replied.

As Jock walked away, Sandy asked, "You know that guy?"

"Nah. Probably recognized me from the show. I get that alla time. Hey, down yer java, we gotta go."

Half an hour later, *LNZ II* entered Mobjack Bay. Rikki said, "Remember guys, we're playing it cool. No accusations, just stick to the story. We're trying to find the captain of that drake tail who might've picked up a cooler that Murph lost overboard when the two collided the other night."

Lindsay and Casey nodded, but Murph stared straight ahead from his spot at the helm. "Murph?"

Finally, he nodded, "Yeah. I got it."

Murph clearly wasn't happy about it, wanting a more direct approach, but begrudgingly yielding to Rikki. Five minutes later he throttled back at the mouth of Talbot Creek, dropping their speed to a fast idle. In a couple of minutes, the woods that had been lining the left shore gave way to farmland.

"Would you look at that!" Lindsay exclaimed. In the fields, a couple of dozen workers were harvesting crops. But what was unusual about them was they all were wearing the conical straw worker's hats usually associated with farmers in mainland China.

"The innkeeper wasn't kidding about it being a Chinese vegetable farm," Murph said.

Rikki looked worried. Casey asked her, "What's the matter?"

"It's not very common to see Chinese migrant field hands in Virginia. But one of the Chinese triad's businesses is human trafficking. Once the smuggled people reach the US, they're forced to work off their debt. Many of the younger and prettier women are placed in brothels, the others work in restaurants and menial jobs. They're kept in hidden dormitories and fed just enough to survive. If they last for five years, they may be released. Or not.

"I know of a case in Charlottesville where a Chinese woman owned several restaurants. The basement of her home was more of a dungeon than a dormitory, with thirty trafficked people living in it. These were her restaurant workers. She paid the triad a fraction of what she would have had to pay legal workers. Her restaurants were very popular, and because of the cheap labor, she made a small fortune.

"When a neighbor got suspicious of the vans coming in and out at all hours, her house was raided. They found a lot of those same types of hats that the people had brought with them when they arrived. I'm wondering if this farm isn't a triad setup. We need to be very, very careful if I'm right."

"What happened to those people and that woman?" Lindsay asked.

"The workers were rounded up by ICE and put into the system. The woman avoided capture, but later her body was discovered tied to the front door of one of the closed restaurants. She'd been beaten to death. A warning from the triad to the other restaurant owners they deal with to be more careful than she was, or the same thing would happen to them." Ricky said.

The next couple of minutes went by silently until they went around the last bend in the creek. Ahead on the right was the inn with its old deadrise tied up at the dock. Over to the left was the large boat shed and dock. Both were empty, with no sign of the drake tail. There were, however, several "No Trespassing" signs at the opening of the dilapidated-looking shed and the end of the dock. As they got closer, however, they could see the shed was in good repair but had been painted in a way to make it look old and abandoned.

Murph pulled the outboard into the shed, then Lindsay and Casey handled the dock lines, tying them up to a finger pier. It connected to a small dock at the back of the shed which looked like it had recently been scrubbed and bleached.

Rikki caught the other three's attention, and said quietly, "We're on candid camera."

There were two cameras, one above the small door to the left at the back of the shed, and another in the middle of the back wall, facing down the creek. Both looked like they were infrared types, the kind that worked in daylight and at night. As the four of them climbed up onto the finger pier, three Asian-looking men burst through the back door. The one in the lead said loudly, "You trespassing. You go now."

Murph said, "Oh, hey! I'm looking for the captain of the deadrise that was here the other night. He ran into my rowboat, and I lost my best cooler. I want to see if he found it."

"You wrong. That boat over at hotel. You go now."

"No, not that deadrise, I'm talking about the round stern one. A drake tail."

"No boat like that here. Over at hotel." The man insisted.

Murph decided to try another tactic. "I heard it might belong to a guy named Robert Outerbridge. Do you know where I can find him?"

The reaction was swift. The man's eyes squinted as he motioned to the two men behind him and suddenly pistols appeared in their hands. "No boat like that ever here. Never hear of that man. You go now, you trespassing!"

Murph replied, "Well then maybe we need to call the cops and report the collision."

"No police! You go now... while you can." The guns raised higher and were now pointed directly at Murph. The look on the man's face now said he was serious. Deadly serious.

Murph raised his hands in front of him as they all edged back and climbed into the boat. The pistols stayed pointed at him as he cranked up the engines.

"You tell Robert that Murph is looking for him." The men

remained silent as Murph backed out of the shed. As he spun the boat around, he spotted Red in the cockpit of the deadrise behind the inn and changed course for that dock.

Red looked up as they approached, recognizing Murph. "Hey there, Murph! Looks like you've got not just one but two good-looking boats. I got a peek at your sailboat when it was here."

Murph pulled up alongside the deadrise and introduced Casey and Rikki. "Thanks, Red. Yeah, this one gets us where we're going a little faster than the *Peggy T.* Speaking of that, we were just over at your neighbor's, trying to catch up with a guy in a drake tail that almost ran me over the other night. They're not very friendly over there."

Red's face clouded up, "Nope, you won't find a lot of friends across the creek. They want to be left alone, and frankly, that's fine with me. We don't see much of 'em unless they're harvesting up near the creek, but it's a pretty good-sized farm.

"About that drake tail, I've gotten a look at it twice, both times on moonlit nights. Always runs without lights. Lucky we don't get a lot of traffic on the creek, or there might've been a bad accident before now. Glad you said he *almost* hit you."

"Yeah, it was close. Hey Red, do you know a guy named Robert Outerbridge?"

"Can't say I've ever heard that name before. Sorry, I'm not much help today."

"That's okay. Anyway, good to see you again. We enjoyed that cruise the other night, and we'll have to do it again, maybe in the fall."

"Anytime! I'll be here."

Murph put the engines in gear, and they idled slowly away. As they went down the creek, Rikki stared over at the farm. "You guys notice anything strange over there?"

The other three scanned the fields and Casey said, "I don't see anything."

"Exactly. The people have all disappeared. Looks like they stopped harvesting only a short way into it, and now they're gone. Are you guys getting the same idea as me that we weren't supposed to see any of them?"

Casey said, "And we got guns pointed at us when Murph mentioned Outerbridge. I'm glad none of y'all went for your guns."

Rikki said, "If we had, at the very least we'd have been in big legal trouble since we were technically trespassing with firearms, and that's a felony. Though he freaked when Murph suggested calling the police. Yeah, things aren't at all like they seem over there."

"I don't know about that," Lindsay said. "That one guy was majorly creepy, even without a gun. That's how the whole place seemed to me."

"HOLD ON CHO, slow down, I can barely understand you. What outboard are you talking about?" Outerbridge was in his office in the warehouse when Cho called, completely irate. "*LNZ*? And he knew what? His name was *Murph*? And he said he got rammed by the deadrise? No, no, don't worry about this, I'll handle it. I *said* I'll handle it, damnit! And don't talk about this on the phone again!"

He hung up the phone, his real phone, not the disposable he'd used when he dealt with Murph. That one was already at the bottom of the Chesapeake. Then he stormed across the yard, making a beeline for the Merritt's slip. He found Jerry and Danny in the salon, having coffee. They looked up as he burst through the door, obviously angry.

"All right bloke, anything you want to add to your report about your latest trip over to the farm?" Robert stared at Jerry.

"Uh, no?"

"Nothing about running into some rowboat?"

"Oh, that. I didn't run into him, I only got kinda close. I didn't see him until I was almost on him, but I turned just in time. I didn't think it was important."

The veins were now standing out on Robert's neck as he began shouting, "You got close enough for him to identify the drake tail, and you didn't think that was important enough to tell me about it?"

Jerry was confused. "Him? Him who?"

"*Murph*, damn it, he was the guy you ran into! And now he knows about the deadrise and the farm."

"I swear, Robert, I didn't run into him! I didn't see who it was, an even if I had, I don't know Murph. That's why I never told you, 'cause if I'd ah known, I woulda told you!"

Danny sat back in his chair with his arms crossed. As a long-time associate of Outerbridge's, he knew that loyalty and truth were two of the things Robert demanded of everyone who worked for him. Jerry hadn't been with them all that long, and now he'd violated both of these things. He was sure the guy's days were numbered.

Danny knew that nobody left Robert's organization and lived to be able to rat them out. In his mind, Jerry was as toxic now as the chemicals they'd had him dump. Which was fine with him, since the guy had seen him take the gun from the houseboat, directly disobeying Robert's orders himself. So far he'd kept his mouth shut, but Danny couldn't trust him not to try using this information to save his skin with Robert.

Robert said, "Just get the damn boat ready to go. We need to leave in five minutes. Danny, come with me."

The two walked in silence across the yard. Danny knew Robert was formulating a plan. He also knew not to interrupt his train of thought as they went.

They walked through the warehouse, passing the tanks filled with chemicals and dollar bills that were soaking. Along one wall was a line of commercial laundry dryers, tumbling and drying the bills. Another, mostly automated line oriented, reprinted, and scanned each bill for quality, then stacked and strapped them in groups of fifty which were assembled in bunches that were finally shrink-wrapped and ready for shipment to Cho's farm.

A similar but much smaller line was set up inside an enclosed room with special air filtration. As they passed the window which overlooked that line, he could also see the equipment that produced the Rescentol powder. A thick-walled cabinet held the special element they got from Cho that was used in the powder's manufacture. Some of that powder was also mixed into the bleaching and rinsing agents for these special bills which were carefully sealed in airtight bags.

The worker in this room was wearing a hazmat suit with its own air supply to avoid any contact with either the Rescentol or Cho's element. And the sealed bills were carefully handled so they stayed safe, and so none of the crew could come in contact with them. These were to be shipped to the farm once the first order was finally completed. Unlike the other line in the warehouse which produced only fifties and hundreds, this one made fives, tens, and twenties.

Danny didn't know the reason behind making these lower denomination bills and was certain he didn't want to. To him, it made no sense, but Robert paid special attention to these, so there had to be something to it. Frankly, the hazmat suit scared the hell out of him, and he avoided being near the room whenever he could.

Danny followed Robert into his office and shut the door behind them. Robert motioned for him to sit in an upholstered chair as he took the matching one across from it.

"Is there anything more that Jerry's not telling me?"

"Not that I know of, Robert. But I wasn't on the boat when the lights got flipped on that night. If I knew any more, I'd have told you already."

"What about ramming Murphy?"

"Again, I wasn't there, and this is the first I've heard about it."

Outerbridge stared at him, apparently trying to decide if he was telling him everything he knew. Danny was trying not to squirm and look nervous as he thought about the roll of coins, the pack of bills, and the pistol. Finally, Robert appeared satisfied.

"Okay, here's the deal, we're going fishing offshore, but only the two of us are coming back. Jerry has seen all of the operations and knows what's in my safe. I know I can't trust him any longer. It was my mistake to trust him at all, and yours as well." Robert again stared at him to see if he had any hesitation that might show some kind of alliance between Danny and Jerry. Again, he saw no sign of it.

He stood up and went over and opened a safe behind his desk. Danny could see the stacks of gold coins, several times the amount he'd brought back from Murphy's. Robert reached in and pulled out a Glock nine-millimeter for himself while handing Danny the silenced .22 caliber he'd carried with him to Murphy's.

"The serial numbers on both of these are removed. Remember, if you use yours, toss it over the side. No taking a chance of a ballistics match. Make sure the casing goes over, too."

Outerbridge closed the safe and stood up. "Let's go."

15

HE'S GOT TO GO

As they ran back across the Chesapeake, Lindsay wasn't happy. "So, we're no closer to finding Outerbridge today than we were yesterday."

Casey replied, "I wouldn't say that. We know for sure that drake tail is involved and that it's owned or at least connected to Outerbridge. You said he was taking the Merritt to his private dock that was already prepared for it. A boat that big needs shore power at the dock, and there wasn't any place for it to plug in there. So he's keeping it someplace else. Maybe the same place where that drake tail docks. We just need to find it and follow it home."

"That's like finding a needle in a haystack," Murph said dejectedly.

"It won't be that hard," Rikki replied. "There's some reason that boat visits the farm, apparently always at night, from what your friend Red says. Whatever that reason it probably hasn't changed, unless your telling that guy you are looking for Outerbridge scares him off. We just need to anchor in Mobjack Bay at night, then use our radar to watch for boats going into Talbot Creek."

"But that isn't the only boat that goes back up in the creek," Murph argued.

142

"True. But it's probably the only one that will be running without lights. If we see the blip on the screen, but no navigation lights on the boat, that's probably it. Then we wait for it to come back out and follow it. We won't use our running lights either. Two can play at this game."

~

"Are you sure 'bout this, Robert? I mean, showing up in their backyard'll just keep us on their radar," Jerry said.

He was uncomfortable, for several reasons. Robert was running the Merritt, and once again making him take the companion seat rather than the one at the helm. If that wasn't enough, both Robert and Danny had stopped making eye contact with him; it was like he no longer existed. That was the creepy part, he thought, feeling invisible. They'd never done this before, and it rattled him.

Robert turned and looked at him for the first time since they'd pulled out from the dock, fifteen minutes ago. "You need to quit thinking and just do what I say, do you understand me? And when I ask you something, you need to tell me everything, not just the parts that make you look good. Being successful is all about knowing and taking care of all the details, even the smallest ones."

Jerry saw that Robert's eyes had closed down to two slits, something he knew only happened when Robert was extremely angry. Then Robert turned back toward the bow, again ignoring him. Jerry had an image of that missing crewman flash into his mind, and his blood ran cold. Was he now one of the details that needed taking care of? He knew that like Danny, he had no family, no one to report him missing. It was like that with everyone who worked for Robert. He purposely hired loners.

Knowing Danny kept that Python pistol along with the roll of coins, and worse, knowing that he lied to Robert about all of it, meant he was now a liability to him. Just how much of one was the first question, and what was he planning to do about it was the second. Make that what *they* were planning to do about it. About him.

Robert gave him a quick side glance, noting that he seemed deep in thought. He didn't want Jerry to think too hard and figure out what was going to happen. To put his mind at ease, Robert said, "There's a good reason I want Murphy to see us at *Mallard Cove*. It makes us seem less likely to be guilty. He wouldn't expect someone who was involved in him losing his home and gold to show up at his marina, so that's what we're going to do. Today and every few days for a while. We'll keep fueling up there instead of our tank back at the dock."

Instead of easing Jerry's suspicions, Robert had inadvertently amped them up even higher. He only explained things when he felt like it; never because he was questioned. Otherwise, everyone was expected to follow orders without question. Jerry had taken a real risk by bringing up the subject.

"Got it, Robert."

"When we get there, we will pull up to the fuel dock. Danny will go to the bait shop and purchase some trolling baits. I phoned in a lunch order to the restaurant. You will need to pick it up and bring it back." He reached into his pocket and pulled out some bills, handing them to Jerry. "And put your pistol in the locker under the starboard bench. I do not want anyone in the restaurant spotting the outline through your shirt. Unarmed people are far less likely to have been involved in what happened to Murphy."

"What about Danny's gun?" He winced when he saw a brief flash of anger on Robert's face.

But instead of a rebuke, Robert said, "Good point. Danny put yours in there with Jerry's. We don't need any of us to draw attention."

The look Danny shot at Jerry was not a happy one as he pulled the weapon out of his waistband, putting it away with Jerry's. But he saw that instead of Danny's usual nine-millimeter carry piece that he loved, this was the small .22 caliber pistol with the tiny silencer attached. Jerry remembered what Robert said about how quiet it was, and how a head shot would "take down anyone who might get in the way." And that he should throw it overboard after he used it. This is an expendable gun, to be used on expendable people. Apparently, he was one of them now. On the outside, he looked calm, cool, and collected. But on the inside, he was trying hard not to panic.

$\sim$

Murph turned into *Mallard Cove Marina*'s inlet, intending to drop Rikki off by where she'd parked her car. But looking straight ahead he exclaimed, "I don't frigging believe it!" Their old Merritt was tied up at the end of the fuel dock, and Robert Outerbridge was in the cockpit, manning the fuel hose. Danny was nowhere in sight. Before Rikki could stop him Murph yelled, "You've got a lot of balls showing up here, Outerbridge!"

Robert put on his best offended face as the outboard pulled up alongside. "What are you talking about? I thought you would like to keep me and your old boat as a customer. I am even buying food and bait."

"Yeah, and I'd like to have kept my gold and my house, you son of a bitch! You stole those coins and burned down my boat!"

Murph jumped onto his gunwale then leaped across the three-foot gap to the Merritt's covering board and then down into its cockpit.

Outerbridge looked shocked as he released the fuel hose handle and turned toward Murph, who was now charging across the deck. "I have no idea what you are talking about..."

Robert's denial was cut short by a right cross from Murph. Taken off guard at first, Outerbridge now began hitting back. Half a minute later reinforcements arrived as Casey boarded the Merritt, backing up Murph by grabbing one of Robert's arms. Danny came running down the dock and also jumped aboard, pulling a fish gaff out from the rack under the covering board. Casey had to let go of Robert to deflect the shaft of the gaff as Danny tried to impale him with its large hook-shaped head.

Suddenly Danny's face was introduced to the rock-hard, teak covering board. Stunned, he dropped the gaff and his arms were then pinned behind him. Rikki had joined in the fracas, taking Danny down from behind. When he tried to twist around or say anything, she yanked both wrists, and the knee that was planted in his back became excruciating. He quickly learned to stay still and quiet.

Casey turned back to Murph and Outerbridge but found that Murph was doing just fine by himself. Outerbridge was tiring, and now getting the worst of the battle. With one last fist to the jaw, Outerbridge dropped to the deck in a sitting position, his back against the varnished teak bulkhead.

"Where are my coins!" Murph was still raging, fist cocked back and on the verge of hitting the now defenseless Outerbridge, who was spitting out blood.

"I have no idea what you are talking about. I gave them to you. If you lost them, it's your own bloody fault."

"You burned down my home!"

"I did nothing of the sort! Just when was I supposed to have done this?"

"You had it done when we were having dinner together!"

"You are deranged. How am I supposed to have done this when we were together?"

"Casey saw your other boat waiting to pick up your diver and my gold!"

"What other boat?"

"Your deadrise. The one that makes the runs over to the Chinese vegetable farm."

"Again, you are deranged. This is my only boat, and I don't know anything about any Chinese farm. And since this is my boat, you are welcome to get the hell off it. All of you! And you, let my man up." He glowered at Rikki.

"I'll be happy to. Just as soon as you or he tell us where the coins are."

"You are all mad. Let him go, or we will press charges for assault with Bromwell. We are leaving, and I'll never spend another cent in this place."

. . .

JERRY WAS on the way back with lunch. As he walked down the ramp that led to the transient boat slips and the fuel dock out on the end, he opened the bag to see what they were having. Inside were two cheeseburger boxed lunches. Not three, just two. The implication hit him like a lightning bolt. Now there was no doubt in his mind, that he was never supposed to come back from this "fishing trip." He dropped the bag, the contents spilling out onto the dock.

As he looked back up, at the end of the dock he saw several strangers aboard the Merritt. He couldn't see Robert or Danny, but one of the strangers appeared to be talking to someone down on the deck, just out of sight. Now one of them boarded an outboard that was lying alongside the cockpit. He saw Robert getting to his feet unsteadily, turned toward the other boat, shouting at the retreating strangers. Jerry realized this was his chance, maybe his only chance to escape. If he tried running back up the dock, Robert could spot him. Looking over to his right he saw a large blue sailboat with no one out on deck. There was a cabin boat next to it blocking the view of the Merritt, which was several slips away.

Jerry quietly boarded the sailboat, passing through the opening in the cable safety rail, and trying the latch on the hatch. Better to have to deal with the intruded-upon sailboat owner than Robert. As he descended the steps inside the hatch, he couldn't see anyone inside. A quick search revealed the boat to be empty. Maybe if his luck held, he could stay hidden long enough for Robert and Danny to leave, and then he could come up with a plan. He'd no sooner sat down at a table amidship when his luck changed, and the hatch opened.

AFTER BREAKFAST, Jock moved *Mistral* from the tee end of the fuel dock over to a transient slip the dockmaster had picked out for him. He'd told the man he'd be there a week, maybe two. The dockmaster had an island accent, and so Jock took the time to pick his brain. He wanted to find a place "down island way" that would fit his needs, or rather, his and Andrea's. Private, off the beaten path, but quaint. As it turned out, the man whose name was Barry, knew just the place.

Barry then had to go deal with the owner of a sports fisherman that had finished fueling, so Jock headed back to his boat. Halfway down the cabin steps he was shocked to see a strange man seated at his table. What was worse was Jock's pistol was in his cabin, all the way up in the bow. He'd need to pass by the man to retrieve it. But like any good confidence man, he realized his best weapon was his voice and his words.

"Who the hell are you, and what are you doing on my boat?"

The man looked frightened, "I don't mean no harm, mister. There's some guys in the marina that're after me. I just need a place to hide 'til they're gone."

"No, you need to get the hell off my boat, or I'm calling the cops." Jock pulled out his phone and started to dial 911.

"No wait, please don't! I'll pay you to let me stay in here for a bit. If you call the cops or throw me off the boat, those guys'll kill me."

Jock hesitated because he didn't want to get the police involved either, and was willing to play this out, especially if there was profit in it for him. "How much?"

Jerry reached into his pants pocket, bringing out the change from lunch and placing it on the table. Jock looked at the small bills and scowled, then went back to his phone.

"Wait!" Jerry was desperate as he reached back into his pocket again, this time bringing out one of the two Krugerrands and placing it on top of the paper money. Jock canceled the call.

Jerry said, "It's a Krugerrand, and worth a lot of money."

"I know what it is." Jock paused, recalling the conversation he'd overheard earlier at the restaurant. What was the chance that this was unrelated to what he'd heard? He took a shot in the dark. "So, where are the other thousand that were stolen along with it?" He watched the color drain from Jerry's face.

"Uh, whaaat other thousand?"

The reaction on his face, along with the stammering, just confirmed that this coin had to have been part of that bunch. And no denial of the theft. This guy would make a terrible confidence man, he thought.

"The other thousand Krugerrands you stole from that couple. The ones whose boat you burned. This is why I'm betting you really do have people who want to kill you. I'd say they have two million reasons why give or take a hundred thousand. Did you hide them somewhere?"

"No! I didn't steal no coins, and I didn't burn their houseboat. I just have some gambling debts I can't pay off."

Jock smiled and sat down across the table from Jerry, but not before picking up the coin. "Nice try, but who said it was a houseboat? I only said 'boat.' And a gambler behind on his debts wouldn't have a Krugerrand left in his pocket. You are a terrible liar. And I bet you don't even play poker, am I right?"

"I heard around the docks it was a houseboat. And that was my lucky coin. No, I don't play cards, what's that got to do with anythin'?"

"Then I'd say that coin's luck has run out. And if you played poker, you would know how to bluff. So, you have those other coins, and that's why that couple is after you. They want them back."

Jerry shook his head, "No! They're not after me, I don't even know them!"

"I'm not buying what you're selling. You either come clean with me, or you can get off my boat."

"I'm telling you, there are other people that'll kill me for sure if I get off your boat and they see me."

"They'll kill you for the coins."

"No! I don't have them!"

"But you know who does."

"What? Uh, no, I don't know!"

"You are lying. Look, I know you are scared and I am willing to work with you here. Since you don't have them, all you have to do is tell me where those coins are, and then you can stay aboard until it's safe. Even better, we can sail to wherever you want that's safe, and I can drop you off there." He paused, looking at a very frazzled Jerry, realizing he was making some headway. The guy desperately needed a friend or at least some ally who wasn't out to kill him.

"You have to give me something. If you don't have the coins, you know who does."

"He'll kill me!"

Bingo, Jock thought, now we're getting somewhere. "I thought he was already going to kill you." Again, he was playing a hunch, but his other hunch had already gotten him this far. He watched as Jerry mulled things over silently. Jock knew the second Jerry caved; he could see it in his face before he even said a word.

"Robert Outerbridge. He's got Murph and Lindsay's coins, and it was his guy Danny that stole them for Robert. Burning the houseboat was an accident."

FINALLY CONVINCED that they couldn't get any more out of Robert or Danny, Murph, Casey, and Rikki got back aboard *LNZ II*. Murph shouted at Robert that he needed to get out of his marina, and never come back.

"Trust me, I would never come back here! You accuse me of being a thief when you're the real thief at what you charge for fuel! This is the last place I'd ever take my business," Robert yelled across the water. Then he turned to Danny, "Where the hell is Jerry? I want to get out of here. I'll go settle up for the fuel and then we'll cast off."

Robert stormed up the dock to the office, but halfway there he saw the bag with the hamburgers. As he picked it up, he looked around for Jerry, but of course, didn't spot him. "Damn coward," he muttered.

After paying for the fuel, he looked around but still didn't find Jerry. Returning to the boat he asked Danny, "Did Jerry come back?"

"No, I haven't seen him."

Robert thrust the bag at him. "Take these. He must've run off instead of coming down to help even the sides. Coward. I doubt he'll show up here now, we'll have to hunt him down. Let's get back to the dock and I'll get the sheriff working on finding him. Then we'll do what we set out to. All right, get the dock lines."

16

HIDE AND SEEK

Murph and the crew waited patiently just out of sight behind Fisherman Island for the Merritt to appear. He rubbed his jaw and said, "It was almost worth getting hit by that guy to have him land in our laps like this. I just hope he's not out fishing for long before he heads in."

Suddenly they spotted the big white hull exiting the marina's inlet. But to their surprise, instead of turning left to run offshore, it turned right, heading for Fisherman Inlet Bridge and the open bay. Murph turned on *LNZ II*'s radar, which would allow them to follow the Merritt from several miles away, hopefully well out of sight.

Murph slowly edged out from behind the island as the Merritt started to disappear behind the other end. He let Outerbridge stay just out of sight, as he made his way down Fisherman Inlet Channel. Finally, Outerbridge made the turn north just beyond the southern tip of ESVA, heading up the bay.

Murph took his time pulling out into the bay, wanting to give Outerbridge plenty of time for a head start so they wouldn't be spotted. With his radar set on the six-mile scale, he knew they wouldn't have any trouble identifying the large signature of the sport fisherman. As they rounded the tip of the peninsula, there it was on the screen, moving at cruising speed. Murph stayed at idle after making the turn north, not wanting to risk catching up to them. They all watched the screen as the Merritt passed Kiptopeke State Park, with its iconic breakwater made of several sunken cement cargo ships from World War II. The ships had an even larger radar signature and were a great reference point, about three and a half miles distant. A mile after that, the Merritt slowed and turned toward land, disappearing a minute later after its blip merged with the shoreline.

Murph exclaimed, "What the heck?"

"Must be an inlet up there or a creek," Lindsay remarked.

"I know that stretch of coastline well, and there's nothing there other than a dry creek bed," Murph replied.

"Not anymore," Rikki said, having pulled up a month-old satellite picture on her phone. "It looks like that's been dredged and opened up into this little cove."

"That looks like a boathouse," Casey pointed out.

"And an uncovered slip next to it large enough to hold the Merritt." Murph began advancing the throttles.

A little less than ten minutes later they saw that the dry creek had indeed been deepened and widened enough for the Merritt to get through. Murph turned in but hadn't made it two hundred yards before having to stop to avoid hitting the thick steel cable that stretched across it, with warning signs about trespassing.

"What the heck," he exclaimed.

Rikki studied the cable and the signs and peered back into the heavily overgrown banks where the cable ends disappeared. "Motorized. See how wet those signs are? It drops into the water to let authorized boats pass, which doesn't include us. No way to get under that heavy cable."

"Not in this boat, anyway." Murph had been studying the cable height and noted how it sagged slightly in the middle. It rose up as it got closer to pilings driven in by the water's edge, where the cable ran through pulleys before disappearing into the thick brush.

Casey looked at him, "You have an idea of how to get past that?"

"I do." But right at that point, his phone rang. The caller ID showed it was Baloney. "Hey Bill, I'm kinda busy right now."

"Yeah, well, I think yer gonna wanna make time ta talk ta this guy."

A stranger's voice came onto the phone. "Hello, Mr. Murphy. I understand you lost some things recently. Small things, but of high value. Over a thousand of them. I think I know where they are, and how you can get them back."

"I'm listening."

"I'd prefer not to talk about this over the phone."

"Who is this and where are you?"

"I am at your marina, with your friend Bill, aboard his boat. I'll be happy to introduce myself, but only in person."

"Stay there. I'm fifteen minutes out."

ONCE JOCK HAD GOTTEN Jerry talking, the story had come flooding out. Con men are called that because they have a gift of gaining the confidence of others. Once comfortable, the mark feels they can trust and or share anything with them. The story Jerry told was hard to believe, and if he hadn't overheard the conversation this morning about the stolen coins, Jock probably would've dismissed it as a fantasy.

But the relief Jerry exhibited at the end could have only come from having finally shared a secret that had become a huge burden. He wasn't cut out to be a drug smuggler or a thief; he'd originally been hired to run and take care of Robert's boats. Too late he'd discovered the world he'd gotten himself into, and by then there was no way out; Robert even owned the county sheriff. And the pay was better than great, as he made more in that first month than he'd ever made before in a whole year. But money wouldn't do you any good if you weren't around to spend it, and his was all hidden back at Robert's dock. Even though he was now technically broke without it, he wasn't willing to risk his life by going back for it.

Jock leaned back, digesting everything Jerry had told him. A plan had begun forming in his head, and he smiled. "I think we can make a lot of money, partner." He stuck out his hand for Jerry to shake, but instead of extending his own, Jerry instead looked dubious.

"Whatta you mean, 'partner?' What do I have to do for this money? I'm not going back to Robert's, and I'm through running drugs and counterfeit money. Those China guys scare the crap out of me, and Danny's a friggin' psychopath."

"Relax! It's not what you or I have to do for the money, it's what others will want to do. The most valuable commodity out there is information. You have quite a bit of it, but it's only valuable if you know where to sell it and how to negotiate the best price. You lack the last two of those three things, and that's where I come in. We're not going to risk our necks; we're going to let others do that for us.

"You know that Outerbridge will have the sheriff on the lookout for you. So, you need to either lay low, or get the heck out of the county, or out of the state for that matter. Kind of hard to do without any money."

Jerry looked at Jock, trying to decide whether or not to trust him. Not that he had much of a choice. Jock smiled and stuck his hand back out again.

"Partners?"

Jerry nodded and shook his hand. "Yeah. Partners."

MURPH and the three others arrived in the salon on *My Mahi*, the flagship of Baloney's two-boat charter operation. Jock stood as they came in, but Baloney stayed seated like a self-anointed king. The smile on his face let Murph know he was about to owe him a huge favor after this. His cigar was even missing, meaning this was a huge deal.

"Murph, Lindsay, Rikki, and Casey, meet Jock Danville. We met this mornin' at breakfast, an' he's got somethin' you wanna hear. Tell 'em, Jock."

Jock was shocked when Rikki walked in, though he tried not to look it.

Rikki said, "Mr. Danville and I are already acquainted. I'm surprised that you're not still up at *Bayside*."

She and Lindsay sat down on the large curved built-in couch, after which the three men did too. However, Murph was sitting at the edge of his seat.

"Circumstances change, Rikki, and please call me Jock."

"I thought it was Jacques like you were French." She stared at him, looking for his reaction.

"It doesn't matter how it's pronounced, either the European or the American way," he shrugged.

Typical con man, she thought. She knew her instincts had been correct up at *Bayside*.

"Well, I happened to overhear at breakfast that you had lost some coins. But you didn't mention that you also lost a pistol in a soft-sided case."

Rikki mentally kicked herself for not noticing him at breakfast. She had been so focused on Casey. It wasn't a mistake she'd repeat.

Murph's eyes narrowed, "How did you find out about all that?"

"The same way that I found out exactly where the coins are, who took them, and how you can get them back."

"I'm listening."

"That's all I'm going to say until you agree to my finder's fee."

"Your *what*? How about you tell the cops instead, for free."

Jock sighed loudly, "That's not going to happen. Mostly because the person behind the theft owns your sheriff. If he gets wind of this, those coins will be long gone and neither you nor I will ever see a cent out of it."

Rikki had moved over next to Murph and put a hand on his arm. She asked, "How much do you want?"

"Fifty percent of what was stolen."

"*Fifty percent!* You're on drugs," Murph yelled.

"Insulting me isn't going to get you anywhere."

"How about ten percent," Rikki said.

"Are you nuts too, Rik? How about no!" Murph insisted.

"I'm not an unreasonable person, Mr. Murphy. But if you don't deal with me, I can merely send in someone else to retrieve those coins. Then I can keep them all for myself."

Before Murph made another outburst, Rikki tightened her grip on his arm. "Right now, you aren't complicit in any crime, Jock. But if you were to do that, you would be guilty of a major felony. Our crooked sheriff loves publicity, and he can only dream of headlines like the ones that would come from that."

"As I said, I'm not unreasonable. Thirty percent."

Rikki countered, "Fifteen."

"*Fifteen?* Rik, this isn't Monopoly money we're dealing with here!" Murph was exasperated.

Jock said, "Twenty-five."

Lindsay, who had been silent up until now said, "Twenty percent. And that's our final offer."

"Linds! Twenty percent? Really?" Murph pleaded.

"Yes, Murph, twenty percent of what was stolen, and not one point higher." She stared directly at Jock when she said that last sentence.

Jock nodded. "Twenty percent. Deal." He stuck out his hand, which Lindsay shook before a reluctant Murph did the same.

Lindsay told Murph, "Eighty percent is better than zero, which is what we've got now, babe."

"And what we're willing to pay up front. Zero. No recovery, no pay," Murph stated emphatically.

"I wouldn't ask for anything up front. As I said, I'm reasonable," Jock replied.

Murph snorted. "You've got a funny way of showing it. Okay, so where are my coins?"

"First we need our agreement put down in writing, and witnessed by everyone here. Then we'll get to the details."

After the paperwork was finished, Murph said, "Now?"

"Right. A man named Robert Outerbridge had them stolen by another man named Danny while Outerbridge took you two to dinner. They're in the safe in his office at his warehouse a mile north of Kiptopeke State Park. One day my associate happened to observe Outerbridge opening the safe, so he knows the combination."

Rikki had been "reading" Jock, and knew there was more to this than he was telling. Not unexpected, coming from a con man. With a hint of sarcasm, she said, "And you didn't go after the coins all by yourself because you are such an upstanding citizen?"

"Uh, no. I didn't go after them myself because it's a bit more complicated than that. According to my associate, there are booby-traps and remote actuated barricades that make it difficult to get to the warehouse from the road."

Murph said, "We already saw the cable across the creek."

"That's one barricade, but there are also booby traps in the scrub between the warehouse and the bay. All these things are about what you'd expect from one of the largest counterfeiters in the country, as well as the inventor and manufacturer of the drug called Rescentol. Have you ever heard of it?"

Rikki was stunned. "Rescentol. Is being made here. On ESVA."

"Yes. I just found out about it myself. Your friend Outerbridge is a murderous monster."

"Youse guys are never boring, ya know that?" Baloney said as he sank farther back into his chair and put a fresh cigar in his mouth.

17

———

"GO TIME"

Jerry was still sitting at the table when the hatch opened again. Jock was the first one through, making an "okay" sign with his hand as the others followed him down the steps. This time he didn't offer introductions.

"We have a deal. Ten percent to you, Jerry, and ten percent to me, as agreed."

Murph exploded, "Wait! You had already decided to take twenty percent before we talked? What was that bit about fifty percent!"

"Negotiations are always the fun part. Had you accepted the fifty percent, I'd have known you probably weren't sharp enough to pull this off, or you wouldn't hold up your end of the deal. Being upset as you were, I now think you will."

"As upset as I am, not were." Murph glared at Jock, then turned his anger on Jerry. "So you're the one who ran me over in Talbot Creek, and then stole my coins and destroyed my home? You're lucky there's a table between you and me right now."

Jerry shrank back in his seat saying, "It was you rowing that night? I didn't see you until the last second. And I wasn't the one who stole your gold, I only ran the boat. It wasn't like I had any choice mister, and now Robert is out to kill me because of what happened."

"Robert needs to get in line behind me."

"Murph, let's focus on getting our gold back, not on how we lost it," Lindsay said.

"She's right," Jock said. "Let's focus. Jerry, we need you to draw a map of the area around the warehouse, and a sketch of the warehouse interior, including Outerbridge's office. As well as the location and combination of the safe."

Rikki said, "That's all important, but we'll need more information. When does the last worker leave the warehouse, and what hours does Outerbridge keep? What's the best time for us to get in unseen?"

Jerry shook his head. "You can't get in unseen, that's the problem. There are cameras all through the warehouse, an' the monitors are in Robert's office an' at his home next door. Nothin' wireless or on th' internet, he's scared of the Feds tapping into 'em. There's no recorder, either. There's a big push going on by his China fella, Cho, right now. So the printin' happens 'round the clock. But there's only two guys on the night shift, from seven p.m. to seven a.m. That's the fewest number of people that're ever there, and everybody has a gun."

"And Outerbridge is usually around?" Rikki asked.

"Him and Danny. But they gotta make a big run over to Cho's tonight, making up for th' runs we got behind with the fish kill when the bay was fulla cops. Cho owns that farm over on Talbot Creek."

Murph interrupted, "Yeah, over by where you almost killed me."

Jerry ignored the jab and continued, "The plan was for Danny an' me to go tonight. Least it was afore they decided to take me out. This is the biggest load we've ever done, both the bills and that drug. Robert didn't want anybody else seein' Cho's operation but us two an' him. I think he didn't wanna give any of the printers or the chemist a chance to make an end run 'round him and make a direct deal with Cho.

"Me and Danny don't know how to print the bills or make the Rescentol, so he figured we were safe. But with that big run coming up tonight, Robert'll probably have to go over with Danny. He won't have time to find anybody else before then."

"Then that's when we'll go," Rikki said. "You say the land way in is well defended, as is the scrub along the bay side. That leaves us going straight up the creek, but it's cabled off."

Murph said, "I've got a way around that. You'll see." Then he glared at Jerry. "I can't believe I have to pay the thief to get my gold back."

Rikki said, "That's better than not getting it back. C'mon, we need to go have a talk."

～

Rikki, Murph, Lindsay, Casey, and Dawn were discussing their plan in the pool house after leaving Jock and Jerry on *Mistral*.

"I still say it's too dangerous for you guys to go in there," Lindsay pleaded. "Jerry said everybody's armed. Can't we get Stephanie and that Secret Service guy to send their people in?"

"Not if you want your gold back," Rikki said. "Once they go in, everything will get seized. They'll say the gold was proceeds from the sale of drugs or the bogus bills, which is probably true. So the property, any boats, and everything else will get confiscated. You'll have lost your home for nothing."

"That doesn't seem right. We didn't do anything wrong, Rik."

"I know, it's screwed up, but that's how these particular laws work."

"Just be careful you guys. No amount of gold is worth any of y'all getting hurt."

Murph said, "It's not just about the gold Linds, it's also payback time. I'm gonna do to him what he did to us."

"You don't need to do that, babe."

"You're right. I don't *need* to, I *want* to. We're starting over from scratch with our home, thanks to him. I want to cost him everything. Especially his freedom."

"I'll meet with Stephanie and put that in motion. Have her put together a raid at the farm for when the drugs and phony bills arrive," Casey said. "Then after we retrieve your gold, I'll text and tell her about the warehouse and include the location. Then they can mop that one up, too."

~

THAT NIGHT, *well after dark...*

"These concrete ships are so creepy at night," Lindsay commented.

"But they make a perfect cover since they're such a popular fishing spot," Casey replied.

The five that put together the plan were aboard *LNZ II,* watching the radar screen while anchored next to the ships at Kiptopeke. The *Peggy T* was attached to the outboard by a tow line. Her masts and sails had been intentionally left behind at *Casey's Cove.* She would come into play in due time.

A storm line had blown through right before dark, the winds it packed had really kicked up the waters of the bay. Fortunately, both the wind and the waves had subsided, allowing them to keep their plan in place. They didn't have a backup plan, and those earlier waves would've prevented them from towing the low-sided, heavy wooden boat in those conditions. Plus, lying at anchor would have been unpleasant at best. But now the light breeze that remained cooled down what otherwise would've been a sticky and hot night.

"There!" Dawn pointed to a new blip on the screen, emerging from the shore right where they expected it to.

Murph scanned that area with binoculars, "No running lights. It's gotta be them."

"We'll give them ten minutes, then pull anchor and start that way at idle speed. That should get us well out of their radar range by the time we split up."

A few minutes after they started watching, the boat changed course and they saw the stern running light come on. Rikki said, "Let's go."

Twenty minutes later Casey, Rikki, and Murph transferred to the *Peggy T.* Casey told Dawn and Lindsay, "You two keep your eyes open,

161

and watch the radar for any incoming boats. Text us if you see anything, we don't need any surprises."

"You be careful too, Casey. All three of you be careful," Dawn added.

Rikki pushed off and Murph began paddling toward the creek. Casey texted Stephanie that she was about to have company and to keep her eyes out.

When they reached the cable, Murph's idea proved to be correct. While it sagged a bit in the middle, the sides nearest the shore were higher. But being near the shore meant shallow water. Bad for even small boats with propellers, but no match for a shallower draft rowboat.

With barely an inch of water under the edge of the hull, the low sides of the vintage craft cleared the cable by two inches like a floating limbo dancer. The three black-clothed invaders lay prone on the deck as they passed under the only barrier between them and Outerbridge's operation. They sat back up as Murph silently resumed rowing.

Two minutes later the creek opened into the small basin. The single security light outside of the warehouse was enough to reveal the outline of the Merritt, resting silently in her slip. A little more light spilled through an open garage door of the warehouse, and they could see someone moving around inside. Rikki subconsciously checked her holster for her silenced pistol, finding it safe and secure. Then they all pulled down black ski masks and put on heavy black nitrile gloves.

Murph picked a spot away from the docks at the edge of the wooded area and secured the *Peggy T* against the wooden seawall. The three clambered up onto the gravel behind it, and stealthily made their way over to the dock, watching through the garage door to make sure they weren't spotted. They knew they'd be illuminated somewhat as they got closer to the Merritt, but it couldn't be helped.

This part of the plan had been hard for Lindsay to accept when they all discussed it, but in the end, Murph got her to see why it had to happen. They needed a big distraction to be able to get past the printing crew, and their old Merritt would just end up being confiscated anyway.

Murph snuck down into the cockpit, then across to the unlocked salon door. Passing quietly through the sliding teak door, he closed it behind him and then crossed over to the galley. He opened several cabinets, splashing their interiors with charcoal lighter fluid he'd brought along specifically for this purpose. Then he lit two flares that he placed in cabinets before quickly retracing his steps, only this time he left the salon door partway open, allowing fresh air to feed what was now a growing fire.

The three raced across the open ground and around the corner of the warehouse, crouching down against the wall on the darkest side, away from the light. From here they had a perfect view of the cockpit and stern of the Merritt. They watched through the partly open door while the fire grew as more of the interior became involved. By the time excited shouts began coming from the warehouse, flames were already escaping through the door and reaching the flybridge overhang.

Three men came racing out of the building, startling Murph. Jerry had said there were only supposed to be two. He hoped that this was all he was wrong about tonight. The three men began trying to put the fire out using water hoses and a single fire extinguisher, their focus now completely on the boat. Rikki led her two friends around the corner to the large open door, then into the building. Even she was taken aback at the size of the operation.

The stench of the chemicals hit all three, who realized why the large door had been left open. Even with several large exhaust fans running, there was no way to get ahead of the awful odor emanating from the open tanks, where thousands of former one-dollar bills were soaking.

Having committed the sketch Jerry had drawn to memory, Rikki was able to lead the group quickly to Outerbridge's office. She used a "bump gun" to pick the lock on his door, and they went quickly inside. Using a penlight, she located the safe that had been built into a credenza behind his desk. She held her breath as she punched in the code, silently praying that Outerbridge hadn't thought or had time to change the code after Jerry's escape earlier. She breathed a sigh of relief when she heard the double chirp, signifying that the code had been entered correctly. Opening the door after she turned the handle, she was shocked by what she saw...

~

DANNY WAS glad that Robert was at the deadrise's helm since it kept him occupied and not dwelling on Jerry getting away. He'd been in the worst mood Danny had ever seen, verbally lashing out at everyone in sight. No doubt part of it was due to his having to face Cho tonight, after Murphy and his friends made that unexpected visit to the farm. But he'd not said a word since they left the warehouse boat shed, which was fine with Danny.

As Robert slowed the boat within sight of the farm, he said to Danny, "I want to make sure we get unloaded, reloaded, and gone as fast as possible. I don't want to be around Cho any longer than necessary, got it?"

"Got it, Robert."

He seemed satisfied with that, then moved out of the cabin back to the cockpit controls. He backed the boat into the boat shed as Danny opened the tank's top that was covering their two and a half pallets' worth of cargo. Then he threw dock lines to two of Cho's waiting men, who made them fast to cleats on the shed's dock.

Cho was also waiting on the dock, scowling down at Outerbridge. "About time. I want you out of here quick."

"Not as much as I do," Outerbridge replied, in an equally unfriendly tone.

He and Danny began passing the plastic-wrapped cubes of counterfeit hundreds up to Cho's men, who loaded them on the first of two waiting pallets. Then came the special Rescentol laced, redundantly sealed cubes of smaller bills, and finally the thick, sealed bricks of Rescentol powder.

"You and your man load your cargo," Cho said, wanting to send the message to Robert that he was still pissed. Then his men brought in a pallet jack to move that first pallet.

"Prick," Robert said under his breath. Then to Danny, "Let's get this done quickly."

Danny climbed up onto the dock and began passing the cubes of straps of singles down to Robert. They'd only loaded two cubes before the inside of the shed was bathed in bright light.

"FBI! Nobody move!" The voice came from a megaphone in a boat outside the shed opening.

The reaction from Cho's men was instantaneous as they opened fire in the direction of the voice and the light. Danny ducked down behind the pallet of special bills and bricks of Rescentol as the FBI began to return fire. Danny saw Cho turn, completely enraged as he took aim and screamed at Robert, "You fault!" But before he could pull the trigger, one side of his head became deformed and a large portion of the back ripped away. One of the FBI's Critical Duty nine-millimeter bullets had bored through his cheek and exited the back of his skull, taking a lot of brain tissue with it. Cho was dead before his body hit the dock.

Though Danny was tough, the sight of this happening unexpectedly to another human made him freeze. Unfortunately for him, he was behind that pile of Rescentol bricks when another of those wicked nine-millimeter bullets exploded the brick that was closest to his face. His startled reaction caused him to suddenly inhale, taking in enough of the airborne powder to subdue and ultimately kill an elephant. He sat down hard, leaning heavily against the pile of drugs and bills. His mind now experiencing the most intense fireworks show ever produced. In less than a minute the seizures started, and by then not even Narcan could have saved him from Rescentol's effects.

Robert ducked down behind the tank. He had the boat's hull, the big diesel's cast iron block, and finally that tank shielding him from the FBI's return fire. He heard Cho yell at him and looked up just in time to see the final second of his life. He looked around for Danny, but couldn't spot him. More bullets were flying from the dock as well as from out in the creek. While he was temporarily safe, he knew it was a matter of time before the FBI overran the shed, and if he stayed put then he'd be captured and on the way to prison.

Keeping the tank between the FBI and him, he crawled to the stern of the boat. He slid headfirst down that angled drake tail transom into the water, the noise of the splash being covered by all the gunfire. He was now in the shadow of the boat's hull, the FBI's lights illuminating most of the rest of the boat shed and the water inside it. About ten feet away, the outer wall of the shed reached down to almost water level. He drew a deep breath and then submerged, swimming for all he was worth. He swam under the wall and then surfaced about twenty-five feet beyond the shed, out of the spill of the FBI's spotlights. He estimated he was a bit over 250 yards away from that deadrise at the inn. He'd aim for that, and hide in or beside it, he'd figure that part out when he got there. He took another breath and submerged.

"Holy crap!" Murph looked over Rikki's shoulder into the safe which was loaded with rolls of gold, many times more than the fifty-four Danny had stolen.

"Looks like you won't be out of pocket replacing your boat after all," she said. Then she started loading roll after roll of the coins into one of the three black backpacks they'd brought along. When she'd loaded as much weight as she deemed to be comfortable and still be able to move swiftly, she started on the next pack. Finally, after loading the third pack she started closing the safe's door.

Murph said, "Wait! You didn't get half of it!"

"Don't get greedy Murph. These packs are already heavy enough, and Stephanie will get credit for it when they bust this place. We left enough to make it look like they didn't get hit." She closed the door and turned the handle, hearing a muffled click.

Murph nodded reluctantly, agreeing with her logic. Then he picked up a bag and swung the first strap over his shoulder. "Whoa!

You were right. Wouldn't want to fall in the drink wearing one of these."

Casey closed and locked the door, shushing them both as he came over to pick up his pack. Quietly he said, "There's a guy coming this way. He grabbed a fire extinguisher by the open door, and he's looking for more." He swept his penlight beam over the wall beside the door where a large red cylinder hung. No sooner had he done that when the doorknob started rattling.

Rikki whispered, "Everyone down behind the desk."

A few seconds later the doorframe splintered, the door swinging open wildly and crashing against the drywall beside it. Rikki had her silenced pistol out and ready in case he decided to come this far into the room. But he'd spotted what he came for, ripping it off its holder, then raced back into the warehouse.

"Let's go before he comes back looking for another one," Casey whispered.

Fortunately, no other workers were left in the shop as the trio retreated over by the big door. Rikki peered outside, seeing that the three were busy fighting the fire with both the hoses as well as the newly collected extinguishers. While it had now involved much of the cabin's structure and spread across the flybridge, surprisingly the trio was beginning to gain control of it.

She motioned to the others to follow her as they dashed for the darkened edge of the woods, then made their way over to where they'd left the *Peggy T*. Loading aboard, Murph then paddled silently around the edge of the basin and out into the creek. They all breathed a sigh of relief once they were out of sight of the dock.

Back aboard *LNZ II*, Casey texted Stephanie about the warehouse's location, warning her to approach only from the water. He also told her to bring a cutting torch for that cable. Murph re-rigged the *Peggy T* for towing, and Lindsay took the helm for the trip back to *Casey's Cove*.

Robert surfaced a final time on the dock side of Red's deadrise. From the muted light of the solar dock lights, he could see an empty boat trailer behind a blacked-out government SUV parked on the inn's boat ramp. An identical rig was parked ahead and to the side of it. So, that's how they snuck up on us, he thought. Cho had always prepared for an assault coming straight down Talbot Creek from Mobjack, not from the other side of the creek itself.

Quietly as possible he pulled himself over the side of the deadrise's cockpit, then made his way up into the small cabin. Hopefully, everyone at the inn had been warned by the FBI to keep away from the windows and walls that faced the creek. But the gunfight was subsiding, and he knew the owners and their staff would start preparing for breakfast service in a few short hours, just before dawn. Hopefully, they would be trying to get some sleep between now and then.

A half-hour before he figured the staff would start moving about, he intended on hot-wiring the deadrise and casting off about the same time most other commercial fishing boats would be leaving their docks. With any luck, the FBI wouldn't be pulling their boats out at the ramp before then, and hopefully, they didn't know he had been at Cho's and start searching for him.

Peering from the dark cabin out through the small cabin window, he could see a swarm of blue and red lights on land across the creek. None of them were going anywhere, and no searchlights were scanning the surface of the water. So far, his luck was holding.

18

GOLD FEVER

Back aboard Lady Dawn, Rikki began emptying the backpacks onto the salon table. It ended up being 113 rolls, slightly more than double what had been stolen off OCT. Murph took over the disbursement at this point, making a pile at one side.

"Fifty-four rolls to replace what was stolen, and two more to cover what we lost that wasn't covered by insurance. Ah, make it three for all the hassle of the robbery. And speaking of robbery, five rolls and eight coins for each of those two robbers over on that sailboat. I can't tell you how much it chaps my butt, having to pay one of the guys involved in burning our boat as well as some damn opportunist."

Lindsay smiled and reached out for his hand. "Babe, it's okay. We got it all back and then some. And that leaves over fifteen rolls for each of you guys for helping us." She looked at their three friends, smiling in gratitude for them being willing to put everything on the line to help her and Murph.

Rikki reached over and slid fifteen rolls into a separate pile. "That's a lot of money, guys. Thanks, but I'm not one of the ones who suffered a loss here, I was just helping out friends. That's not something you accept money for, especially knowing how Outerbridge is in the first place. So, I'm not comfortable taking any of it. But I would

169

be comfortable putting it to good use for others. I'm donating this to 'Rev,' and 'Rut' for the Watermen's Fund."

"Rut" was Sean Rutledge, a boatyard owner and head of a small foundation that benefited local watermen who needed a hand up. "Rev" was the Reverend Eddie Jones, a former waterman turned preacher at the *Watermen's Church of ESVA*. Both Rut and Rev were members of *Casey's Crew*. Rev knew everyone around the docks and was very familiar with which watermen were trying but having a hard time making a living. He was an advisor to the foundation Rut managed that gave anonymous grants to these fishermen. With the recent decrease in the local shellfish and fish populations, and now with the huge hit the ESVA fisheries had taken from the fish kill, this year the need for these grants had outstripped the available funds.

Dawn said, "Add Casey's and my coins to that pile. Since we're pretty certain the fish kill was caused by Outerbridge, it's only right that these should go to helping the folks who were hurt the most by it."

Lindsay said, "I don't mind taking back what we lost, Murph, but that's like fifty-five rolls, not fifty-seven." She tilted her head slightly as she looked at him in a silent challenge. He sighed, then nodded as he shoved the two extra rolls over with the rest of the pile.

Lindsay continued, "Losing *On Coastal Time* and having everybody here offer to help us has gotten me thinking, Murph. I don't want a big wedding up at *Bayside* in front of a bunch of our business contacts. I want to get married here, up by the pool at *C2*, with only our friends and family around us. They're the ones that truly matter to me. And instead of looking for a replacement houseboat, let's use the money that would've gone to a bigger wedding to build exactly what we want. Carlton Albury's boatyard did such a great job building *Tied Knot* for Kari and Marlin, let's get him to build one for us."

Ordinarily, Murph would've kept arguing over the wedding venue and size, but he looked at the coins and then around the table at his friends, and he realized Lindsay was right. Not just about that, but also about not taking the extra gold. He realized what a lucky guy he was to have her, partly because she helped give him the balance that he needed.

He said, "We'll go see Carlton in the morning. Meanwhile, I guess I need to go pay those vultures."

"How about I go do that for you, since I don't have the emotional investment in this that you do, so I'm less likely to hit one of them and end up in jail." Casey offered.

Rikki spoke up, "I'll go with you, and then I'm going to head home from there."

ON THE WALK over to *Mistral*, Rikki told Casey what had happened up at *Bayside*. "I had a bad feeling when I met Danville, and I was going to have my office check him out, but then he took off. I got the feeling then that he was more of a gigolo and con man than an extortionist.

"I only wanted to protect Eric and felt pretty certain Danville was more interested in fleecing Andrea Coyne, Eric's annoying neighbor. So, I ended up not pursuing it after he ran out on her. That was a shame because she and Danville deserve each other." Her voice oozed with sarcasm. "Now, as Murph said, I'm adding 'opportunist' to his resume."

Casey said, "I'm just glad that Murph and Lindsay got all of their coins back, and that Danville and his pal's 'finders fees' didn't have to come out of them. That's not something I could have done, collecting two hundred grand for sitting on my duff while sending someone else to do the risky part. Opportunist is right, he fell into the information. But I have to hand it to him, he was smart enough to figure out who to sell it to." He paused a moment, thinking. Then he continued, "Kind of a matchmaker when you think about it. Getting paid for twelve hours of no work at all." He turned toward Rikki, smiling. She looked curiously at him.

"I know that look, Case. What are you thinking?"

"That it's our turn to play matchmaker." He outlined his plan.

· · ·

AT *MISTRAL'S* TABLE, Jerry and Jock had arranged their respective rolls and loose coins in front of them. Jerry looked up at Rikki, who was addressing him.

"The FBI and the Secret Service are flooding into ESVA as we speak, mopping up everyone connected to Outerbridge's operation. Without a doubt, your name is going to come up, and you'll be high on their 'wanted list.' How do you feel about Indonesia?"

Jerry's eyes widened, "Huh?"

"Indonesia. Great climate, plenty of good fishing, and with what you have there," Rikki indicated the coins, "you can live like a king."

"Why would I wanna go there?"

"Because if you stay in the US, I can pretty much guarantee you'll get caught, they'll take that gold and throw you in jail. And when that happens, you'll want to trade information on our little group's visit to the warehouse to the prosecutor for a lighter sentence. Not something we can let happen, which means I can also guarantee you'll have a 'jailhouse accident' before you sing."

"No, I wouldn't..."

"Yes, you would, after you give it enough thought."

"But why Indonesia?"

Rikki smiled, "No extradition treaty with the US. I have an associate who owns freighters that regularly run from the west coast to Indonesia, and I can get you passage on one. No chance of your gold being spotted and seized by the TSA at an airport, and my associate's people can help you get set up when you reach your destination."

"Why should I trust you?"

"Jerry, if I wanted, I could kill you right now and take back that gold and never lose a minute's sleep. Don't look a gift horse in the mouth."

Staring into her ice-blue eyes, he realized she was serious, and that this was a huge opportunity. "Okay."

She nodded, "Good. One of my people will take you to the bus station in Richmond in the morning where you can buy a ticket to

San Diego. He'll also convert however many of those coins you want so that you have some cash."

"Thanks."

Danville had been watching the interaction between the two. While he looked calm on the outside, his mind was racing as he tried to figure out the extent of his exposure, as well as his next move. The comment about killing Jerry now had unnerved him since Rikki sounded so casual when she said it. She turned to him next.

"Looks like we are both in the same position, waiting for the all-clear after Jerry here steps off that freighter in Indonesia."

Jock nodded slowly. "So it would seem."

"There are worse places than *Mallard Cove* to have to wait it out. But we do need to have you stick around until then while we can keep an eye on you and let things settle down. If you try to run, that would just make us nervous, and I can guarantee you wouldn't get far. Also, it wouldn't be a bad idea for you to become a known commodity around here, rather than the mysterious guy who showed up then suddenly disappeared right after the Feds flooded ESVA." Rikki carefully watched his reaction.

"I was planning on spending at least a couple of weeks here anyway. But what about that Baloney character. He knows most of it since he was there when we talked, and he's not exactly a quiet kind of person."

Casey said, "Bill can be trusted, especially with things like this. I'll have a talk with him in the morning. But if you happen to run into him in any of the bars or the restaurants here, picking up his beer tab would go a long way toward making friends. Which will help keep him quiet, and on your side. Plus, he can help you blend in with the rest of the regulars.

Casey said, "And by the way, we have a private facility over beyond that east tree line. We'll be having a small get-together and cookout there this Saturday evening. We'd love to have you come as our guest to get to know our group."

Quite a switch of gears, Jock thought. He didn't hesitate long. "I'd love to." He didn't know what more might be behind the invitation, but he was willing to find out.

THE FOLLOWING morning Stephanie stopped by *Lady Dawn*. Casey poured her a cup of coffee, then they sat on the covered aft deck.

"So, where's your sidekick?" Casey asked.

"Overseeing the processing of both crime scenes."

"Shouldn't you be there with him?"

"I'll get back over there soon enough. But the boy wonder was quick about claiming the credit, so he can put in the most sweat equity that goes with it. I'll get plenty of credit for busting the drug operation, which turned out to be international in scope. Big connections over in China as well as the triad here. Not only were Outerbridge's group counterfeiters, but they were also manufacturing the Rescentol for them as well. But they didn't stop there. They were also soaking legitimate bills in a solution containing Rescentol. This stuff is so powerful that holding one of those bills for any amount of time would transfer the drug through your skin. Contact with one bill could transfer the equivalent of several Fentanyl-laced oxy pills."

"Why would they want to do that?" Casey asked.

"It has a huge addiction factor, even after only the first exposure. You wouldn't necessarily know how you had become addicted; you'd only know that you needed to find something to continue the high. The withdrawal symptoms from this stuff are vicious. So, imagine putting a few of these bills in each of the ATMs in a town. People who wouldn't ever consider using drugs would be exposed. Then they planned to supply the local street dealers with Rescentol-laced pills after getting the word out. Not only would they expand their user base exponentially, but they could also target areas that contain certain military bases and intelligence units."

Casey whistled. "Effectively taking out the effectiveness of a base or an intel unit without firing a shot."

"Exactly. Crippling the functionality of those stationed there, from the top brass on down, even if only for the short term."

"Wow."

"Yeah. So, I wanted to thank you in person for those 'anonymous' tips. Do I want to know how you found out about it?" She took a sip of coffee, looking at him over the cup's rim.

"Uh, negative."

"I kind of figured that but thought I'd ask anyway. In Outerbridge's office, we found and confiscated millions in gold coins. There's a good possibility of a hefty reward if you decide to come forward."

Casey shook his head, "You keep it."

"Hah! Wish I could, but the bureau frowns on its agents trying to 'double dip.' Same pay, just a different day."

"Well, I guess your reward is in getting Outerbridge out of ESVA."

"Outerbridge? You didn't hear? We missed him. He snuck out in the middle of the gunfight at the farm. Then somebody stole the deadrise from the inn across the creek, which was more than likely him. We're looking for it now."

"I'll tell Murph and Lindsay to keep their eyes open for him," Casey said.

"Yeah, and their firearms loaded. If he figures out they had anything to do with us busting his operation..."

"I get it. We'll all be watching out for him."

"Oh, and somebody burned that sportfish last night that those two sold him. So that wasn't an option for him to use to escape, at least from ESVA. You wouldn't know anything about how that happened, would you?" She asked in a sly tone.

"Me? Why would I, Stephanie? Wow, what a shame, that was a beautiful boat. Did it sink, too?"

"No, it didn't quite burn to the waterline, but the wheelhouse and the flybridge are gone. It got put out before it got any farther. Some counterfeiters make good amateur firemen, too."

She searched his face for any hint of a reaction. When she didn't see any she winked and said, "Thanks for the coffee."

As she stood up, Casey said, "Cookout Saturday night, if you're up for it."

"Wouldn't miss one, Casey. See you then."

HALF AN HOUR LATER, Rev came in. He was a man of average height, a few years younger than Casey, with salt and pepper hair. His wavy mop was a tad longer than you'd expect from a preacher, but this was ESVA after all, and there were a lot of unexpected things here.

"Hey, Casey."

"Hey, Rev, coffee?"

"All coffee'd out already this morning, but thanks. Interesting voicemail you left, 'It'll be worth your while to stop by the boat.' I'm always happy to stop by, you know that. It's always worthwhile chatting with you, my friend."

"I appreciate that Rev. But this isn't so much a social chat as it is business. Did you hear about what went on last night up by Kiptopeke?"

"I did. Hard to believe it was happening in our backyard without anyone knowing about it."

"There's more to it. That was the guy Murph and Lindsay sold the Merritt to. He paid for it in gold coins, then had one of his guys steal them back and burn their houseboat."

Rev whistled, "I heard a boat there got burned, too." He suddenly realized how this might be connected. "Probably not a good idea for me to know any more of the details."

Casey agreed. "Probably not. Except one. That outfit was likely responsible for the fish kill. And I know your grant money has been stretched pretty thin this summer, so this should help." He picked up the backpack that had been beside his chair and placed it on the table, opening the zipper.

Rev was stunned. "It sure would. But if it's dirty money..."

"You know none of us would ever be involved in an operation like that. However, paybacks are a whole different subject. Those folks you watch over need help getting through this season, and this is the kind of payback I like. One that helps good people without the bureaucrats skimming off the top."

"In that case I thank you, and we'll gladly take them. Now I need to figure out a way to change these into cash. I'm assuming that it wouldn't be a good idea for a bunch of watermen to be flashing these around."

Casey chuckled, "I'm getting this vision of a scene from a pirate movie. No, that wouldn't be a good idea. But come to Saturday night's get-together at *C2*, and I'll introduce you to someone who can help you with that."

19

EXILE

Sheriff Bromwell felt his phone vibrate; he'd been expecting this call. It wasn't his department-issued phone, instead, it was the one Outerbridge had given him. After hearing what went on with the Feds the night before, and the fact that Outerbridge had gotten away, he knew it was only a matter of time before he reached out for help. He hit the answer button.

"Where are you?"

"Oh, I guess you think I should trust you enough to tell you that after what happened last night? No, I don't think so. Instead, I need some information from you. First, I need to know if you've found Jerry. The second thing is, have you heard anything about Danny? Plus, I need a rundown of exactly what happened at the warehouse."

"No luck on Jerry, he's still in the wind. And according to the Feds, Danny's dead. One of Cho's guys was the only survivor from the farm's boathouse, and he may not make it. Two FBI agents were wounded, so the Feds are not in a happy mood today. They're looking everywhere for you."

Outerbridge had suspected that Danny didn't get out alive, but it was still a blow to have the death of his right-hand man confirmed. "Well, you keep looking for Jerry, this had to be his doing."

"I don't think so, Robert. He'd have never had the balls to burn your new sportfish."

"Wait, what? Someone burned my Merritt?"

"An hour before the Feds hit the warehouse. The boys were finishing putting it out when the place got hit. They didn't have a chance to torch the shop and destroy the evidence."

This last bit of news wasn't completely unexpected either, but still, it was the worst possible outcome. As he crossed the bay, he had seen a boat with blue lights sitting at the mouth of the warehouse's creek. He knew then that property was compromised, and there would be no way to get back into his office to get at that gold.

His boat having been set on fire was no coincidence; he figured that was a message from Murphy, and maybe a distraction for something. Murphy had known about Cho's farm, and somehow he also found out about the warehouse. Maybe Jerry told him. Then again, maybe Jerry never left *Mallard Cove*. Or he might be right next door, at Murphy's private marina.

"Jerry must have told Murphy about everything, and this was his doing. I'll take care of Murphy, but first, we need to find Jerry. If he's still on the Shore, there's a good chance he's around *Mallard Cove*."

"I don't think he's still around, Robert."

"Oh, you can be so sure about that and are willing to just write him off? I'm not. Don't forget, he knows all about you and Cho's girls, and that you are on my payroll. You don't want him talking to the Feds about any of that."

Bromwell swallowed hard at the thought. "Don't worry, I'm not writing him off. The Feds have him listed as armed and dangerous, and I've told the boys to treat him that way."

"Excellent. Now go give *Mallard Cove* a good shakedown and find him. That's one loose end neither of us can afford."

After he hung up, Outerbridge scanned the room for the umpteenth time since he arrived, knowing that he would be stuck in here for the foreseeable future. After he cranked up the deadrise early this morning he'd used it to cross the bay, intending to get to his Merritt which was the focus of his escape plan. He had specifically chosen that boat not just for its beautiful design, but also for its speed, range, and size. It could easily make Bermuda on its own bottom, and it would fit in with the large fleet of modern sportfishing boats based there. Once there it would be camouflaged by being in plain sight.

But after spotting the blue lights by the warehouse, he'd had to switch to an alternate plan. Turning north, he ran along the coastline of the bay for several minutes, then throttled back and set a course back toward the southwest. He knew the hydraulic steering should hold the boat's rudder straight, though he was counting on the current and the wind to determine the actual location where the boat would finally end up grounding itself across the bay. The important thing was that its course not be a straight line, leaving the Feds with an accurate starting point to begin looking for him.

He bailed over the side, then began swimming the hundred yards to shore. Outerbridge aimed at the security light behind a house he knew on the beach. He remembered there was a pathway next to that house the locals used to access this strip of sand. Outerbridge also knew he had to hurry, because he needed to be inside his safe house in the center of the peninsula before the sun came up, and it was a mile inland. He made it just minutes before the first slivers of the dawn began to brighten the sky.

But now here he was, stuck in a prison of his own making. Like a "prepper" anticipating Armageddon, over the last year he'd tried to stock it with every need and contingency he could imagine. Enough food to last him a year, as well as guns, ammunition, more gold Krugerrands, and even a supply of burner phones. A local lawyer paid the utility bills and taxes from a trust account, which had a large enough balance to last several years. Though he didn't plan on being cooped up here for anywhere close to a year. He'd hired the attorney by mail, using a fake name and cashier's check, so he knew he was safe until he could make a break for it.

From the outside the place looked like a small derelict farmhouse, hidden from the side road by numerous overgrown trees and shrubs. Vines were growing up the exterior walls and across the shuttered windows. An old satellite dish attached to the back eaves was the only indication that someone had lived here at any point during the past twenty years. The a/c unit was even camouflaged to look ancient, and there were tiny cameras up in the eaves and in other places on the property that covered every potential avenue of approach. He was well set to begin his life as a fugitive, though he'd always hoped it wouldn't become necessary. At least now he would have plenty of time on his hands to figure out what to do moving forward. One thing he was sure of was that he'd make certain Murphy would pay dearly for this disaster.

MURPH AND LINDSAY spent part of the morning renting a safety deposit box at their bank and filling it with most of the Krugerrands. Then they stopped by *Washington Coins* to convert a couple of coin rolls into cash for the deposit on a new house barge. Their final stop before returning home was at Carlton Albury's to get the new build started.

Pulling into *Mallard Cove*, the two were surprised to see several cars from the sheriff's office in the parking lot and a handful of deputies working their way up and down the docks. Even more surprising was finding the security gate open at *Casey's Cove*, and more sheriff's vehicles parked over by *C2*. Casey was standing outside of the pool house, holding a sheet of paper. He didn't look happy.

"What's going on, Casey? The docks are crawling with deputies," Murph said.

"They have a warrant to search for some guy named Jerry, and an additional warrant to search your rooms for anything connected to some counterfeit and drug ring that was busted last night." He'd intentionally said all of this loudly, for the benefit of any deputies who might be within earshot.

"What? They think we're counterfeiters or drug dealers? That's crazy," Lindsay exclaimed angrily. "Who is this Jerry guy? And I wish they'd have taken this much interest in finding whoever robbed us and burned our houseboat."

Lindsay started for the door but was blocked by a big deputy who said she had to remain outside. It didn't help her temperament, as she then rejoined both men.

"From what I saw through the sliding glass doors, they're making an absolute mess of the place! Isn't there something we can do?"

"I know one thing I'm going to do, and that's siccing our lawyer on the judge that signed this warrant. As far as I know, they didn't have any probable cause to have this issued. I want to know why they're doing this to us." Murph was about as mad as he gets.

Casey lowered his voice as he said, "Remember how the sheriff got very forceful when he heard you mention Outerbridge's name after the robbery? I think Rikki's suspicions about those two being tied in together might be dead on. After our visit to the farm, and you telling that guy who you were and to give Outerbridge your message, you can bet he knows you were behind the Feds finding out about it. This is payback. I only hope they aren't planting evidence they can arrest you for."

A few minutes later a very smug-looking sheriff emerged from the building, holding two clear plastic evidence baggies. Each contained a Glock pistol.

"Hey! Those are our guns! You've got no damn right to take them," Murph shouted.

"Watch your mouth, boy. I got every right in the world. We're gonna have these checked out to make sure they ain't stolen, and that they haven't been used in the commission of any crime, like that shootout on the other side of the bay last night."

"In that case, sheriff, I'll take them." Stephanie had arrived, accompanied by Dawn, who had called her about what was going on.

"Like hell! These could be evidence from a crime, and my department confiscated them." He clearly was unhappy to see the FBI agent.

"Casey, let me see that warrant." She read it quickly and then looked up. "Just as I thought, this warrant is for any evidence related to that counterfeit and drug ring, both of which are under federal jurisdiction now. This is a total overreach by you and some local judge pal of yours, Sheriff.

"Since no shots were fired on this side of the bay in connection with this case, you don't even have any probable cause to have those weapons checked for ballistics. You are dangerously close to stomping on this couple's Constitutional rights if you haven't already. Fortunately, I'm here to save you from having them file a huge and very winnable lawsuit against you. Now hand over those evidence bags."

"They reported these as stolen in their burglary if there even was one. More likely it was insurance fraud, and that crime *is* under my jurisdiction," he replied.

Stephanie shook her head. "I seem to remember these were discovered at Albury's in their boat's safe after the fire. I also recall they reported only one pistol stolen, a Colt Python. Which I'm here to tell them was discovered this morning in a storage locker at Robert Outerbridge's warehouse. The serial number matched. So it would seem their suspicions about him were correct. A safe filled with the type of coins they reported as having been stolen was also discovered on the premises. So, I'll take those bags."

The sheriff stared daggers at her as he reached out with both bags. Stephanie unsealed each one, then made a call. After reciting the serial numbers stamped on the side of the receivers she waited a minute, then thanked whoever was on the other end of the call. She handed the weapons to both Murph and Lindsay while telling the sheriff, "Legally purchased, and neither ever having been reported as stolen.

"And as to your warrant and search for this Jerry character, if either the FBI or Secret Service decide we need your help in finding him, we'll give you a call. But right now you need to pull your deputies out of both of these marinas. And I think you can expect a call soon from the State's Attorney asking some questions about how and why you were able to obtain that warrant in the first place. You and your deputies need to vacate these premises, right now."

The sheriff didn't say another word to her, though his eyes spoke volumes, and none of it was good. He turned to his deputies who had been gathered by the door. "Leave it, let's go."

As they surveyed the mess left behind by the deputies, Stephanie said, "It probably would be a good idea for you guys to stay well under the speed limit driving around in this county. He looked like a man who knows how to hold a grudge. I'll refer that warrant to the State's Attorney, but that will no doubt put an even bigger burr under the sheriff's saddle."

"Well, he just put a whole stalk of 'em under mine," Murph said. "You know he had to have been sent here by Outerbridge."

She nodded. "I don't think he's got balls enough to make that kind of an end run around the bureau without someone pressuring him to do it. So if he'd have found this Jerry guy, I'm willing to bet Jerry wouldn't have survived the encounter. Then publicly, we'd have been forced to thank him for his assistance, whether we asked him for it or not. A pretty good way to get rid of a witness before he gets interrogated when you think about it."

"So, you also think he's being paid by Outerbridge," Dawn asked.

"I wouldn't bet against it. That, or Outerbridge must be holding something against him, and the two are still in contact somehow. I mean, how could he know about this Jerry character? We only found out about him this morning from one of the guys we interrogated at the warehouse. There weren't any deputies around then, so Outerbridge had to have told him. All of you need to watch your backs until we find Jerry and get everything sorted out."

"Don'tcha think you're in the wrong bar?" Baloney asked as he walked up to the *Cove Beach Bar & Grill* table where Jock sat alone having lunch.

"Wrong bar? What's wrong about it," Jock asked.

"Well, I'm just sayin', most of youse blow boat types like stickin' around the *Catamaran Bar* next door." He jerked a thumb over his shoulder at the other adjacent beach bar.

"Maybe some do, but I kind of like this place. And from the sound of it, I probably couldn't talk you into letting me buy you a beer over there."

"Ya got that right. I only been in there a couple times, when Murph or Casey dragged me with 'em. Wait, did you say you're buying?"

Baloney pulled out a chair opposite Jock and pocketed his ever-present unlit cigar as he sat down. He motioned to the server that he needed a beer. She didn't even need to be asked which kind, or if she should add it to Jock's tab.

Jock said, "Thank you for helping me get in touch with Murph and Lindsay. Buying you a beer is the least I can do to show my appreciation."

"Yeah, it is. So, you can buy me lunch, too. Hittin' those kids up with that 'finder's fee' was a real crappy thing ta do, I wanna tell ya."

"Maybe from your point of view. But I don't know them as well as you do, and I do know there's a lot of inherent risk in having told them what I did. And it's not like what I charged them is going to put a crimp in their lifestyle. I mean, look at this place." He swept an arm around, indicating the bar and the rest of *Mallard Cove*.

"Hey! Lemme tell ya something, those kids have worked for every cent they got! I met 'em when they first bought this place, an' it was a pig sty. Busted down docks, a restaurant that'd been closed for years, and fuel pumps that took all day ta fill yer tanks. They put every cent of their tournament winnings inta this place and worked their butts off ta make it what it is today. They didn't hold somebody up for information."

Jock countered, "And bought a two-million-dollar sport fisherman along the way."

"You don't know squat. They bought old boats and fixed 'em up in between doin' tourneys up an' down the coast. They traded for the Merritt as part of a bet in a tournament down south. The country singer that had her wanted their Rybovich real bad, and bet them for the difference between the two, and they got lucky. Everything they got was by taking risks, having guts, and using their brains. It ain't 'daddy's money' or nothin' like that. Those two are the real deal. An' it's because ah them I met the folks that own *Tuna Hunters* and started makin' some real money myself. I owe alla them a lot."

"I admit I didn't know any of that. But maybe they will tell me more tomorrow at the get-together next door."

"Wait, what? You got invited ta that?"

"Casey Shaw invited me. Why, didn't you get an invitation?"

"Ah, *course* I did. I'm just surprised he invited ya too, seein' as he doesn't know ya, and he can't be happy about what you pulled on the kids." Baloney was confused as well as surprised.

"Maybe he's looking at it from my perspective. As I explained to Murph, I could just as easily have gone after all the gold myself, but I didn't. Instead, they recovered eighty percent of what they lost, which most people would be very happy with. I'm sure that's much higher than the average recovery rate from a burglary. And it was because I was able to extract the information from Jerry by gaining his confidence. Not everyone could have done that. I seriously doubt he would have admitted anything to you. Nothing personal, but you seem more inclined to talk than listen."

"Yeah, says the guy who's been flapping' his gums ever since I sat down. If ya want to make friends tomorrow, ya need to listen more and talk less."

"The pot is giving the kettle advice."

"Whaaa?"

Jock grinned and held up his beer. "Here's to you, my well-named new friend."

"Don't get ahead of yerself with that 'friend' talk, but yeah, here's to me."

20

NEW ACQUAINTANCES

The next afternoon...

JOCK PUNCHED the code Casey had texted him into the gate's keypad, then followed the concrete path through the narrow woods. Breaking out into the open, he was surprised by *Casey's Cove*. While not huge, it still held a variety of different boats, and all the slips but one were occupied. He'd learned that Casey had been the driving force behind the creation of *Bayside*, and he could see that same level of attention to detail here.

He followed the directions in the text and found Casey in his outdoor kitchen, unloading a smoker filled with amberjack, bluefish, and Mahi.

"You're just in time to help me mix up some Chesapeake Crack, Jock."

"What in the world is Chesapeake Crack?"

"Only the finest smoked seafood dip you'll ever put in your mouth." Rikki had walked up behind him.

"In that case, I'll be happy to help."

Baloney arrived a few minutes later, and Casey quickly enlisted his help even before he had a chance to grab a beer from the cooler.

"While Rik and Jock bust up the smoked fillets, you want to give me a hand bringing the rest of the ingredients and bowls from the pool house kitchen, Bill?"

"Sure." Once they were out of earshot, Baloney asked him, "Case, why'd ya invite that guy? I mean, I know it's your place and all, but *him*? Really?"

"Oh, I don't think he's all that bad, Bill. You might even find that he can be entertaining."

"Entertaining? That guy? Are you *serious*? He's a stiff, and he ripped off the kids! Not that bad? When Murph sees him here, he'll blow a gasket."

"Oh, Murph already knows he's coming. And I think you are underestimating his ability to forgive and forget."

"*Murph*? Ya gotta be kiddin' me!"

"All right, maybe then you are underestimating me. I had Rik do some digging, and we amended the guest list by adding one more. Let's just say the floor show should be starting soon."

Baloney stared at him for a minute then said, "I know that look, Case. And I trust ya. I hope ya got plenty ah beer, this sounds like it's gonna be a fun afternoon then."

"Let's hope so."

HALF AN HOUR LATER, Casey had the brick pit loaded with oak that was well on its way to becoming coals, and he was loading the grill with chicken and beef. The crowd had grown considerably and now included Rev and his girlfriend, also Carlton Albury, and his wife. Rut Rutledge and his girlfriend Cammie arrived soon afterward and headed straight for Casey. Cammie worked for Casey and Dawn's real estate management company, and Rut owned *Mockhorn Boat Works*, which was located a few miles north of Albury's. While Carlton's business focused mainly on the sportfish and yacht crowd, Rut's yard mostly repaired the workboats of watermen. But his main job these days was overseeing the Watermen's Fund.

"I wanted to thank you, Casey. Rev told me about your huge donation to the fund, along with Dawn's and Rik's."

"You're welcome. I hope he told you to keep it in confidence."

"He did, and you know I will. I heard a little bit about how it got into your hands. And about how you're still sticking your neck out for your friends. Seems to be a less common thing to find these days, friends that are willing to go to such lengths for others."

Casey nodded. "True, except for most of the people here this afternoon. Like-minded, good-hearted folks who don't just believe in the way things ought to be, but are willing to do something about it. All but one or two have put their butts on the line for one or more of the others. You know, just as you have." He grinned at Rut.

Rut chuckled. "I owe so many of the people here, not the other way around, which you know all too well. And I won't hesitate if any of them need me." He paused, then reached out to shake Casey's hand. "You've done so much for this area already, and you keep on helping. Like this donation, it came at a great time in a very tough year for the local watermen. I only wish they could know about the part you're playing."

Casey took his hand saying, "Um, nothing personal Rut, but I don't even want you to know the whole story. Some things are better left unsaid."

"Amen!" Rev had walked up, smiling after he heard the last bit of their conversation. "What you don't know can't come back to bite you in the butt in court. And for the record, I trust you two completely, so I don't need nor want to know everything."

Rikki joined them. "Well, I think we're about to know a bit more about someone. Our latest arrival will see to that." She pointed over toward the basin's inlet where a massive sailing sloop was making the turn in.

"Geeze, Case, another blow boat? Tell me they got lost and ain't gonna dock here," Baloney bellowed from fifty feet away.

Everyone watched as the beautiful ninety-foot Pendennis yacht came to a stop in the middle of the basin. Then with the help of a pair of powerful bow thrusters, it began a slow 180-degree pivot, eventually backing into Murph and Lindsay's now vacant slip. Even at this distance, they could tell there was a woman at the helm, with several crewmen manning the dock lines. She handled the massive yacht with ease, though fitting into that slip she had little room to spare.

As interesting as it was to watch the boat, a few in the crowd were more interested in watching the reaction on Jock's face. His color faded a bit as he stared at the yacht's captain whom he recognized. He turned and came over to the group, addressing Casey.

"Do you know the woman who is running that sailboat?"

"No, but Rikki and Eric do. He mentioned to her that we were having a get-together, and suggested she come down in her boat and stay here a few days."

"*Her* boat? That Pendennis is hers?"

Rikki said, "Yes, didn't you see it when you were up at *Bayside*? It's kind of hard to miss."

Ignoring her sugary tone he answered, "Of course. But I had no idea she owned it or any other boat."

"And I thought you two knew everything about each other," she said sweetly.

Suddenly it dawned on him that Andrea Coyne's arrival was not a coincidence. He glared at Rikki, completely speechless. His mind raced as he tried to figure out what her angle was, and what his next move should be.

Murph smiled at him saying, "Looks like you'll be the one paying the most for that finder's fee you charged me."

Five minutes later Andrea appeared at the end of the path, scanning the crowd for any familiar faces. Her jaw dropped when she saw Jock, who came hurrying over to her.

"Jacques, what are you doing here? Not that I should even be talking to you after you left in the mid..."

Jock interrupted her, "Andrea, I'm so glad that you got my message!"

"*What* message?"

"To meet me down here, of course. I can't wait to introduce you to my new friends." He wrapped his arms around her, pulling her close and whispering, "Please just follow my lead. There are some here that I cannot trust, starting with that Rikki person."

She pushed him back. He could see by her face that she was a mixture of angry, confused, and surprised. After a moment she nodded slightly. He took her arm and began introducing her to those in the crowd that he knew. After a few minutes of small talk, she pulled him aside.

She said, "I thought you had to be so wary of new people."

"No, I said I could only raise funds from those I knew. People that also know my cause to be trustworthy. And back at *Bayside*, I thought you said you did not own a boat. I saw that Pendennis in the marina up there, and now you show up with it."

"No, you asked me why I didn't own one, and I said I had a friend with one. You. I never actually said I didn't own a boat myself. So, yes, I own *Temptress*. But I enjoy trying out other boats, like *Mistral*. I thoroughly enjoyed sailing her, and I thought if you found out that I did own *Temptress*, you would rather go sailing on her. Besides, it was a lot of fun watching you figure out that I already knew how to sail."

"What else haven't you told me about yourself," he said sarcastically.

She smiled. "A woman needs to have *some* secrets. And what about you, sneaking off in the middle of the night because you didn't want to put me in danger. Really? That's the best you could do as an excuse?"

"It's true. I wanted to find a place, a safe place where we could be together and spend some time."

"Where is *Mistral* now?"

"Next door, at *Mallard Cove*."

Her nose wrinkled. "That's where you thought I might like to go with you? A place full of loud tourists and smelly fishermen?"

"No, it is just a safe stop on my way to an island that I have learned about, and which will be my destination. Hopefully *our* destination."

"Looks like a lover's quarrel happening over there," Rikki said to Casey, nodding toward where Jock and Andrea were standing off to the side.

He agreed. "You said this might end up being an interesting afternoon, and it's starting to look that way. He certainly did not see this coming."

"Neither did she." Rikki's face had a look of total satisfaction. "Eric is going to get a huge kick out of this. Speaking of which, where is he?"

"Said he'd be a little late, but he'll be here soon enough."

"Have you found Jerry yet," Robert asked.

"No, an' I've got my hands full right now. Not only your mess but some lawyer a little north of here got himself tortured and his body dumped out on the road so it'd get found. Looks like the work of your China buddies. He had a triangle with some Chinese writing inside it carved on his chest," Bromwell said.

A chill went down Outerbridge's spine. "This lawyer, what was his name?"

"Hugh Baskin. Why?" There was dead silence on the phone. "Outerbridge? Did you know him?" The sheriff looked at the phone's screen and saw it was disconnected. He dialed the disconnected number but got no answer.

Bromwell wasn't a man who worried about much, but the triad was different. If Outerbridge and Baskin were connected in some way, the triad must have seen him as a loose end after they had gotten whatever information they'd come for. Which meant that he and Outerbridge were now loose ends as well.

Since Outerbridge was rabbiting, it must mean the lawyer had known where he was hiding. And somehow the triad had found some kind of connection between the two. If that was true, then they knew about him as well, and being sheriff meant he was higher profile, and very easy to find. Meaning he was going to need protection, which wouldn't be easy to hide. It was hard to believe that everything could go so far south so darn fast.

ROBERT HUNG up the phone and raced over to his floor-to-ceiling shelf unit that held his "go bag" backpack. Inside was a lot of cash, numerous rolls of Krugerrands, two pistols, and several fully loaded magazines that fit both weapons. He grabbed the bag and glanced at the video monitor which displayed the multiple feeds from his hidden cameras. There was movement on the one that was mounted in a tree up by the road. A black-windowed SUV slowed slightly as it passed by the driveway entrance.

"Damn it, time to go," he thought, toggling a hidden latch in that same shelf unit and swinging it away from the wall. In the recessed concrete shaft behind it was a ladder that dropped straight down about fifteen feet into a dark hole. He flipped a light switch and the floor at the bottom came into view. Pulling the shelf unit back into place, he started down the ladder. At the bottom of the shaft, a horizontal six-foot diameter black plastic pipe was attached, leading away from under the house.

He ducked slightly and started into the pipe. After fifteen feet he passed through a steel bulkhead and hatch that had been salvaged from an old freighter and cemented into place. Once through the hatch, he closed and locked it behind him. This bulkhead was intended not just to slow or stop any pursuers but to also camouflage the fact that just beyond it the pipe made an immediate ninety-degree turn, heading over toward the woods. Hopefully, it would send his pursuers above looking in the wrong direction, in the open field instead.

Suddenly the lights in the tunnel went out for a split second before a series of battery-powered emergency floodlights came on. The triad had reached the house and cut the power. He figured he had maybe four minutes before they discovered the shaft and tunnel. Hopefully, all their attention would then be focused on the tunnel and getting through that hatch.

Two minutes later he reached the end of the pipe, which dumped out into a matching concrete shaft and ladder. Above was a square steel hatch that was hidden back in the woods, flush with the ground and covered in pine straw. He pushed it open slowly, peering out and around as he did. There was no sign of movement in the woods surrounding the hatch, so he climbed out and made his way over to a low mound of pine straw. He cleared it off the blue tarp underneath and pulled out the mountain bike it had been concealing. He glanced around again, then hung his backpack on the handlebars and started pedaling down a trail through the trees.

21

PAYBACKS

"He doesn't seem all that upset about seeing her," Murph said. He was standing with Rikki, Cindy, Dawn, and Casey, covertly watching Jock and Andrea. Those two had moved to the far end of the pool and were now sitting side by side in a pair of patio chairs.

Rikki replied, "A real pro wouldn't show that much emotion, and that's what he is. A pro. I still think he'll take off again, and when that happens she'll be humiliated and won't want to show up around Eric's anymore. So, his annoying neighbor problem will be solved, which was my intention in inviting Andrea."

"Remind me to never, ever tick you off, Rik," Murph said.

"Ever? You mean 'again' don't you?"

"Either."

The sound of a helicopter interrupted their conversation and their attention turned to Eric's approaching Sikorsky S-76. It descended over the waterway and made a perfect landing on the pad. Eric, Missy, and Candi climbed out of the big helicopter with two other people, who turned out to be Claire Fisher and her husband, Charles. Eric led the group over toward Casey, but as he did, Claire

195

and Jock spotted each other. It was hard to tell which of the two was more surprised. Or more worried.

Andrea asked Jock, "Isn't that..."

"Yes," he interrupted. "The last person I wanted to find me. She must have learned I would be here from Eric."

"It's too late now, she's seen you."

"I know."

For the second time this afternoon, his mind was racing, trying to decide how to play this. Fortunately, the group continued past them, going over to say hello to Casey and Dawn first, but not before Claire shot him a look of both anger and hurt. At least she didn't confront him yet, gaining him precious thinking time before that happened.

Andrea said, "I still say you must be mistaken. She is the sweetest person, there's no way she could be who you think she is."

"Professionals like her easily hide their intentions. No, there's no mistake. You saw how she recognized me."

"Maybe it was me she recognized."

He was trying to think and come up with a plan, but for the first time in recent memory, he was drawing a blank. Probably because he couldn't recall a time when he had to deal with two marks at the same time, with each being face to face with each other as well as him. Jock decided to trust his instincts and deal with things as they happened. Any plan could easily be derailed, and he'd end up working this way anyhow.

After introducing them to Casey's group, Eric led the Fishers around, introducing them to everyone else that was there. Fortunately for Jock, he and Andrea would end up being two of the last they would reach.

"Am I the only one who saw the look that Claire Fisher gave Jock and Andrea?" Dawn asked.

Rikki replied, "No, and now I'm very curious as to what was behind it, although I can guess. I knew that having Andrea here would throw him off his game, but it's pretty obvious now that he and

Claire Fisher know each other, too. Probably in the biblical sense, I'm guessing. With both of them here together, it seems this might get even more interesting pretty fast."

"Sheriff Bromwell, I would appreciate you meeting me in thirty minutes behind the closed convince store on US 13 in Painter." The caller had a slight Asian accent, but his diction was perfect.

"Who is this?" Bromwell wasn't happy about getting a call from a blocked number on his cell phone. "And what is this about?"

"I am someone who knows the details of your arrangement with Robert Outerbridge. All of the details. So I assume that you would rather meet in person. Or, if you prefer, we can discuss this over the phone..."

"No! Okay, fine, I'll meet you, but I can't make it in an hour, I'm busy right now." He was shaken by the call and wanted to stall so he had time to think.

"Fine. In that case, make it twenty minutes. I do not like to be kept waiting. Of course, I can call the FBI and leave the details anonymously if you are still too busy to meet me."

"I'll be there."

"A wise decision." The phone disconnected.

Bromwell was sweating now. That caller had to be with the triad, they were the only ones who might know about his arrangement with Outerbridge. But if he was a loose end like Robert, why ask for a meet rather than ambush him in a sneak attack? He'd know in a few minutes.

THE PRIUS WAS in the old abandoned garage, just as Outerbridge had left it. He grabbed the backpack as he ditched the bike inside, then locked the old wood doors after pulling the car out. He'd picked this make of vehicle carefully, then had the windows tinted and added a couple of eco-friendly bumper stickers on the back. Not too many to draw attention, just enough to make it fit in.

It was probably the last car someone would expect him to escape in. But he wasn't planning on taking it too far. The Bridge-Tunnel had cameras he wanted to avoid, and there were too many miles of the peninsula with only one main traffic artery to the north. But neither of those was his destination. He had unfinished business somewhere else to attend to, and he figured he could steal another mode of transportation at his destination.

Murph had caused all this, and he was going to pay dearly for it. If everything went well, part of that payback might be him taking Lindsay along for the ride. She was one hot-looking woman, and it was going to be a long boat trip. Right before he puts a bullet in Murph's brain, he'd tell him what was going to happen to her. It wouldn't repay all of what he'd done by tipping off the FBI, but it would be a nice down payment.

Now he turned south on 13, heading for *Mallard Cove*. He smiled to himself at the thought that Murphy would be dead in less than an hour.

BROMWELL PULLED behind the closed convenience store where a black Escalade with limousine tinted windows sat idling. A young Asian man dressed all in black emerged from the driver's door and opened the door behind his. Through the open door, he saw another similarly dressed young man in the front passenger seat pointing a large caliber automatic at him. This earned him a rebuke in Chinese from a third man in the seat behind him. He lowered his gun.

The man in the back said in English, "I am sorry, sheriff, my associate is still upset at the loss of my operation, and he tends to be impulsive. Please climb in so that we may speak in private." Again, he said something to the front passenger who reluctantly got out and closed his door, taking up position outside his boss's door.

Bromwell climbed in, and the other apparent bodyguard closed the door behind him. The man next to him wore a grim smile.

"My name is Fong." He didn't offer to shake hands. "It was been a very unprofitable two days for both of us. I lost my operation, and you lost your rather lucrative side job. It seems that these losses are not all the two of us have in common, we have a loose end which could affect both of us in a very bad way."

Bromwell felt slightly relieved since he hadn't been lumped in with Robert as a "loose end." He figured if he was going to be killed, it would have happened before he'd gotten out of his vehicle.

"Yeah, we do. Really bad."

"Tell me, are you interested in getting that side job back?"

"Well, yeah, but you said that operation don't exist anymore."

"This is true, but I learned quite a bit from it about this place you call ESVA. There is a lot to be said about the privacy and water access that can be found here. Reprinting money and manufacturing Rescentol are only two of my interests, and I will find other, more suitable locations to restart those businesses. But Outerbridge's property intrigues me. It will be seized, of course, and at some point, there will be a government auction. I intend on buying that property, which means I will need some security for my operations. Not just there, but all around Northampton County." He let the implication sink in a moment before continuing. "Are you interested in the job?"

"It depends on the pay. There's a lot of eyes on my department now, since the Feds think we didn't know what was goin' on right under our noses."

"I know what Robert was paying you, and I'll add thirty percent to that."

"Fifty percent."

Fong smiled. "Done. But you will need to do something first for me. If Robert is dead, that auction I spoke of will happen a lot sooner since there will be no court entanglements to delay it."

"Yeah, but he's vanished."

"I assume that you know about the death of his lawyer."

"Baskin was his lawyer? That explains a lot," Bromwell said.

"One of his lawyers. He paid the bills on a certain property, and my men missed him there by minutes. But he also had a gray Prius car that was at Robert's disposal. Here is the tag number. My men have been looking for him up north of here by Cape Charles and down at the Virginia Beach end of the Bridge-Tunnel. He has to still be somewhere on ESVA. Perhaps looking for a way to escape to his Bermuda home."

"That's likely. But there's one score he'd want to settle first. And maybe kill two birds with one stone."

"I don't understand."

"Well then it's a good thing you hired me, ain't it. 'Cause I got a good idea where to look."

BROMWELL CRUISED SLOWLY through the parking lots of the restaurants, bars, hotel, and bait business at *Mallard Cove*, but without any luck. He had one lot left, on the far side of the boat storage barn between it and the fence at what they call *Casey's Cove*.

He cleared the corner of the building and spotted the gray Prius with the matching tag numbers. He scanned the area but didn't see any sign of Outerbridge. Both the vehicle and pedestrian gates into Shaw's compound were closed and locked. But Bromwell remembered from his previous search that the fence changed from this tall security fence to a regular four-foot-high hog wire fence a little farther north. He set off in that direction and climbed over where the lower fence started. The sheriff made a beeline for the cover provided by the boathouse and crept up toward the pool house where Murphy and his girl were staying. He had almost made it to the far corner of the boathouse when he heard a shot and a scream.

AFTER CLIMBING OVER THE FENCE, Outerbridge scanned the area for any sign of Murphy on or around the boats and docks. All looked deserted. The sound of an approaching helicopter made him race over to the shelter of the boathouse doorway, wanting to get out of sight. The door was unlocked, and the interior was mostly dark except near the open end. He stepped inside and saw a single engine outboard moored in the shaded slip.

From this new, shadowy vantage point he was able to see the slightly elevated helipad and some of the pool area beside it. He watched as the helicopter landed and several people got out. They walked over to join a small crowd that was already assembled on the pool deck. Originally he'd hoped to find Murphy and Lindsay alone, eliminate him in private, and take off with Lindsay on their outboard. He'd spotted *LNZ II* tied up along the bulkhead, and remembered that Cho said it was the boat Murphy had been aboard at the farm.

But now this gathering had blown his original plan, though the helicopter might do as a backup, he'd have to think about that. Suddenly the boathouse door opened, and a big man stepped inside with a cooler as he turned on the overhead lights.

"Whoa! Who are you and what are you doing here," Rev demanded.

"I might ask you the same thing."

"Casey sent me over to get more ice." He indicated the commercial ice maker on the dock behind the outboard. "And you didn't answer my questions."

Outerbridge pulled both pistols out of his go-bag, pointing each of them at Rev. "I'll give you one out of two answers, but first, put up your hands. I'm here for Murphy, and now you're going to lead me to him."

OUTERBRIDGE MADE sure that Rev stayed just far enough in front of him to ensure he couldn't spin around and grab one or both of his pistols. They walked out slowly and took the concrete path up to the pool area.

"Everyone stay where you are and raise your hands. Do what you are told, and no one will be hurt," Outerbridge said. Then he focused on Rev. "You, get over there with your friends."

Rev complied, but Charles Fisher wasn't one to be bossed around, even by someone with a gun. He kept his hands down and said, "Are you insane? There are two dozen people here! You can't shoot all of us before we can get to you."

"You are probably correct. And I'm guessing that you would be the first to come after me," Outerbridge said, a second before he shot Charles Fisher in the chest. Claire screamed as her husband fell to the ground.

Outerbridge nodded grimly. "Anybody else thinks that you can get to me before I run out of bullets? I'll gladly demonstrate how wrong you are about that."

Like many of the others that were there, Rikki and Stephanie were usually armed, but today each had left her pistol locked in their cars. Everyone here knew that at these cookouts, they all tended to drink a bit more alcohol than usual and firearms were left at home. Not that surprising since before today there had been a sense of complete security here. So Outerbridge was the only one who was armed.

At the far end of the pool, Jock and Andrea had stood up, but now Jock stepped between her and the gunman. Outerbridge noticed that and said, "Ah, a chivalrous gentleman. Both of you, come over here. In fact, all of you get over here, we're going to walk together over to that pool house. You two as well." He pointed one of the guns at Claire and Dawn who had both knelt to help Charles.

"And you, Murphy, you've cost me almost everything. Now I'm going to take from you even more than what you cost me. Lindsay and I are going to take a little ride, and she's going to be my entertainment on the trip if you know what I mean. But unfortunately, there won't be any room for you to go with us, or anywhere for that matter. Say goodbye, Murphy."

Outerbridge pointed one pistol at Murphy's head and a shot rang out. But instead of hitting Murph, this bullet went into Outerbridge's skull, both scrambling and removing a large portion of his brain tissue as it exited the other side of his head. Most of them turned to look in the direction of the shot, and there stood Sheriff Bromwell. His pistol was still extended out toward where Outerbridge had stood. He raced over and picked up Robert's guns, putting them in his waistband. Then he knelt next to Charles Fisher, assessing his condition.

"We need to get him to a hospital right now. The nearest level one trauma center is in Norfolk. That thing have fuel in it?" He pointed to Eric's Sikorsky.

Eric nodded. "Yes, and my pilot is here," pointing to a man over by the aircraft.

"Help me get him aboard."

Within minutes of the helicopter taking off with Charles Fisher, Claire, and Eric on board, *C2* was crawling with law enforcement officials, both local as well as federal. Since Outerbridge was wanted for federal crimes, Bromwell gave a statement to the Feds explaining he was acting on an anonymous tip that led him to the Prius, and ultimately to Outerbridge. He also said he had warned him to drop his weapons before he fired that fatal shot. While no one remembered him saying that, none of them were willing to argue the point either. Outerbridge was dead, and that was all that mattered.

Eric returned less than an hour later without Claire. Charles was in surgery, but because they had gotten him to the hospital so swiftly, his chances of living were substantially improved. Candi took Dawn's SUV to go be with Claire while she waited.

"I knew from the start what you were, by the way," Andrea said to Jock. They were back in the same two chairs at the pool's far end.

"What do you mean?"

"That you are a con man, out for money."

"What? Why would you..."

She held up a hand, stopping him mid-sentence. "Just... don't. You did something that showed a lot of character a little while ago when you stepped in between me and a gun-wielding maniac. I never expected that from you. But there's nothing like a near-death experience to bring things into focus. That guy even called you chivalrous, and he was right. But you're also a swindler."

He started to say something but the hand went up again. "I'm not through. I'm guessing that it really was you that Claire recognized, and she might have been one of your marks. Poor Charles, I bet he has no idea. But here's the deal Jacques, I don't care. What's behind both of us is just water past the transom, and nothing to worry about.

"What you need to know going forward is that I'm not going to fall for your line of garbage, and you aren't going to be able to con me out of a cent. But you were enough fun to be with that I'm willing to ignore all of that. So, here's the deal. I've decided I'm going to St. Barts for the winter. I can either take *Temptress* alone with my crew, or we can go together on *Mistral*. Your choice. Or, we can go our separate ways, that's up to you. Give it some thought and let me know what you decide."

Hours later after law enforcement had cleared out, Casey, Dawn, Murph, Lindsay, and Rev were sitting around the fire pit finally able to have drinks and relax. Lindsay said, "Rev, would you marry Murph and me here this fall? We need to let things settle down a bit and get past what happened, but we still want to do this here, with all our friends around us."

"I'd be honored to. You guys have been through a lot, and I think y'all are meant to be together. I'm glad that you aren't going to let what happened today spoil this place for you. I've got a lot of good memories here."

Murph nodded. "Us, too. And there'll be a lot more to come from now until Outerbridge is nothing but a faded memory."

"We're going to be too busy before the wedding to worry about him, there's so much to do," Lindsay added.

"What? All I have to do is go to my bachelor party and show up on time, right?"

Casey laughed. "Oh, I think the girls will find you plenty to do before then."

"Speaking of things to do," Rev said, "I found this in the boathouse after I went back for the cooler. What do you want to do with this?"

He opened the cooler and took out the black go-bag that Outerbridge dropped when he'd pulled out the pistols. When he opened the top they could see the rolls of gold coins and numerous straps of bills.

Casey said, "I vote we add it to the Watermen's Fund. Let a little more good come from all that bad. All those in favor say aye..."

EPILOGUE

Andrea looked at the mountains rising in the distance out of the deep blue water. "This is where *Mistral* belongs, Jock. Just the two of us aboard, island hopping with no set itinerary." She looked up at the sails, filled with the warm trade wind.

"I thought you would be tired of me by the time we hit the Turks and Caicos Islands."

"I would have if you hadn't come clean about your whole con game. If you had kept playing that stupid role with me."

"It wasn't stupid; it was well thought out. It worked so well for so long. I just worry that we might run into one of my past marks down here. I wouldn't want to get caught and ruin our trip."

"How would that happen when you have your loyal courtesan with you to back up your story? Two can play that role, you know."

～

"I still can't believe nobody was around *Casey's Cove,* and it was a regular ghost town. They knew we were due home today, and I'd have thought they would've wanted to greet us," Murph grumped.

"You know there must be a good reason, babe. I mean, it's not like they've forgotten us; our honeymoon was only two weeks long."

"Yeah, but we were there for Case and Dawn when they got back."

"Don't worry about it, I'm sure they'll show up by tonight. Besides, I can't wait to see how our new house barge is coming along."

The two were just pulling into *Albury's Boat Works*. It was a crisp fall Saturday, and the boatyard was mostly quiet except for a few boat owners working over on the concrete do-it-yourself side known as "the slab." But their new home was taking shape in a shed on the other side of the 'yard. Built less like a boat and more like a conventional home, the construction was coming along fast.

The pair wandered through the build, checking on all the little details. They'd just about finished when they heard the loud engine of the travel lift crank up over at the slab.

Murph commented, "Carlton's hauling a boat on the weekend? Must be an emergency."

"Maybe someone's sinking. We're through here; let's go check it out and see if we can help."

Walking out of the shed, they saw Carlton lowering the travel lift's slings into the water, getting set to haul an incoming boat. They heard Baloney bellowing before they even saw *My Mahi* entering the turning basin. His cigar smoke was rising from the flybridge even as he was yelling directions.

At first, they worried that My Mahi was the one headed for the lift, but then they spotted the tow rig running from her stern. The boat it was attached to was very familiar to them; it was the fire-damaged hull of their old *Irish Luck*. But there was still one more boat attached to this daisy chain. Outerbridge's drake tail deadrise was bringing up the rear, attached to the Merritt's stern, keeping her from swinging as she was towed down the narrow entrance.

"Youse two gonna just stand there with yer mouths open, or are ya gonna make yourselves useful an' catch the lines," Baloney bellowed at Murph and Lindsay.

They hurried over to the ends of the twin travel lift piers that stuck out into the basin. As Baloney gingerly tugged the Merritt in close, they saw that Dawn was on the foredeck. She unhooked the tow line and then tossed them each a line from the bow. They slowly pulled the hull in over the straps as Carlton began lifting it. Dawn dropped the stern line, and Casey retrieved it on the deadrise. It turned out he'd been the one running the drake tail. He and Baloney then docked their respective boats at the adjacent floating dock.

Baloney went over and held a hand out to Dawn, who stepped from the Merritt's bow onto the slab. He turned to admire the hull, which was now being raised high enough to clear the slab.

He turned to Murph, "Ain't she a beauty!"

"No! She used to be, but now she's not. And I missed you too, Bill."

"Huh? What? Oh, yeah, there's that. Hiya, Lindsay." He rushed around to the stern as Carlton moved the boat over the slab, heading into another shed.

Dawn laughed, "Don't pay any attention to him, you guys. He's been floating on air ever since he won the government auction yesterday."

"He bought our old boat." It was just starting to dawn on Murph.

"And Casey bought that deadrise." She pointed to the dock where it was tied up.

"Okay, Baloney has a history of rehabbing wrecked boats, but what's with the drake tail?" Murph asked.

Casey replied, "Nobody was bidding on it. I couldn't buy a used engine for what I paid for it. So, we've got a few bullet holes to patch, but she runs great! And Baloney almost *stole* that Merritt."

They walked over to look at Baloney's newest charter rig and let him explain to everyone all about it. This, even though they were all far more familiar with the boat than he was.

Finally, Casey said, "Well, we need to get back to the *Cove*. I'm sure these two have a story or two to tell us about their trip."

"Yeah, I'll be there in a while; then they can buy the beer. Great ta have you kids back."

They walked back to the deadrise as Casey explained how he was going to take the tank out and install a table and bench seat, making it more of a cruiser.

Dawn grinned, "Kind of the 'Shaw Family Cruiser.' He's got about eight months to get it all done. You know, before our little one arrives next year..."

FROM THE AUTHOR:

Thanks for keeping up with the *Mallard Cove* crew! Their adventures will continue in Coastal Cruise. Click on this link for more information or to buy this next book.

And if you liked *this* book, please leave a review on Goodreads or Book Bub, since its success depends on garnering great reviews. Thanks again!

AUTHOR NOTES & FACTS

The story about Andorra and the two princes? It's true, you can look Andorra up on the internet. Even the part about the man who claimed to be king, that's also true. I stumbled onto it when I was looking for locations and was blown away by how perfect a fit it was for this story.

Bay Breeze restaurant is a little less than loosely based on *Hole In The Wall Restaurant* on Gwynn's Island. Unless you come by boat the parking is tight, the food is fantastic, and the view is incredible. One of my favorite "dock 'n' dines" around the bay. They consistently rank at the top in many surveys. It's two and a half hours from my land-locked home, and I've driven there and back just for lunch. It's that good.

Talbot Creek is fictional but is based on Tabbs Creek. I stayed at the *Inn at Tabbs Creek,* and that's where I came up with the idea for this story. I can never look at such a peaceful and serene place without thinking of some way of bringing havoc to it on the pages of a book. I don't know if that's a gift or a curse. Oh, and the farm across the way from the inn is actually a dairy; they don't grow Chinese vegetables. That farm was inspired by a dove lease I had many years ago at a Chinese vegetable farm down in Hobe Sound, Florida. It just kind of fit in with the idea of the smuggler's farm.

Mathews is one of my favorite little towns. Great restaurants, fun little shops, and friendly people. Busy in the summer, but idyllic in the spring and fall. A great place to relax and bring a book. One of mine, of course.

Rescentol is fictional, thank God. We have enough of a problem with the flood of Fentanyl coming into the US today. As I write this in mid-2022, that flood has grown to such epidemic proportions that the price has dropped by *half* over the past year. Three-quarters of the opioid deaths last year were due to Fentanyl.

<u>Update</u>: a week after I wrote this note, I learned about the new drug called *ISO* which is now flooding the streets of Miami. It is twenty times more potent than Fentanyl, and many times more deadly.

Then two months after coming up with the idea of Rescentol saturated currency, I learned yesterday that a woman in New York picked up a dollar bill she saw on a sidewalk. Shortly afterward she had to be treated for a Fentanyl overdose. The dollar was drenched in it.

About that group of twenty-four "synthetic elements," I said make up the section of the Periodic Table of Elements that do not occur naturally here on earth? True. All of the original twenty-four were created between 1944 and 2010. The mechanism for the creation of these elements involved human manipulation of their fundamental particles inside a nuclear reactor, a particle accelerator, or an atomic explosion. The twenty-fifth member of this group that's a key component of Rescentol? False. And I hope they don't ever discover it.

Mistral was based on an actual Palmer Johnson sailboat that I sailed on once down in Palm Beach. It was designed and built to be single-handed, just like Jock's. Had that crazy hydraulic table, too.

Claire's Harry Winston bracelet and Andrea's Atocha emerald pendant? Both are real pieces and those are their real prices. Stunning, both of them.

Oh, and those testing tools for Krugerrands? Also real. You can buy them online. The marble shelves on antique cash registers really were for testing gold and silver coins by bouncing them. Maybe not as accurate as the modern methods, but good enough for that time.

One last fact, the *Peggy T* is real. She's mine, but she's not for sale. Don't forget, this book *is* a work of fiction, after all.

GLOSSARY

I grew up on the water in South Florida, and I have an extensive boating background. I've worked on boats, built them, re-built them, and spent a good amount of time in boatyards. I've always loved boats, and ever since I was a pre-teenager, I haven't gone longer than six months without owning at least one. Most of my friends are boaters, too. So it's easy for me to forget that not everyone is as familiar with the jargon as my friends and me, which is something that I've now been reminded of on more than one occasion. (My apologies to those readers that I ended up sending to the dictionary!) To make amends, here's a (growing) list of uniquely nautical terms and words that have been included in several of my books. Bear in mind that these definitions are based on my own usage and experience. Things can be different from one region to another. For instance, you can fish for stripers in Montauk, New York, but here in Virginia, we fish for rockfish. But the true name for the target species is "striped bass."

So, here are the definitions of some of the more confusing words, at least as I know them. We'll start with a half dozen simple ones, then move on to those that are more complex:

- **Bow:** the front of the boat.
- **Stern:** back of the boat.
- **Port:** the left side of the boat.
- **Starboard:** the right side of the boat.
- **Aft:** the rear of the boat.
- **Forward:** (fore) the front of the boat.
- **Bow Thruster:** a propeller in a tube that is mounted from side to side through the bow below the waterline, allowing the captain more maneuverability and control when docking especially in adverse winds and current. Powered by an electric or hydraulic motor.
- **Bulkhead:** boat wall.
- **Center Console:** a type of boat with a raised helm console in the middle of the boat with space on each side to walk around. Most also incorporate a built-in bench seat or cooler seat in the front.
- **Chine:** the longitudinal area running fore and aft where the bottom meets the side. It can be rounded or "sharp." They hurt when the boat rocks and it meets your head when you are swimming next to it. Trust me on that.
- **Circle Hook:** a fishhook designed to get caught in the corner of a fish's mouth. Greatly reduces the mortality of fish that are released or that break the line.
- **Citation:** at an airport, it's a type of jet made by Cessna. But here in Virginia, it's a slip of paper suitable for framing, issued by the state confirming that you caught a fish that's considered large for its particular species. Or it can be a speeding ticket, either on water or land. I like the fish kind better.
- **Covering Board:** a flat surface at the top of a gunwale usually made out of teak or fiberglass, that's used as a step for boarding and for mounting recessed rod holders.
- **Deck:** what floors on boats are called.

- **Fighting Chair:** a specialized chair that can be turned to face a fish. Mounted on a sturdy stanchion with a built-in gimbal, the chair allows the angler to use the attached footrest to use their legs and body to gain more leverage on a large fish. Most of today's fighting chairs are based on the design by my late friend John Rybovich.
- **Fish Box:** a built-in storage box for the day's catch. They can be either elevated in the stern, or in the deck with a flush-mounted lid. Some of the higher-end sportfish boats have cooling systems or automatic ice makers that continually add ice throughout the trip.
- **Fishing Cockpit:** the lower aft deck on a sport fisherman that usually contains a fighting chair, fish box, baitwell, and tackle center. Surrounded on three sides by the gunwales and the stern. The cockpit deck is usually just above the waterline, with scuppers that drain overboard. Can get flooded when backing down hard on a big fish.
- **Flying Bridge (Flybridge):** a permanently mounted helm area on top of the wheelhouse. Can be open or enclosed.
- **Following Sea:** when the waves are moving toward the boat from behind the stern.
- **Gaff:** a large, usually barbless hook at the end of a pole, used for landing fish. They come in different sizes and lengths.
- **Gangway (Gangplank):** a removable ramp or set of stairs attached to the side of larger boats to allow easier access for boarding from a dock. Usually hinged to allow for tide variation.
- **Gear:** marine transmission which has forward, neutral, and reverse.
- **Gimbal:** there are a few types, but the ones in my books are rod holders with swivels built into fighting chairs.
- **Gin Pole:** a vertical pole next to the gunwale usually rigged with a block and tackle and used for hauling large

fish aboard. These used to be quite common until John Rybovich invented the transom door fifty years ago.

- **Gunwale (pronounced gun-nul):** aft side area of a boat above the waterline, also the area on either side of a fishing cockpit.
- **Hatch:** a hole in a deck or bulkhead with a cover that may be hinged or completely removable. On a sport fisherman, the door into the wheelhouse may be called either a hatch or a door.
- **Head:** a bathroom, or a marine toilet.
- **Helm:** the area that includes the steering and engine controls. In many sportfishing boats, the controls are mounted on a helm pod, a wood box with radiused edges that juts out of a cabinet or bulkhead.
- **Keys Conch:** a person born in the Florida Keys. You can be born in Miami and move to the Keys an hour later, then live down there the rest of your life, and you will still NEVER be a Conch. They are usually very tough and independent characters.
- **Lean Seat:** a high bench seat usually found behind the helm of a center console. Designed to be leaned against or sat upon. May have storage built-in under the seat section.
- **Mezzanine Deck:** a shallow, raised deck on a sportfish just forward of the fishing cockpit, and aft of the wheelhouse bulkhead. Usually contains aft-facing bench seating for anglers to comfortably watch the baits that are being trolled behind the boat.
- **Outriggers:** long aluminum poles on sportfishing boats that are raked up and aft from up alongside the wheelhouse. They are extended outward when fishing, having clips on lines that carry the fishing lines out away from the boat, creating a wider spread.
- **Pilot Boat:** a smaller boat designed to handle all kinds of seas, whose sole purpose is delivering and retrieving a

captain with extensive local knowledge to larger boats approaching or leaving a port.

- **Rod Holder:** As the name suggests, a device that a fishing rod butt is inserted into to hold it steady. There are recessed types that are mounted on covering boards, and exposed ones attached to railings or tower legs.
- **Salon:** a living room area of a boat's cabin.
- **Scuppers:** deck or cockpit drains.
- **SeaKeeper Gyro:** a stabilizing gyro that almost eliminates roll in boats.
- **Shaft:** attaches a propeller to the gear.
- **Sheer Line:** the rail edge where the foredeck meets the side of the hull.
- **Sonar/Fish Finder:** electronic underwater 'radar' that displays the sea floor, and anything between it and the boat.
- **Sportfisherman (Sportfish):** a unique style of boat designed specifically for fishing.
- **Spread:** the arrangement of the baits being towed while trolling.
- **Stem:** the forwardmost edge of the bow.
- **Stern:** the farthest aft part of the boat, also called the transom.
- **Tackle Center:** a cabinet in the fishing cockpit or the center console which holds hooks, swivels, leads, and other fishing supplies.
- **(Tuna) Tower:** an aluminum pipe structure located above the house or the flybridge designed to hold spotters or riders, and may or may not have an additional helm.
- **Transom:** stern.
- **Transom (Tuna) Door:** a door in the stern just above the waterline, designed for boating large fish, but also useful for retrieving swimmers and divers.
- **Trough:** the lowest point between waves.

- **Wheel (Propeller):** slang for a prop.
- **Wheel (Steering):** controls the boat's direction.
- **Wheelhouse (House):** the cabin section of a boat which sometimes contains an enclosed helm.

ABOUT THE AUTHOR

Don Rich is the author of the bestselling Coastal Adventure and Coastal Beginnings series. Don's books are set mainly in the mid-Atlantic because of his love for this stretch of coastline.

As a fifth-generation Florida native who grew up on the water, he has spent a good portion of his life on, in, under, or beside it. He now makes his home in central Virginia. When he's not writing or watching another fantastic mid-Atlantic sunset, he can often be found on the Chesapeake or the Atlantic with a fishing rod in his hand.

Don loves to hear from readers, and you can reach him via email at contact@donrichbooks.com

ALSO BY DON RICH

Check my website www.DonRichBooks.com for the current list of all my book titles.

The Coastal Beginnings Series:

(The prelude to the Coastal Adventure Series)

- **COASTAL CHANGES**
- **COASTAL TREASURE**
- **COASTAL RULES**
- **COASTAL BLUFFS**

The Coastal Adventure Series:

- **COASTAL CONSPIRACY**
- **COASTAL COUSINS**
- **COASTAL PAYBACKS**
- **COASTAL TUNA**
- **COASTAL CATS**
- **COASTAL CAPER**
- **COASTAL CULPRIT**
- **COASTAL CURSE**
- **COASTAL JURY**
- **COASTAL CURRENCY**
- **COASTAL CRUISE**

Other Books by Don Rich:

- **GhostWRITER**

Here's A Tropical Authors Novella by Deborah Brown, Nicholas Harvey, and Don Rich:

- **Priceless**

Go to my website at www.DonRichBooks.com for more information about joining my **Reader's Group**! And you can follow me on Facebook at: https://www.facebook.com/DonRichBooks

I'm also a member of TropicalAuthors.com, where you can find my latest books and those by dozens of my coastal writer friends!